TAMA

A cat-eared girl.

A s

SATOU

A twenty-nine-year-old programmer who has been transported to a parallel universe.

POCHI

A dog-eared girl.

ARISA

A former princess of the Kuvork Kingdom. She was Japanese in her previous life.

LULU

Born in the Kuvork Kingdom. She is Arisa's older sister.

DEATH MARCH 6
TO THE
PARALLEL WORLD RHAPSODY

NANA
An expressionless homunculus.

KARINA
The second child of Baron Muno.

MIA
A taciturn elf who loves music.

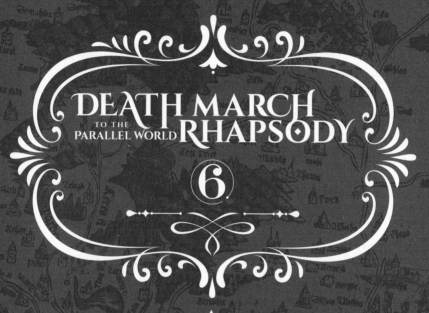

DEATH MARCH
TO THE PARALLEL WORLD RHAPSODY

6.

★ ★ ★

HIRO AINANA
ILLUSTRATION BY SHRI

NEW YORK

Death March to the Parallel World Rhapsody, Vol. 6
Hiro Ainana

Translation by Jenny McKeon
Cover art by shri

© Hiro Ainana, shri 2015
First published in Japan in 2015 by KADOKAWA CORPORATION, Tokyo.
English translation rights arranged with KADOKAWA CORPORATION, Tokyo, through Tuttle-Mori Agency, Inc., Tokyo.

English translation © 2018 by Yen Press, LLC

Yen On
1290 Avenue of the Americas
New York, NY 10104

Visit us at yenpress.com
facebook.com/yenpress
twitter.com/yenpress
yenpress.tumblr.com
instagram.com/yenpress

First Yen On Edition: September 2018

Yen On is an imprint of Yen Press, LLC.
The Yen On name and logo are trademarks of Yen Press, LLC.

The publisher is not responsible for websites (or their content) that are not owned by the publisher.

Library of Congress Cataloging-in-Publication Data
Names: Ainana, Hiro, author. | Shri, illustrator. | McKeon, Jenny, translator.
Title: Death march to the parallel world rhapsody / Hiro Ainana ; illustrations by shri ; translation by Jenny McKeon.
Other titles: Desu machi kara hajimaru isekai kyosokyoku. English
Description: First Yen On edition. | New York, NY : Yen ON, 2017–
Identifiers: LCCN 2016050512 | ISBN 9780316504638 (v. 1 : pbk.) | ISBN 9780316507974 (v. 2 : pbk.) | ISBN 9780316556088 (v. 3 : pbk.) | ISBN 9780316556095 (v. 4 : pbk.) | ISBN 9780316556101 (v. 5 : pbk.) | ISBN 9780316556125 (v. 6 : pbk.)
Subjects: | GSAFD: Fantasy fiction.
Classification: LCC PL867.5,I56 D413 2017 | DDC 895.6/36d—dc23
LC record available at https://lccn.loc.gov/2016050512

ISBNs: 978-0-316-55612-5 (paperback)
978-0-316-55618-7 (ebook)

1 3 5 7 9 10 8 6 4 2

LSC-C

Printed in the United States of America

CONTENTS

Death March
To the
Parallel World
Rhapsody

Ringrande

*Satou here. When I think of **mokuba**, wooden horses, my mind automatically goes to merry-go-rounds. But for some reason, most of my friends think of some card game. Very mysterious.*

"A hooorse?"

"It's a horse, sir."

Tama, a white-haired girl with cat ears and a tail, and Pochi, a girl with a short chestnut bob and dog ears and a tail, were staring at the sky from the deck of the large ship carrying us downriver.

The rest of the group, sprawled on the sofas we'd placed on deck, looked up with interest.

"Hmm? That little white spot there? I can barely see it."

Arisa, her lilac hair hidden by a blond wig, narrowed her violet eyes to squint at the sky where Tama and Pochi were pointing.

"Master, I would like a telescopic vision expansion, I entreat."

Nana's head popped up behind me, her golden hair tied back in a ponytail. She was expressionless as always, but I was starting to get the hang of reading her emotions.

She put a hand on my shoulder, her substantial chest pressing against me. Normally, this would suggest an attempt at seduction, but since she was a homunculus and technically zero years old, it was probably more like a child demanding attention from a parent.

That said, it would be a waste to move away from such a pleasant sensation, so I let her do as she liked.

However, not everyone was so forgiving.

"Too close."

Mia, who'd been playing a gentle tune, stopped to glower at Nana and wedge herself between us.

Her long, pale turquoise pigtails swayed, allowing a glimpse at the pointed elf ears beneath her hair.

I felt a slight tug on my sleeve, and I turned around.

"M-master, does this mean that you prefer...you know, bigger...?"

Speaking to me with tears welling up in her dark eyes was Lulu, a beautiful black-haired girl who could easily pass for Japanese. A girl that lovely could make any expression look good.

I wished I could preserve this moment forever as a painting or something, but I wouldn't let one of the kids in my care stay sad, so I gently wiped her tears with a finger.

If you asked me, it was downright sinful that the beauty standards in this world meant this beautiful girl was considered homely by most.

"Master, it appears that someone is riding the horse," added Liza of the orangescale tribe, standing alert at my side with her magic spear at the ready.

Behind her crimson hair, her dignified profile was just visible. Her orange tail flicked slightly with tension.

"Are we under attack?"

"A single horseman would not attempt to rob a ship."

Miss Karina, the daughter of Baron Muno, brushed back her blond curls before peering at the sky from the neighboring sofa.

The calm male voice that answered her came from Raka, a silver amulet that glowed blue at her breast. It was an "intelligent item" that enhanced the wearer's strength and created a powerful barrier to protect them.

Though most of the group was on the alert, I could tell from the detailed information next to the point on my map that whatever was approaching us from the sky wasn't an enemy.

However, no one would believe this unless I explained the workings of my Unique Skill "Search Entire Map," so I couldn't say anything to my group with the likes of Miss Karina and Raka around. They'd be able to see for themselves soon enough; I decided to just keep enjoying the relaxing boat trip for now.

Still, though...

This peaceful scene made it hard to believe that a demon lord had been resurrected in the depths below the old capital just last night.

It felt like ages ago that I'd met Sara of the Tenion Temple.

Not far from the banks of this peaceful river, the demon lord cult

Wings of Freedom had used her as a sacrifice to resurrect one of the evil creatures. Fortunately, I defeated him, and Sara was revived with help from the head priestess of the Tenion Temple and the Treasure of Resurrection.

According to my map, Sara's current status condition was **Weakened**, but she should be fine, since there were plenty of priests at the temple who could use Holy Magic. *I'll have to go visit her once she's recovered a little more.*

The next "Season of the Demon Lord" wasn't for another sixty-six years; I was planning to enjoy a nice peaceful journey from now on. *Besides, there are supposed to be all kinds of rarities in the old capital where we're heading next, so I think I'll stay awhile and enjoy the sights.*

This would extend the trip to take Mia home to the elf village, but they already knew she was safe, and Mia herself had said that even an extra year or two made no difference to elves. We'd just say she was broadening her horizons before going home.

We'd also be parting with Miss Karina at the old capital, since she had been tasked with delivering a letter from Baron Muno to the royal capital, but with Raka and her two armed maids, I expected she'd be perfectly fine.

While my thoughts were wandering, the ship guards and knightly passengers noticed the shadow approaching from the sky.

The guards began preparing magic and bows to defend the ship, and some of the birdfolk and batfolk among their number took off to scout out the situation.

My group began to follow suit and arm themselves with bows and stones as well, but I quietly stopped them.

"Don't worry. We're not under attack."

I already knew the flier's identity; I'd checked on my map as soon as Pochi and Tama pointed it out.

My "Telescopic Sight" and "Long-Distance Vision" skills meant I already had a clear view.

A white golem shaped like a wooden horse was galloping through the sky. It probably used a similar principal to my "Skyrunning" skill. My AR display labeled the contraption a **wooden Pegasus**.

Riding on its back was a slender knight clad in silver armor. The helmet hid the rider's face, but the feminine outline of the armor hinted at the beauty of its wearer. If the curves of that breastplate were anything to go by, she was probably around an E cup, too.

Her name was Ringrande Ougoch. Level 55. Judging by the configuration of her skills, she seemed more like a magic knight than a mage.

At twenty-two, she was seven years older than her sister—Sara of the Tenion Temple. She was also a follower of the hero Hayato Masaki.

I had no idea why a grandchild of Duke Ougoch, one of the most powerful men in the Shiga Kingdom, would be working for the hero of the Saga Empire, but I was confident she would be a beauty with a strong resemblance to Sara, at least.

Naturally, I kept these high expectations to myself when one of the birdfolk who'd gone to scope out the situation hurriedly returned.

"It's Lady Ringrande!" the scout exclaimed. "The Witch of Heavenly Destruction has returned!" With that, he took off around the ship to excitedly repeat his message.

His beak garbled his speech a little—it sounded more like "Lay-hee Lin-glad"—but I managed to figure it out.

The sailors, ship guards, and even the knights repeated her name to one another. *Sara's sister must be pretty famous.*

"Riiin?"

"Glad, sir?"

The murmurs from all sides set Pochi and Tama on edge; they glanced around uncertainly.

"Lady...Ringrande?" Miss Karina repeated. "The one who travels with the hero?"

Jumping to her feet, she stared at the approaching rider like she was about to meet her biggest idol. She must have heard all kinds of gossip in the hero-crazy Muno Barony.

"Have you met this Lady Ringrande, Arisa?" I asked quietly.

"Never. I must have met Hayato before she joined up." Arisa shook her head, then paused thoughtfully. "But if she knows what Japanese people look like, she might realize where you're from."

"Good point. I guess I'll just say I'm descended from a Japanese hero, like Lulu."

I made a mental note of this new addition to my made-up backstory.

Miss Ringrande and her wooden Pegasus approached the ship.

She removed her helmet, her long hair cascading like silver threads.

Unlike Sara, whose hair was closer to a platinum blond, Miss Ringrande's hair was the color of pure silver. It was so beautiful, it almost didn't look real.

Her face was indeed similar to Sara's, but while the features of the oracle priestess brought to mind a sweetly blooming flower, Ringrande's had the commanding charm of an elegant rose.

"I am Ringrande, granddaughter of Duke Ougoch! I hereby request permission to land on your ship!" she cried with a sharp, booming voice, and the captain quickly granted permission from the stern.

Her voice reminded me of Sara's, too, but it gave a completely different impression.

""""Ringrande!"""" Perhaps stirred by the sound of her voice, the people on board cried her name in welcome. """"Ringrande!""""

Their stamping and flailing were so fervent that I couldn't bring myself to join in.

Overwhelmed by the noise, Tama and Pochi flattened their ears and looked at me anxiously, so I sat them on my knees and patted their heads.

Except for my party and myself, the only passenger who wasn't hopping up and down was Imperial Knight Sir Ipasa Lloyd, Sara's former escort. His gaze was warm, as if he was fondly watching a grown younger sibling.

Little Mayuna, the baby with the "Oracle" skill, was peering out from her mother Hayuna's arms in excitement. Hayuna's husband, Tolma, was still seasick in their cabin.

"Sit."

"H-hey, me too!"

Mia and Arisa sat down on either side of me, snuggling up to me with satisfied faces.

"Sh-she's very popular, isn't she?"

Flushed, Lulu settled onto the soft fur rug laid out in front of the couch. Her excited expression was cute enough to preserve forever, too.

"Master, I desire a plush toy in the shape of that horse, I assert."

"Sure, I'll make you one. There's not much else to do while we're on the ship."

Behind me, Nana stared intensely at Miss Ringrande's wooden Pegasus. A few simple plush toys should take only a half hour or so, even if I made enough for everyone.

"Thank you, master!"

Delighted, Nana expressed her gratitude by embracing my head, her ample breasts pushing against my face.

Of course, the ever-watchful barrier of Arisa and Mia was quick to pull her away, but just a moment in paradise was enough.

I'll have to make the cutest plush toy I possibly can.

"Sir Knight, I apologize for the sailors' noisy behavior."

This apology came from the tour guide who was taking care of us on the ship.

In addition to being the resident guide for our vessel, she was a civil official in the service of its owner, Viceroy Worgoch of Gururian City.

"It's quite all right. Lady Ringrande must be very popular," I said, casually broaching the topic.

Miss Ringrande had landed her wooden Pegasus on the afterdeck and was chatting with Sir Ipasa and the ship's captain.

"Are you not familiar with her, Sir Knight?" The guide, evidently a big fan, approached me with her fists raised to her chest in excitement.

I shook my head politely, and she promptly regaled me with various tales of Miss Ringrande's exploits.

Some of them I already knew from reviewing her information on the map, but the story went something like this:

Miss Ringrande was the eldest daughter of the next duke and a princess of the Shiga Kingdom—making her the granddaughter of a king as well as a duke. This didn't give her the right to inherit any throne, as it turned out, but she still came from an impressive bloodline. On top of that, she was a prodigy who entered the royal academy at just ten years of age and graduated within two, and she'd mastered both Wind and Blaze Magic to advanced levels. After graduation, she even became a researcher at the academy, and by the age of fifteen she'd revived the lost arts of Destruction Magic and Explosion Magic. During the course of her research, she brushed up on her magical techniques in the Labyrinth City Celivera.

"She was granted the rank of honorary baroness as thanks for defeating a floormaster in Labyrinth City."

"Did she do that all by herself?"

"Not even Lady Ringrande could do that on her own!"

The tour guide explained that she had the help of Holy Knights from the royal capital.

Because of her accomplishments, when the beloved prodigy turned eighteen and left the Shiga Kingdom to work with the hero of the Saga Empire, the kingdom went into an uproar. I didn't care about that part so much. I just nodded along without really listening.

I did learn, however, that this was the first time she'd returned in four years.

The *clink-clank* of armor heralded Miss Ringrande's approach, along with Sir Ipasa.

It seemed rude to stay seated, so I stood up to greet her.

At the urging of her maids, Miss Karina rose to her feet, too, her knees knocking with nerves.

"Nice to meet you. I'm Ringrande Ougoch, follower of Hero Hayato Masaki." Introducing herself, Miss Ringrande bowed politely to Karina.

"N-n-nice to meet you…"

That was as far as Miss Karina's introduction went before she stammered to a halt and turned bright red. I stepped in to give her some backup.

"Pardon my intrusion. This is Karina Muno, the second daughter of my lord Baron Muno. It seems she is so overwhelmed with emotion at the chance to meet you that she has forgotten herself; allow me to apologize on her behalf."

"Oh, not at all! Baron Muno—you mean Uncle Leon, right? Why, that would make us second cousins, then. The books he wrote back when he was a researcher were the reason I decided I wanted to work with a hero! Please treat me as an equal."

Miss Ringrande gave Miss Karina a warm smile.

Like a fan whose favorite singer had smiled at her, Miss Karina was so red that she could have been on the verge of fainting.

Picking up on this, Miss Ringrande tactfully shifted her gaze toward me. "Might I ask your name, then?"

"Certainly. I am Satou Pendragon, an honorary hereditary knight and vassal of the Muno Barony."

Miss Ringrande's eyes widened at that. "You're Uncle Leon's vassal? Haven't you heard the rumors about Muno Barony?"

"Yes, of course. But the curse that was afflicting the barony has been broken now."

Naturally, I left out how the one who removed the curse was the "silver-masked hero."

Since she worked for the hero Hayato, bringing up the appearance of a new hero would probably result in a lengthy explanation.

"Well, that's splendid news. Who was the one who…?"

Before Miss Ringrande could finish her question, I shifted my gaze toward the tour guide, who appeared to be itching to say something.

"What's the matter?"

"Well, we'll be entering the Dreamglow Cavern shortly…"

The Dreamglow Cavern was a man-made tunnel about two miles long in the middle of the river and ran through the Grapevine Mountains.

The cavern was just wide enough for one large ship to pass through, while the main current of the river took a wide detour around the mountains and merged on the other side.

As the tour guide had explained earlier, this was one of the most famous sightseeing spots in the Shiga Kingdom and was especially popular as a honeymoon destination for nobles.

I found out later that Miss Ringrande, too, had boarded the ship in order to take the shortcut through the harsh Grapevine Mountains.

"Oh my, I apologize. I would hate to disrupt anyone who's never seen it before. Might there be a seat for me as well?" Miss Ringrande said. I saw Miss Karina's eyes dart furtively toward the three-seat sofa where she'd been sitting.

I tried not to meddle too often, but it might be good for Miss Karina to make a new friend.

"Lady Ringrande, if you please, the spot next to Lady Karina is open. Why don't you have a seat there?"

"Is that all right?"

"Y-yes, of course! H-h-have a seat."

Obviously unbothered by Miss Karina's stammering invitation, Miss Ringrande sat down lightly on the sofa.

Watching the situation unfold with a grin, Sir Ipasa interfered even further.

"Rin, would you mind scooting over a little? I'd like to sit and look at the Dreamglow Cavern, too."

"Ah…certainly. Pardon me."

Miss Ringrande drew close enough to Karina that their shoulders touched, causing the latter to turn red enough to boil.

Miss Ringrande chatted with her in a friendly tone, but Miss Karina could give only short responses like "Yes" and "That's right."

Fortunately, Miss Ringrande didn't seem to take any offense.

If this continued, I might have to help Miss Karina work on her interpersonal skills a bit more when we arrived in the old capital.

"All right, everyone, please close your eyes for the moment. Don't open them again until I give the word, if you wouldn't mind."

As we perched on the sofas, we all followed the tour guide's hushed instructions. She sounded like a veteran staff member at a theme park.

The suggestion to close our eyes was probably to help our vision adjust to the dark inside the Dreamglow Cavern.

"Our batfolk navigator Meru will be steering the ship for the captain as we pass through the caverns."

After the introduction, a batfolk woman gave a bow. It was the same lady who was in charge of patrolling at night. I'd assumed she was a guard, but evidently she was a navigator as well.

I surmised the switch was because a batfolk person's echolocation would make it easier to proceed in the dark of the tunnel.

"Sound echoes inside the Dreamglow Cavern, so please refrain from making any loud noises."

At this warning, Tama and Pochi covered their mouths with both hands. Because they were covering their noses, too, I shifted their hands downward so they wouldn't suffocate.

There was a docking station in front of the tunnel's entrance, and a small boat left it to enter the cavern just ahead of our ship. As it did, it flashed a signal light to the other end of the tunnel.

After a few short moments, another light flashed back in response from the end.

Then, the small boat left the tunnel, and our ship folded its sails and proceeded inside. The tunnel was wide enough for only one ship; the signals must have been for traffic control.

I felt a warm breeze from the tunnel. It was like the kind of thing you'd find in a fairy tale where the tunnel leads into the stomach of some enormous beast. But of course that wasn't the case.

Instead, the ship advanced into the passageway safely, and the light from the entrance gradually dimmed.

Now, I was the only one observing all this with my eyes cracked open. Everyone else obediently kept their eyes closed as the guide had instructed.

Thanks to the "Light Intensity Adjustment" skill, I was able to adapt to the darkness right away. Now, that was handy.

Whoa!

As my eyes quickly adjusted, I was met with an incredible scene.

Although she couldn't have sensed my inner surprise, the tour guide chose this moment to give the signal.

"Now, everyone, please open your eyes slowly! Welcome to the famous Dreamglow Caverns of the Orcs!"

Though I'd been a step ahead of everyone else, it really was a sight to behold.

From the ceiling of the cavern down the walls on either side, luminous moss emitted a pale light in all the colors of the rainbow, creating a mystical gradient that enveloped us. The exposed crystals flecked across the walls reflected the lights, adding extra variety to the scene.

It was like a painting that brilliantly captured the starry sky.

That alone would have been beautiful enough, but there were also countless firefly-like lights flickering and dancing in the air.

I've seen decorative lighting before, but this really takes it to the next level.

"Sparklyyy? Floatyyy!"

"Amazing, sir! Master! Look, it's 'mazing!"

Sitting on my left and right, Pochi and Tama grabbed my sleeves and shook them vigorously. They seemed to be a little overstimulated.

"It's beautiful."

"I've never seen anything like it…"

On the carpet, Arisa and Lulu gazed at the fantastic display as if their souls were leaving their bodies.

Though I don't think they were doing it on purpose, the way they were both grabbing my legs was a little painful.

"It's pretty, isn't it? It's so very lovely. Truly…"

Watching the lights dance in the air, Mia murmured almost deliriously. That was more talking than she would usually do in a whole day.

After a dull *thud*, I turned to see that Liza had dropped her spear against the back of the sofa.

The sound brought her back to her senses, and she quickly picked it up again. For a moment, everyone else turned toward the source of the sound, but the tunnel quickly stole their attention again.

Liza ducked her head and apologized, then returned to her characteristic stiff pose; she was clearly embarrassed. Her usual gallant manner was admirable, but it was nice to see her cute side occasionally.

"Master, I lack the vocabulary to describe the scene. Recommend installation of language set two, I request."

What on earth is "language set two"?

"Don't worry about that, Nana. Just the word *beautiful* is enough."

"Understood, master. Beautiful."

Nana gave a little sigh of admiration as she gazed at the dancing lights.

It occurred to me that Miss Karina was uncharacteristically quiet. I glanced over and found her gaping in astonishment at the scenery around her, absolutely captivated.

Eventually, the ship reached the exit of the Dreamglow Cavern. Even the length of two miles didn't feel like nearly enough.

Maybe I can come back to see it again with Zena sometime.

◆

"Goooo, Princess!"

"Captain, now!"

Miss Ringrande attempted to take off as soon as the ship left the caverns, but the knights begged her to spar with them first.

She defeated her opponents with ease, then explained to each of them their weak points and how they could improve.

And now, she was in the middle of her final match, this one against Sir Ipasa.

The difference between the level-55 Miss Ringrande and the level-33 Sir Ipasa was clear, but since it was a practice match, it ended up being a pretty close fight. Miss Ringrande's flashy techniques were a sight to behold.

By comparison, Sir Ipasa's swordsmanship seemed plain. However, he was actually very steady and efficient with his movements, so he was surprisingly strong on defense. I wished Tama and Pochi could learn to use a sword like him.

Just watching seemed like a waste. I decided to try imitating him a little.

I fell back from the circle of spectators and copied Sir Ipasa's moves, pretending to hold a sword in my hands.

...Hmm.

Trying it out myself clarified the meaning behind things like his stance and center of gravity that I couldn't figure out just by sight. Pretending I was him myself, I fought an imaginary Miss Ringrande with my nonexistent sword.

> Skill Acquired: "Imitation: Martial Arts"

To my surprise, I acquired a handy-looking skill in the process, so I activated it right away.

With the help of the skill, I found I could copy Sir Ipasa's movements more precisely than before.

I wanted to keep experimenting, but I had no choice but to stop when the pair's fight ended. Too bad.

While I was lamenting the end of my practice time, the circle of people opened, and Miss Ringrande appeared. For some reason, she was advancing on me with an unsettling smile.

Please don't look at me like a lion that's just spotted its next prey.

"You seemed like you were up to something fun over here. Won't you be my next opponent?"

"This man was a savior in the defense of Muno City, you know. And he defeated a lesser hell demon in Gururian City without a scratch! Even you might be in trouble if you're not careful, Rin."

Sir Ipasa popped up behind Miss Ringrande, supplying extra information that only added fuel to the fire.

"Oh? Sounds like I can look forward to an exciting match, then." To my dismay, Miss Ringrande licked her lips.

I considered running away on the spot, but this was a rare opportunity to learn from her swordsmanship. I decided to try my hand without giving myself away.

"Master, your fairy sword."

"Thank you, Lulu." Lulu seemed anxious as she handed me my

sword. I whispered, "It's all right" and lightly patted her head to reassure her.

The crowd cheered as I poured magic power into the fairy sword. My main goal was to keep the sword intact, not to strengthen it.

I could invoke Spellblade if I wasn't careful, so I paid close attention to how much magic I used.

"...■■■■■ ■ ■■■■ *Light Defense Hikari Bougyo*."

When Sir Ipasa's incantation finished, white light enveloped my and Miss Ringrande's bodies.

Guess this is a defensive spell to ensure we don't hurt each other.

I thanked Sir Ipasa with a bow.

Then, my "Sense Danger" skill kicked in. Letting it guide my instincts, I flung myself to one side to escape.

"Ho-ho. You looked like your guard was down, but apparently not. Why not use that to lure in your opponent and then counterattack?"

As she advised me, Miss Ringrande drew her arm back from her thrust.

With a smile as my only reply, I focused on her eyes and footwork, trying to copy her fighting style.

It was clear to me now why the demon lord I fought claimed that my attacks "rang hollow."

Using one's gaze and footwork to tempt the opponent into attacking, then countering while their guard was down seemed to be an effective strategy.

To take full advantage of this opportunity, I tried various feints to see what she would fall for, drawing out new tactics with different actions so I could fully understand her fighting style.

Red sparks flew each time my fairy sword clashed with her magic blade.

The sparks made it harder to track her. On top of that, my radar and log windows obstructed my vision, making me even more distracted.

Just as I attempted to turn off the menu display, Miss Ringrande used my momentary lapse to thrust at my blind spot. I might've been able to defend against it, but I was concerned that I might break her sword if I did. I took the hit and awaited Sir Ipasa's refereeing verdict.

"Winner: Ringrande!"

A chant of "Ringrande! Ringrande!" echoed from all around.

"You're not half bad," Ringrande remarked, sheathing her sword as she approached.

A bit of sweat shone on her forehead, and her slightly ragged breath was rather sexy.

I couldn't help suspecting that Sara, her younger sister, might grow up to be a similarly sensual beauty.

"Oh, I still have a great deal to learn. Thank you for your guidance."

I shook Miss Ringrande's extended hand as I thanked her.

Just then, she gave a little tug, pulling me closer to whisper in my ear.

"Your black hair and eyes, your features—you're Japanese like Hayato, aren't you?"

So she really did know how to recognize a Japanese person.

"Yes, that's correct." I answered honestly, then elaborated. "My ancestors are Japanese. The name Satou, which originally belonged to a hero, has been passed down through generations. Though his name might not be listed in the hero records of the Saga Empire…"

This was the backstory I'd been brainstorming since I first learned that Miss Ringrande was a follower of the hero Hayato.

Nothing I said was a lie, either. My ancestors really were Japanese, and I'd used the character name throughout generations of games. And, of course, there was no Satou recorded in the history of the Saga Empire.

"I'm told the black-haired girl who travels with me is the great-granddaughter of a Saga Empire hero, as well." I waved at Lulu, who was looking in our direction with concern.

"…I see. I thought you might be a summoned hero, but it seems I was mistaken." Miss Ringrande nodded slowly, ostensibly convinced as she surveyed my group. "Oh? You have a pair of beastfolk children and even an elf—why, it's the sort of party a hero might have."

Ringrande smiled pleasantly at the girls.

From what Sara had said, I'd gotten the impression that there was some distance between the two sisters, but as far as I could tell, she was a kind and friendly girl. It'd be nice if they could get along, but I'd rather not stick my nose where it didn't belong. That only ever led to trouble.

After our match, Miss Ringrande joined us for a lip-smacking lunch of my homemade shrimp tempura. Then she took off for the old capital on her wooden Pegasus with a jaunty wave.

Banquet at the Duke's Castle

Satou here. It's always nice to share a delicious dinner with a big group of friends. Personally, I prefer to be involved in the eating rather than the cooking.

"Master, bridge-shaped monster sighted, I report. We should prepare for battle, I advise."

"Oh nooo!"

"Dangerous danger, sir!"

Alarmed by Nana's declaration, Pochi and Tama started to panic.

"Calm down, you three. That's just a special kind of bridge called a drawbridge."

A hundred-foot section in the middle of the vast area across the river was raised in the air so the ship's large sails wouldn't crash into it.

The river was over half a mile wide, so it didn't look like a very big gap, but in reality, it was similar in scale to the Tower Bridge in London. The architecture of this world was impressive, too.

As I gazed at the drawbridge, my AR display informed me that the moving section was actually a kind of golem. Our curiosity must have awakened the tour guide's instincts, because she came over with an explanation.

"It's said that this bridge was created by the gods a thousand years ago..."

She went on to inform us that the bridge pier included barrier posts so that aquatic monsters couldn't approach the outskirts of the old capital.

Downstream, I could see ten or more barrier posts erected in addition to the bridge.

As the guide talked us through the sights, our ship traversed a harbor docked with numerous boats, traveled up a tributary along the edge of the city, and entered a harbor for the exclusive use of nobles.

The whole city seemed to be in a heightened state of revelry, no doubt thanks to the martial arts tournament going on.

As the ship was being unloaded, I looked up the latest information about the city.

There were a lot of high-level warriors about, probably also because of the tournament. Miss Ringrande seemed to be the highest at level 55.

I didn't see any reincarnations like Arisa, people with the Hero title, demons, possessed individuals, or anything like that.

There were still about thirty members of the demon lord–worshipping cult Wings of Freedom left in the old capital: nine in the lower parts of town, fifteen lurking below the castle of a noble called Count Bobino, and four detained in the dungeon of the duke's castle.

The last two were inside the castle itself: the third son of the duke, who was also Sara's uncle, and his right-hand man.

Count Bobino himself wasn't a Wings of Freedom member, but evidently the count before him had been in its upper echelons.

Because the last thing I wanted was another demon lord or the like being summoned, I'd have to report these names and hiding places to the duke under my hero alias.

That being said, most of the members were killed during the demon lord incident I'd thwarted, so I doubted they'd be able to pull off another large-scale plan like that anytime soon. Still, better to be safe than sorry.

"Sir Satou! The carriage my brother sent for me has arrived! I'll be taking my leave now."

Tolma seemed to have recovered from before and called out to me as soon as I disembarked.

Amazingly, the carriage behind him didn't have a horse. Though it was shaped like a normal carriage, it was actually a magic item called a golem car.

A closer look at the wheels would reveal the artificial hands there to turn them. Now, that was a fantasy carriage if I'd ever seen one.

"Did you have plans for where to stay in the old capital? If not, you should stay at our house! With the martial arts tournament going on, I doubt there'll be many open rooms left."

"I appreciate the offer, but we're all right. We'll be staying in the house of the esteemed Count Worgoch."

Count Worgoch was the viceroy of Gururian City. After I defeated the lesser hell demon that attacked his territory, the count offered to let us stay in his parents' mansion here in the old capital.

We waved to the Tolma family as they entered their vehicle, then took our own carriage and horses to Count Worgoch's mansion.

Thanks to the tour guide's cart leading the way, we wouldn't get lost.

"This is quite a comfortable ride."

"Yes, it's amazing to be able to speak so easily in a moving carriage."

Miss Karina and her maid escort Pina marveled aloud.

"Well, of course! Our master enhanced it with love!"

"Mm. Love."

Arisa and Mia spoke proudly with me between them.

I was pretty sure it was because I enhanced it with technology not love, but I decided to keep that to myself.

Except for our driver Lulu, the other girls were riding in front of and behind the carriage.

Tama and Pochi were riding the runosaur, their ears and tails hidden by hooded cloaks, while Liza and Nana were armored and on horseback. Erina, another one of Miss Karina's maid escorts, was riding a horse next to the carriage.

After we left the Dreamglow Cavern, the temperature had risen to a springlike warmth. The hooded cloaks were probably pretty warm.

As soon as we passed through a large set of gates near the harbor, we were in the middle of the aristocratic quarter of the city. We were stopped just inside the gates, but the guide in front took care of things, so all I had to do was show the silver plate that was proof of my nobility.

The streets of the aristocratic district were paved with stone, and the buildings resembled concrete.

According to what I learned at the banquet in Muno Castle, this area was built with a special kind of Earth Magic called architectural magic. A noble called Count Hohen who lived there in the old capital was apparently a master of the art.

Most of the maids hurrying to and fro on the streets were in the same kind of outfits I'd seen in Muno Castle: plain dresses.

I'll have to popularize maid outfits in the old capital, too.

As I mused on these ambitions, the cart arrived in a quiet neighborhood where the wealthiest aristocrats lived.

On the map, I saw that other high-ranked nobles like marquises and counts lived near the duke's castle.

Each of the mansions was as big and spacious as Tokyo Dome. If anything, it might be more apt to describe them as "palaces."

Arisa quickly tired of viewing the houses and lobbed a question at Miss Karina instead.

"Are you staying with Count Worgoch, too, Lady Karina?"

"I-indeed. I was planning to stay at Orion's boarding house, but as it seems several other young men are staying there besides him…"

Right. It would probably be too much for someone as uncomfortable around men as Miss Karina to stay there.

I had planned to accompany her there so I could meet Orion myself, but from the sound of things, that might have to wait until another day.

Orion was Baron Muno's eldest son, five years younger than Karina at age fourteen. He was studying abroad in the old capital.

According to Viscount Nina from the Muno Barony, he had chosen this over the esteemed academy in the royal capital because the nobles there objected to his visit, owing to the barony's reputation as a "cursed territory."

Eventually, the carriages slowed their pace not far from the duke's castle.

Once we arrived at Count Worgoch's impressively mansion-like estate, the viceroy's parents—the previous duke and his wife—greeted us. Once we'd exchanged pleasantries, they directed us to the count's private house.

Here we parted ways with the guide, who went off to the duke's castle to deliver a report along with a letter requesting my introduction to him.

The viceroy's house was a large three-story mansion, complete with stables and separate lodging for the servants. It was even more impressive than the guesthouse where the beastfolk girls and I had stayed in Seiryuu City's local castle.

When we stopped our carriage in front of the entrance, twenty or so servants were waiting for us, led by a thin older gentleman with gray hair.

"It's a pleasure to meet you. I am Sebaf, the supervisor of this house." The man bowed politely, as did the staff behind him.

"Aw, man...," Arisa muttered behind me, and I privately agreed. If only his name were Sebastian, it would have been perfect.

"I am Satou Pendragon, a hereditary knight. Thank you for having us, Mr. Sebaf."

"Please, you may simply call me Sebaf."

I nodded at the mild-mannered man, then introduced Miss Karina as well.

After Sebaf guided us to a living room and we relaxed awhile, I asked him for a tour.

"This will be your room, Sir Satou."

This suite had several smaller chambers, including a bedroom, a study, and a dressing room. There was an extra-large bed in the center of the bedroom, big enough to fit our entire group.

There were private rooms for everyone else, too, but since several of my kids didn't like to sleep alone, I suspected that the rooms other than mine and the living room wouldn't see much use.

However, Miss Karina's party was staying on a different floor, so I didn't see an "accidentally got into the wrong bed" type of event in the cards.

After the tour, I let the kids explore the mansion freely.

"It's Tamaaa?"

"And Pochi, sir."

"What a beautiful mirror. The reflection is quite different from that of a copper mirror."

I heard voices from the dressing room next to the living room.

Beyond the open door, I found the beastfolk girls standing in front of the glass mirror inside, gleefully waving at their reflections.

As I flopped down on the bed to organize our plans for our old capital visit, Arisa and Lulu returned from touring the kitchen.

"We're back!"

"Master! The kitchen here is amazing!"

Flushed with excitement, Lulu told me all about the cooking-related magic tools there.

Sebaf gave us permission to use the space, so we could prepare our own meals as long as we let them know in advance. He added that meals were generally cooked in the kitchen of the main building; this one was mainly for preparing light fare and snacks.

"There was even an oven and a refrigerator!"

"Guess what! There was milk and fruit in the refrigerator. You should bake a cake or something!"

"Good idea. Maybe I'll try making a sponge cake."

At that, Arisa gave a shriek of delight.

Tama and Pochi had been peering out from the dressing room, but they came rushing over at the mention of food.

"Caaake?"

"Sir!"

Both of them joined Arisa in jumping for joy.

If it would make them that happy, the effort of baking a cake would be well worth it.

"Letter."

"We have received two messages from the elderly man, I report."

Mia and Nana had returned from their exploration of the grounds.

The letters in question were from the former Count Worgoch and Duke Ougoch himself. The count was inviting us to dinner that evening, while the duke was accepting the request for a meeting the tour guide had delivered on my behalf. According to the letter, he would meet with me tomorrow.

Both invitations were directed toward only Miss Karina and me, so I told the other girls to relax and enjoy the mansion.

Dinner that evening came in the form of many trays of small but extravagant delicacies to delight the palate, several of which seemed reproducible. I decided I should cook them for the others during our stay in the old capital.

The next day, Miss Karina and I went to Ougoch Castle for our audience with the duke.

Duke Ougoch was a sturdy old man with an abundance of gray hair, especially his beard. My first instinct was to classify him as a jolly old man, but the powerful glint in his eye said otherwise.

"Welcome, daughter of Leon. Ipasa has told me all. I have heard that you fought valiantly on the front lines in the defense of Muno City and even took on a demon in Gururian City. I commend your bravery."

Leon was Baron Muno's first name. *Oh yeah, I guess the duke and Baron Muno are related.*

Normally, this would be where Miss Karina gave a demure response, but instead she just acted nervous. *Her social anxiety must be kicking in again.*

I would've liked to back her up, but for all intents and purposes, I was just a tagalong lesser noble. It would be rude to speak without the duke's permission.

Instead, Raka spoke up for her, glowing blue on Miss Karina's chest.

"I accept your words with gratitude on behalf of my master."

"Oh-ho, a magic tool that understands human language? It's just like the invincible armor that my parents spoke of in legends."

"Indeed."

The response came from a slender consul who was standing nearby the duke.

His slitted eyes resembled a snake's as he observed us appraisingly, but because he didn't have nearly as powerful a presence as the duke, I paid him no mind.

"Grandfather!"

I heard the sound of familiar footsteps along with the cry, and sure enough, Miss Ringrande entered the room.

"Rin...this is official business. Leave us."

"Not likely! I heard that Miss Karina and Satou were here, so I came to rescue them before you put them through the wringer."

Ignoring the duke's complaints, Miss Ringrande looked around at the armored knights stiffly lining the audience room.

"Honestly. What sort of a welcome is this for the heroes who saved Gururian City? Besides, it doesn't seem to be intimidating the person you wanted it to."

Ringrande gazed right at me as she spoke.

Wait, he was trying to intimidate me?

Given their formal stance and perfectly polished armor, I had assumed that the knights were supposed to be some sort of honor guard giving us a warm welcome. Walking down the line of armored knights was honestly a pretty exciting experience. I felt more like thanking him than complaining, really.

"I can't get anything past you, Rin."

The duke raised a hand to signal the officer standing nearby, and the knights marched out of the room.

Other than us, the only people who stayed in the room were the council, the haughty-looking level-50 military officer, and a few knight guards, including Sir Ipasa.

As well as some maids and other servants, of course.

"Now, is that good enough?" the duke grumbled to Miss Ringrande.

Then he signaled to the consul, who took a rectangular tray from a nearby servant and carried it over to us.

"As thanks to Lady Karina Muno and Sir Satou Pendragon of Muno Barony for their heroic service in protecting Gururian City from demons, Duke Ougoch hereby bestows upon thee the Ougoch Duchy Sapphire Medal."

Laid on the tray were two heavy-looking medals and two velvet sachets chock-full of gold coins.

If I had to guess just by looking at the sachets, there were probably about a hundred coins in each. Miss Karina, unaccustomed to seeing this much gold, had sparkles in her eyes.

"So that's the Sapphire Medal...," Sir Ipasa murmured in admiration, which I was able to pick up on with my "Keen Hearing" skill. Given his reaction, this medal had to be a pretty rare and valuable object.

"Please accept these gifts. They are well deserved for your achievements." The duke had evidently mistaken Miss Karina's rapture at the sight of the gold coins as reluctance to accept them. "You may not have heard, but lesser hell demons like the one in Gururian City have been attacking in every city in the duchy."

I hadn't seen any signs of a demon attack in Zurute City, where we stayed on the way here, but that could have been because it was nighttime and our stay was short.

At the request of the duke, the consul elaborated. "Gururian and Sutoandell are the only two cities where damage was minimal. The rest may take years to fully recover."

Huh? The greater hell demon I fought beneath Seiryuu City was one thing, but there should be enough people of high enough level to defeat a lesser hell demon in pretty much any city...

Well, I suppose the damage might've been done before anyone strong enough to do that showed up. Now I understood why the viceroy of Gururian City gave a low-ranking noble like me such generous treatment.

But did that mean the short horns had shown up in other cities? I referred to the map and discovered three of them in a hidden safe in the duke's office.

The short horn was an item that could change humans into demons. I hadn't mentioned them to the viceroy in Gururian City out of fear of starting a panicked witch hunt, but maybe that didn't make much difference.

The amount of used short horns I had didn't match the number of demons I'd beaten. I concluded it wasn't an item they dropped every time.

As for the used short horn I'd gotten in Gururian City, giving it to the duke at this point might just have been stirring up a hornet's nest, so I decided to feign ignorance for now.

As I followed this somewhat negative train of thought, the meeting with the duke continued.

Once we'd accepted the medals and rewards, the next item on the agenda was the letter from Baron Muno.

"It's signed from Leon, but I don't doubt it was Nina who wrote it. She always did know how to make a troublesome request sound like an easy favor."

I was a little surprised to hear Duke Ougoch refer to Viscount Nina by her first name. Then I remembered that he was the one who recommended her as consul for Muno Barony.

Still, what could she have requested?

"Not only is she asking for a loan and extra supplies, she wants us to lend civil officials, military officers, and even engineers? Impossible."

Sounds like quite a wish list.

Knowing Viscount Nina, they probably only truly needed the supplies, while the manpower would be a nice bonus, added to make the rest sound more reasonable.

From the duke's expression, he understood this as well. Then his face suddenly turned mischievous.

"How about this? Sir Pendragon, if you become my vassal, I will grant all these requests. I can even make you an honorary baron if you wish."

Trading me for all those resources? I'd imagine any ordinary statesman would accept immediately.

As I was contemplating how to respond to his jest, someone else went ahead and overreacted.

"Y-you mustn't! S-Satou is a vassal of my father. E-even you cannot take him away, Your Grace!"

Lady Karina leaped in front of me, spreading her arms in a childish attempt to hide me from the duke.

Her bewitchingly large bust was enough to win me over under normal circumstances; such fierce protective instincts from her almost made me fall head over heels. Especially considering how nice her curves looked from this angle.

"Hmm. No luck, huh?"

"C-certainly not!" The duke smiled drolly at Karina's furious response. Apparently, she had managed to charm him into a good mood. "Very well. Daughter of Leon, worry not. I will not steal away this person you hold so dear."

"D-d-dear…?!"

At that, Miss Karina turned bright red and just about fainted dead away, and I quickly caught her.

"Your Grace, Lady Karina is quite purehearted, so I beg you not to tease her too much."

"I suppose. She is Leon's child, after all."

As the duke chuckled, Miss Ringrande whispered into his ear.

…*Huh?*

When she was finished, the duke called Sir Ipasa over, and they exchanged a few quiet words.

They had to be using some kind of magical counterintelligence-type device, because my "Keen Hearing" skill couldn't pick up their conversation.

"Hmm, a miraculous dish, you say…"

However, my "Lip Reading" skill did manage to catch the duke's words, since I could see his mouth.

"Sir Pendragon. Ipasa tells me you made a remarkable dish called 'consommé soup,' and Rin spoke highly of your 'tempura.' I am hosting a banquet tonight for the highest nobility of the city, and I would like you to cook these dishes for my guests and me. If they are satisfactory, I shall give Nina the aid she requested."

Tempura was one thing, but the pseudo-consommé soup that Ipasa described as a "miraculous dish" could be a bit of an issue.

"I would be remiss to refuse a request from Your Grace, but I must

confess that preparation of consommé soup is a lengthy process, so it would be impossible to make in time for tonight's dinner."

"Very well. Then we shall make do with the tempura for tonight. I shall host an evening party for the nobility three days from now; you may prepare the consommé soup for that occasion."

"It would be my pleasure."

A real aristocrat might resent being treated like a chef, but as an ordinary citizen who ascended to nobility out of nowhere, I was actually pretty proud to hear that someone would want to eat my cooking for such a reason.

A young maidservant led me to the kitchen of the duke's castle.

Several maids were looking after Miss Karina while she was unconscious. I told them to send her back to Count Worgoch's place on the carriage that brought us here once she was feeling better. Hopefully, she wouldn't come charging into the kitchen.

As we walked through a long corridor, I used my "Search Entire Map" to see what ingredients were in the castle.

They were a little short on a few things, so I expanded the search area to include all of the old capital and looked up shops that were selling what I needed. As always, the map skill was super convenient.

The room was three times the size of an average classroom and bustling with activity, like the galley of some luxurious hotel.

"I'll go and fetch the head chef. Please wait here, Sir Knight."

The maidservant who guided me here slipped in among the busy cooks, heading for the red-bearded head of the kitchen.

"The duke is ordering us to let some noble whippersnapper take care of the main dish?!"

"Ch-Chef, please! Not so loud! Do you want to be arrested for speaking out against the duke?!"

Sounded like the head chef and his assistant were arguing about me. Was I going to have to make a dish to prove myself worthy, like in a cooking manga? That could be fun.

"Hmph! This is an important banquet. I'm not letting some noble mess things up on a lark!" the head chef bellowed.

"I-it'll be all right!" The maidservant who guided me here piped up with an exaggerated gesture. "Sir Ipasa of the Lloyd family personally vouched for the taste!"

This made him pause. "…What? The Lloyd family…?"

As it turned out, Sir Ipasa came from a line of famous gourmets. This seemed to be enough to satisfy the chef.

"All right. Open up the back kitchen. We're not helping him, but he can use whatever ingredients he wants."

"But Chef, wouldn't it be better to have a few sous—"

"Fool! If this noble's main course fails and we have no backup dish, it'll bring shame on the duke! We'll make our main dish as planned. Surely this noble can call on his own vassals to help him."

The head chef and second-in-command wrapped up their conversation, and the latter approached me with the maidservant to apologetically sum up what I'd just heard with my "Keen Hearing" skill.

The head chef, clearly not a fan of taking orders, must have delegated the task of negotiating with "the noble" to his assistant.

"I understand. As long as there are ingredients and cookware I can use, I can supply my own assistants."

At that, the assistant head chef looked as if I'd taken a huge weight off his shoulders.

I guess middle management is tough in any world.

"Could I trouble you to deliver this letter for me?"

"Certainly, sir."

Before setting out to secure the ingredients, I asked the maidservant to contact Arisa and the others back at Count Worgoch's mansion. She gave a signal, and a maid standing in the hallway quickly took the letter and hurried away with it.

"Thank you for waiting. Allow me to bring you to the ingredient storehouse."

Along the way, the maidservant explained that her role was to be the aide of a lesser noblewoman, and that she therefore ranked higher than ordinary maids. According to her, it was a popular job in the duchy, thanks to the perks it provided of teaching courtly manners and helping in the search for potential marriage partners. And here I assumed it was just a synonym for *maid*.

I showed the authorization slip that the assistant head chef gave me to the guard in front of the ingredient storehouse, and he stepped aside to let us in.

"Whoa, this is impressive."

I wasn't just being polite; I was genuinely impressed. Even on earth, I had never seen so many ingredients and spices in one place. There were dozens of varieties of soy sauce alone, all with different flavors or places of origin.

The maidservant brought me a small dish for tasting, and I sampled them one by one, noting the differences with my menu's memo pad feature.

Unlike in the Shiga Kingdom, where I'd seen only ordinary tallow, there were several varieties of vegetable oil here.

We went through the room-temperature, refrigerated, and finally frozen storage, collecting the ingredients one by one.

They even had the likes of green beans, sweet potatoes, and lotus root, none of which I had seen on my journey so far. These seemed to be available in the marketplace of the old capital, too, so I'd have to stock up during our stay.

Wait, is that tofu? If I made tofu hamburg steaks, even Mia should be able to eat them.

My mind was full of possibilities as I finished collecting the necessary ingredients and spices. As I started to carry them back toward the kitchen, the maidservant quickly summoned someone to take them for me.

"You must let the help take care of manual labor like that," she scolded me lightly.

…I'm sorry. I'm still new to all this nobility stuff.

Because I'd never heard of some of these ingredients, I decided to taste the different oils while I was preparing to cook.

The kitchen was chock-full of incredibly useful magic cooking tools. Once I realized the stove was a bit wonky, I did a little magic plumbing to clear the channels, like I always did.

If they were letting me use all of this handy equipment, it was the least I could do.

"Mm, this lotus root tempura is wonderfully delicious."

"The sweet potato is very good, too… I think I liked the pumpkin better, though."

"Wouldn't white fish make delicious tempura, too?"

When I had the maidservant do some taste testing for me, I soon noticed a gaggle of maids and pageboys watching enviously. I let them know they could help, too, as long as they didn't get in the way of my work.

Many of them turned out to have surprisingly discriminating palates, so this ended up being a good call.

Eggplant tempura, for instance, was surprisingly poorly received, while they loved the thinly sliced carrot tempura for some reason.

But eggplant tempura is so good…

"Master! We brought the goods!"

"Satou."

"Sorry for taking so long, master."

At the chorus of lively voices, I turned to see Arisa, Mia, and Lulu entering the kitchen.

"Pochi and Tama gathered the green *shiso*."

"Pickled ginger."

"I couldn't find the 'pike conger' eel you requested, so Arisa told us to buy garden eel, fanged eel, and sweet eel."

"Thanks, that's a huge help."

After thanking them, I sorted through the ingredients they brought.

The pickled ginger was a light pink, not the red kind I was expecting. *They must not color it with red* shiso *here.*

I decided to make it into tempura instead of using it as a garnish. I'd only ever seen pickled ginger tempura in Kansai tempura shops, but I found it surprisingly addictive. Maybe it'd be a big hit in this world.

"Lulu, could you help me with prep?"

"Of course!"

"Arisa and Mia, you two charge the magic tools."

"Okeydoke."

"Mm."

Everyone went into action.

This time, we chose nine types of tempura: shiitake-like mushrooms, pumpkin, carrots, green beans, shrimp, green *shiso*, pickled ginger, lotus root, and fanged eel, which was closest in taste to conger eel.

I wanted to add eggplants and sweet potatoes, too, but since they weren't very well received in the taste tests, I decided to hold off this time.

For the base of the special tempura sauce, I used Gururian-made mirin and a light soy sauce from a famous artisan in the royal capital. To that, I added a pinch of high-quality Sutoandell white sugar and a few drops of pure Shigan sake from the old capital. Including *dashi*, too, seemed to detract from the flavor of the sauce, so I used only a small amount. The result was a light but agreeable flavor.

Next, I fried the tempura with a special mixture of a few different kinds of vegetable oil, with sesame oil from Zetts County as the base.

Once I'd cooked up all the delicious-looking tempura, I arranged it on a tray to drain the excess oil.

Then it was Doctor Mia's turn.

"Mia, you're up."

"Mm… ■■■ ■ ■■ ■■■ *Steam Loop: Tempura Jouki Junkan: Tempura.*"

When Mia chanted the spell, the extra oil was removed from the tempura coating.

I'd designed this cooking spell in my spare time back on the ship specifically for this purpose, making the tempura both healthier and crunchier to boot. Taking out too much oil resulted in a loss of flavor, so it took a long time to find the perfect balance for maximum crispiness.

"Thank you, Mia. It's going to be two hundred percent more delicious now."

"Reward?"

Mia offered her head expectantly, and I stuck my hand under her hood to pat her on top of her silky hair, but that made Arisa and Lulu envious. I'd have to do the same for them later.

"Sa… Sir Pendragon! I've come to help you!"

Suddenly, Miss Karina came charging into the kitchen. Thanks to inertia, it took her mystical breasts a moment to come to a halt after the rest of her stopped moving. As always, it was a sight to behold.

"Guilty."

"Grr, damn those supernatural boobs…"

I bonked Mia and Arisa gently on the head to reprove them before speaking to Miss Karina.

"Are you sure you're feeling all right?"

"But of course! I'm perfectly healthy! Now, let us combine our powers for the greater good of all people!"

Miss Karina's eyes sparkled, and her fists were clenched with eagerness, but alas, the cooking was already done.

"I will do whatever it takes! Anything at all!"

At those promising words, I was tempted to shift my gaze back toward her bosom, but I managed to control myself.

"Sorry, but—"

"In that case, I have an important task that only you can carry out, Lady Karina."

Before Arisa could say we were already finished, I clamped a hand over her mouth. I didn't want to let Karina's enthusiasm go to waste.

The young noble awaited my assignment rather nervously.

"I'd like you to sample this tempura and tell me if there's anything wrong with the texture or flavor, please."

"Understood. I'd be happy to assist!"

Relieved, Miss Karina let out the breath she'd been holding and brought the shrimp to her mouth with an intense expression. Her glistening lips parted, and her perfect white teeth bit tentatively into the shrimp tempura.

With each movement of her jaw, her serious countenance softened into a blissful smile.

"How is it?"

"It passes with flying colors, Satou! Without question, the most delicious shrimp tempura I've ever eaten in my life!"

Miss Karina beamed as she responded. She didn't even seem to realize that she'd called me by my name for once.

Her reaction indicated success, and the waiters and waitresses gathered around. Clearly my turn was just about up.

I plated the tempura on gorgeously colored dishes and entrusted them to the waitstaff. Normally, I would've liked to grate some daikon on top, but I refrained thanks to a notion among the people of the old capital that daikon was unlucky. From here, all I could do was entrust my fate to the heavens (and the tastes of the nobles) and start cleaning up.

After a while, my "Keen Hearing" skill alerted me to delighted cries from the upper-class nobles, so by all appearances, I'd succeeded.

Most of all, I was just happy they appreciated my cooking.

The waitstaff streamed back into the kitchen with brilliant smiles.

"Sir Knight! You're a huge hit! The guests all send their highest compliments!"

They were as happy for me as if I were one of them, which improved my mood further.

I thanked the waitstaff for letting me know and apologized to the head chef for causing a fuss in his kitchen.

Of course, I had to thank my kids for their hard work, too.

"Good work, everyone."

"Whew, I'm staaarving!"

"Mm, hungry."

"Hee-hee. We did work quite a bit."

I thought I'd made plenty of extra tempura for them to "taste test," but evidently it wasn't enough.

Scanning the kitchen, I saw whole piles of vegetable scraps.

"Is it all right if I use some of these vegetables?"

"Certainly."

After checking with one of the chefs, who had just come in to make rice, I gathered some of the vegetables.

"What are you going to make?" Arisa curiously inquired.

"Oh, nothing big."

It really wasn't anything special, so I tried not to get her expectations too high.

I diced onions and carrots, panfried them lightly, mixed them with some cut greens, rolled them in the tempura batter, and tossed them into the oil.

"Oh! Vegetable fritters!"

"That's right. Arisa, could you take these bowls and see if you can get some rice for us?"

"Okeydoke! Mia, help me carry them?"

"Mm."

Arisa followed the smell of fresh rice over to the young chef, who agreed to share some with us.

I cut each fritter into quarters and put them on the piping hot rice, then topped them with the tempura sauce, which I'd boiled to make it a little thicker. With that, the *kakiage don* was complete.

"Mm, tasty!"

"Yum."

"It's so crispy and hot… It's wonderful."

"Delicious! I think I might enjoy this even more than ordinary tempura."

The four girls dug into their bowls with gusto. My three were using chopsticks, but Miss Karina used a fork and spoon.

After watching them fondly for a moment, I put together an extra bowl.

"Here you are." I handed it to the maidservant.

"For me? Are you sure?"

"Absolutely. You've been a great help today, so please allow me to thank you with this."

At first, I'd figured such a meal might be too inelegant for someone who worked closely with nobility, but I could tell she wanted to try it and decided to offer.

Next, I made two more bowls for the head chef and his assistant.

I'd need to use this kitchen again for the evening party three days from now. A little late-night snack might help my standing with them a little.

"Thank you for letting me use your kitchen today."

"Bah, I should never have doubted you, you—"

"I'm terribly sorry if we seemed mistrustful of your abilities, Sir Knight. His Grace the duke has sent along his compliments as well."

The assistant head chef was quick to interrupt the head chef before he could be too impolite.

At the same time, he offered up a tray, which held a letter praising the tempura and inviting me to join the dinner guests for a light gathering in the salon after the meal.

"Incidentally, what is that you have there?"

"Oh, this is a simple dish called vegetable fritters. It isn't made with such high-quality ingredients as what we put together for the nobility, but you are more than welcome to it if you like."

"Hey, it looks damn tasty! Thanks, bud."

The two chefs accepted the bowls I offered them and ate with apparent enjoyment.

The envy of the other chefs around us was plain to see. I felt bad, but I didn't have enough batter left for everyone.

"Sir Pendragon! Your tempura is a work of art! That crispy coating on the crunchy shrimp was exquisite!"

"No, no, Marquis Lloyd. The pickled ginger tempura reigned supreme. Nothing else could possibly compete."

"I beg to differ, Count Hohen. Shrimp is the ultimate tempura. That vivid taste and texture were so unlike boiled or roasted shrimp..."

The famed gourmets Marquis Lloyd and Count Hohen were extolling the virtues of tempura to me with such fervor that spit threatened to fly from their mouths.

They had caught me the second I entered the salon, before I even had a chance to greet the duke.

Miss Karina, who never fared well in social situations, had excused herself on the grounds of feeling poorly and returned to the count's mansion with the others.

"Marquis Lloyd, Count Hohen, I am in complete agreement that tempura is delicious, but please give Sir Pendragon some space. At the very least, he ought to be allowed to greet the duke first."

"As you wish, Sir Worgoch."

"Indeed, you make a fair point. Sir Pendragon, let us discuss tempura later."

The former Count Worgoch was the eldest man present. Thanks to his intervention, I was able to go and say hello to the duke.

I felt the eyes of the upper crust following me as I approached.

The nobles present were the pillars of the Ougoch Duchy, all ranked viscount or higher—mostly the heads or former heads of major families. The exact breakdown was one marquis, three counts, and eight viscounts.

Miss Ringrande's father, the next duke, and her younger brother, next in line after her father, were off in Eluette Marquisate. According to Miss Ringrande herself, they would be returning to the old capital within the next few days.

Even Tolma was present, greeting me with a friendly wave and a casual compliment to my cooking. His elder brother, Viscount Siemmen, didn't seem to be around; Tolma was probably here in his brother's place.

At any rate, as a transplant from a different world, I was still having a hard time adjusting to all of these ranks besides "king."

An important aspect of the noble rankings here was the corresponding permission level to use City Cores, so all the people here besides Duke Ougoch, the lord, were probably vassals who had been granted some degree of that power.

And yet only a king could grant any title higher than baronet. How confusing.

I wish my "Shigan Language" skill had translated lord *as* junior king *and* king *as* super king *or something.*

Shaking off these absentminded notions, I kneeled in front of Duke Ougoch to thank him for his invitation.

"…Sir Pendragon. Your cooking was truly delicious, and—"

"Wasn't it?"

With a powerful glare, the duke silenced Miss Ringrande, who was sitting beside him.

"—I am sure the meal at the evening party will be just as pleasing. I shall put out a public call for capable men to send to Muno Barony; in the event that no one comes forward, only then shall I order some to do so."

"Are you certain? I haven't yet completed my end of the bargain."

"I insist. Think of it as compensation for tonight's dinner. If you can impress the nobles at the evening party just as much, then I will permit you to solicit donations and investments for the barony as well."

Wow, this was turning into a bigger deal than I bargained for.

I found it hard to believe that simple tempura was enough to warrant all that, but maybe it was the result of my maxed-out "Cooking" skill.

"Grandfather, those are rewards for Baron Muno, aren't they? Shouldn't you reward Satou himself, too?"

"Hmm, a fair point… What might you desire?"

Thanks to Miss Ringrande, the duke was planning to reward me even further, but I was starting to think this was a little much for some tempura.

"Seeing as you have generously agreed to assist the barony already, I couldn't possibly accept any further reward."

"Oh really? Restraint's not a virtue, you know! You should be accepting it proudly after the excellent dinner you gave us." Miss Ringrande was talking to me like a teacher scolding a naughty student, but once she noticed my discomfort, she grinned and made a joke to set me at ease.

"How about this? Would you like to become the exclusive chef of the hero Hayato?"

Yeah, no thanks. I love eating delicious food and all, but I honestly prefer when someone else cooks it for me. I should probably come up with a request before they give any more weird suggestions.

"Come now, ask whatever you'd like. Do you want Rin as your bride, perhaps?"

"Hey! Grandfather, you know I'm a follower of the hero, so I have no intention of marrying until the demon lord is dealt with!"

...Huh? Do they not know the demon lord is gone from the head priestess of Tenion Temple yet? Maybe I should sneak into the temple later and ask her what the deal is.

"I have no such desires that would be so far above my station. Though, if it's at all possible, receiving permission to purchase scrolls and spell books in the duchy would be a most unexpected joy."

"Hmm. You are truly free of greed, to request not the items themselves but simply permission to purchase them. Very well, I shall grant it."

The generous duke called over a man in a butler's uniform to write up a permit.

Tolma had already agreed to introduce me to Viscount Siemmen, but with the duke's permission, I should be able to get even more scrolls.

"If you ever decide to quit being Leon's vassal, you ought to come here instead. I would hire you as a chef anytime," the duke commented.

"Wait a minute, Your Grace! Sir Pendragon should be the head chef for the Lloyd family instead. He would be wasted as a mere sous chef!" Marquis Lloyd protested.

"It is most unbecoming to attempt to lure away a vassal of Baron Muno, Marquis Lloyd," said Count Hohen. I appreciated his attempts to discourage them from trying to hire me as a chef, but unfortunately, he didn't stop there. "Incidentally, Sir Pendragon, would you happen to be a married man?"

"No, I feel I'm too young for that, and I have no wish to settle down anytime soon."

"Why, then you should take one of my daughters or granddaughters who's around your age. You could become a member of my family, if you—"

"Count Hohen! Are you trying to make our knight into your son-in-law?!"

As it turned out, there were an awful lot of greedy nobles in this duchy.

I thought he was joking at first, but it turned out Count Hohen had upward of forty children and grandchildren combined, at least seven of who were unmarried young women, so maybe not.

Marquis Lloyd and Count Hohen seemed to be good friends; they spent some time jousting over me.

Eventually, Miss Ringrande rescued me. Then I was able to speak to other people as well.

Because a few of them had workshops and studios in the old capital or rare spell books that might interest me, I was certainly amenable to making friends with them.

In particular, it seemed many advanced spell books were hidden away in nobles' collections, so permission to purchase them wouldn't help me there.

I ran a map search on the old capital, but I didn't find any textbooks for advanced kinds of magic in any of the shops.

"Sir Satou, it turns out my brother is in Labyrinth City on scroll workshop–related business at the moment. I'm told he'll return soon by way of the royal capital. Would you mind waiting until then for the scrolls? I don't believe it should be longer than a trimoon, at the very latest."

"Certainly. We plan to stay in the old capital for a while, so that's not a problem at all."

"Whew, I'm glad to hear you say that."

My smile seemed to ease Tolma's apologetic mood.

A trimoon was only ten days; that wouldn't be an issue. I was planning to find out if I could have scrolls made of my original spells. If it turned out to be a lengthy process, I could always come back on my own with "Skyrunning" to pick them up.

"Sorry to come so late at night, Head Priestess."

"Why, if it isn't Mr. Nanashi. You do tend to show up unexpectedly, don't you?"

After I returned from the duke's castle, I donned my disguise as Nanashi the Hero and paid a visit to the head priestess's room at Tenion Temple, in the nobles' quarter.

This was after confirming on the map that she hadn't gone to sleep yet, of course.

She didn't have any abnormal status conditions, but thanks to the mysterious atmosphere of her room, she had an unearthly quality that made you wonder if she wouldn't vanish if you looked away for a second.

"I had a little question for you."

"Oh my, I wonder what that could be? But first, I have something to tell you myself, as it happens. Do you mind?"

"That's fine. What is it?"

I was trying to make Nanashi sound as different from Satou as possible, but I still felt awful speaking so rudely to an older woman like the head priestess. If I wasn't careful, I could easily slip into a more polite attitude.

The head priestess rose slowly from a seat that resembled a rocking chair.

"I have received an Oracle message from Goddess Tenion regarding the defeat of the demon lord. Nanashi the Hero, allow me to offer the temple's thanks in her stead," the priestess said solemnly. Then she broke into a small smile. "Thank you for protecting my beloved old capital, Mr. Nanashi." With a little less gravitas, she added, "Worry not. Priestess Sara is not yet able to leave her bed, but the other two Oracle priestesses have returned to their normal lives."

According to the map, I saw that Sara's status now read **Weakened: Mild**. It had been only **Weakened** that morning, so she must be recovering steadily.

I decided to go visit her as Satou once that status condition was gone entirely.

"I'm glad to hear it. But would you mind if I inquired about something?"

"Oh, certainly. My apologies for going on so. Ask whatever you like."

Maybe it was just my imagination, but the head priestess looked pale. "Standing for so long could bode ill for your health. Please go ahead and sit."

The priestess smiled faintly and returned to her seat.

"I haven't heard anything in the old capital about the demon lord being defeated. Has it not been officially announced?"

"Indeed... I did bring a report to His Grace the duke, but he preferred to wait until the other temples received Oracle messages about it before making an announcement."

The head priestess appeared troubled.

"And the other temples have not received these messages yet?"

"Even with the 'Oracle' skill, the ceremony itself can take several days, depending on the temple."

So you can't just ask the gods questions whenever you want, huh?

"Here at the Tenion Temple, we have this sanctuary, so it's easier to prepare the ritual here than at other temples."

"Oh really? That sounds convenient."

She chuckled. "It is the work of Our Lady Tenion, after all. This sanctuary is the only reason I'm able to move about normally, even so close to the end of my life. Outside of it, I can hardly even sit up without assistance."

So that was what Sara meant when she said back in Muno Barony that the holy woman couldn't leave the sanctuary.

Well, now I had my answers as to why the information hadn't been made public. It was probably time to wrap things up.

"...I understand. Thanks."

"Oh? Leaving so soon? I was hoping we could chat a little longer."

I stood up to leave, but the head priestess stopped me.

All I had left to do for the evening was anonymously report the whereabouts of the Wings of Freedom members to the duke, so I could spare a little more time.

Now that the Treasure of Resurrection had used up its magic power bringing Sara back to life, I offered to restore its charge while we talked. We passed the time with tea and pastries I brought out from Storage, exchanging idle conversation and discussing myths.

Eventually, the priestess's AR display showed her status as **Fatigue: Mild**. I decided to take my leave.

"It seems I've overstayed a little."

I returned the refilled Treasure of Resurrection to the priestess and stowed the Holy Sword I was using as a battery in my Item Box.

"Thank you, Mr. Nanashi. Though I hope that we never have need of this again."

"As do I."

Nodding to the head priestess as she put away the artifact, I left the Tenion Temple.

◆

Hidden by the dark of the night, I used "Skyrunning" and various stealth skills to slip into the duke's bedroom.

As I did so, I felt a slight sense of resistance.

Upon closer inspection, an AR display appeared reading **Ougoch Castle Barrier Wall**. Was this a barrier created by the City Core?

"You got through the castle barrier…? Who are you?"

The duke's status had read **Sleeping** just moments ago; the City Core must have alerted him somehow.

"A hero," I answered shortly as he sat up.

Now that the perceptive duke had met Satou several times, I took care to keep the gender of my voice ambiguous and to speak only in short phrases.

"A hero, you say? And with violet hair… Are you Nanashi the Hero?"

I nodded briefly to avoid letting the conversation go too far, then tossed him a packet of papers tied with a string.

"…What's this?" the duke asked, eyeing them doubtfully.

"Read," I answered simply, taking inspiration from Professor Mia.

"The hiding places of the demon lord cult… Where did you get all this information?"

The map included not only the hideout in the old capital but all the other locations in the duchy. A group like that was sure to make a comeback if they weren't all rounded up at once.

"In Count Bobino's basement of all places, right under our noses… That foolish son of mine…"

The duke seemed stunned that some of his family and chief vassals were included on the list.

"Please allow me to take care of this personally, Sir Nanashi the Hero. I swear on the name of Duke Ougoch that it will be dealt with appropriately."

I had no trouble believing that.

"I will dispatch a band of knights to round up the members in Count Bobino's estate tomorrow. As for the ones in the downtown area, I shall send not knights but individuals who can arrest them quietly."

I tilted my head Mia-style, and the duke explained.

"Just to be certain, we will need assurance that this information is true. We will capture them first, then have vassals use Yamato stones or the Eye of Judgment to ascertain their guilt."

Right, I forgot those handy tools and gifts existed.

If anything, I thought it would be easier to use the City Core to find them, but they probably had a good reason for not doing it that way.

Just to be safe, I pointed out my cautions in the documents regarding the capture of Wings of Freedom members. Namely, to capture them all at once and to be wary of the "short horn" item that turned people into demons. I had written that terrorists could become desperate when chased down, so it was best to deal with them all at once.

No individuals possessing short horns had showed up on my map search, but some of them had "Item Box" skills, Magic Bags, or the like. I couldn't search inside those except for marked objects; I highlighted the names of those individuals on the list.

There weren't any particularly strong ones lurking about, so even if one of them did have a short horn, their demon form would probably be easy enough to defeat. There were at least three knights in the city who were above level 50, after all.

I waited a few seconds in thought before I told the duke, "All yours."

This short-spoken version of Nanashi would probably be harder to identify, but it sure made meetings difficult.

It'd probably be wise to come up with a better dummy personality whose way of speaking and acting would be difficult to connect with me. Maybe Arisa would have some ideas.

The Martial Arts Tournament

Satou here. Rather than kendo or judo, the phrase martial arts tournament *makes me think of a* shonen *battle manga. My only real-life martial arts experience is the judo they made us do in gym class.*

"Good morning."

I yawned as I entered the room where the others were all waiting.

"Good morning, master. I'll go ask Mr. Sebaf to prepare breakfast."

Lulu's smile healed my soul as she cheerfully hurried down the hallway.

"Morning. Don't you look tired."

"Mrrr. Sleepy?"

Arisa and Mia greeted me with noticeable irritation.

"Yeah. I found an out-of-the-way spot to make some arrows, since we were running low after the last battle."

"Huh? So you didn't go off to some establishment with a bunch of pretty ladies?"

"Of course not."

I should've known that was what they suspected.

After my meeting with the duke the night before, I had gone into the labyrinth ruins underneath the old capital to make new Holy Arrows, Holy Short Spears, and so on. I also wanted to make more blue in case we ever ran into another demon lord–class opponent.

However, ten Holy Arrows, two Holy Short Spears, and just one vial of blue were enough to exhaust my supply of dragon powder from the Seiryuu City labyrinth.

I didn't really want to mess around with the corpses in the Valley of

Dragons, so I would have to get my hands on some dragon scales or I might end up in trouble somewhere down the road.

"Sorry for being so suspicious."

"Sorry."

"It's all right. Anyway, where did Liza and the others go?"

I tapped their heads lightly, then asked a random question to hide my feelings of guilt. Tolma had already agreed to show me the night-life of the old capital during our stay. If I didn't let my libido run loose once in a while, I was afraid I might cross a dangerous line with someone like Nana or Miss Karina.

For the time being, my "Poker Face" skill kept those emotions hidden.

Lulu returned, and as we went to the dining room, Miss Karina, her maids, and the vanguard group came in through the door that led to the courtyard.

They'd worked up quite a sweat training outside all morning.

After enjoying a fancy hotel-like breakfast made for us by the chefs of the Worgoch estate, we were sipping cups of blue-green tea when the butler Mr. Sebaf entered.

"Sir Knight, a letter has arrived for you. And you as well, my lady."

I accepted the letter and took a look at the seal.

Mine was from Tolma, while Miss Karina's letter was from her younger brother, Orion.

Tolma's letter said that his brother, Viscount Siemmen, would be returning the next morning. That was much earlier than what he'd said in the salon. He listed times when the viscount would be available to meet, so I wrote back requesting the soonest slot, the next afternoon at two chimes.

"Oh, that Orion!" Miss Karina bristled as she finished reading her letter.

"What's the matter?"

"Why, if he thinks seeing some martial arts tournament is more important than a visit from his far-off sister...!"

She trailed off, too indignant to continue. Large tears began pooling on her eyelashes.

I tried to offer Miss Karina a handkerchief, but I was speedily intercepted by the iron-wall duo.

"Nana."

"Give Lady Karina a hug."

"Tactical commands accepted, I report."

Nana promptly hugged Miss Karina to her chest, mechanically repeating, "There, there," as if comforting a child.

Miss Karina, socially clumsy as always, was too stunned by Nana's sudden action to do anything but sit and accept it.

"It's all right, Lady Karina. At that age, a fourteen-year-old boy is bound to find affection from his family embarrassing. It might be better to keep a little distance—otherwise he's just going to get mad."

Arisa's advice sounded strange coming from someone who looked so young. It was probably based on experience from her previous life.

Once Miss Karina started to calm down, I asked Sebaf what sightseeing spots he recommended in an effort to ease the awkwardness.

"At this time of year, I suggest the stadium where the second round of preliminaries for the martial arts tournament is held. The master of the house says you are welcome to use his family's premium seats."

At the phrase *martial arts tournament*, the beastfolk girls' eyes sparkled.

Even Liza, usually so composed, was clearly excited; her tail was whacking the back of her chair.

"Aside from that, the museum is currently holding an exhibition about the ancestral king Yamato. Cyriltoa the Songstress has an extraordinary voice that will soothe your soul, and she will perform at the concert hall. If you don't mind mingling with commoners, perhaps you would enjoy perusing the unusual wares at the grand market in the harbor ward."

All of these sounded like couldn't-miss attractions during our stay.

But for now, we'll start with…

"Want to go see the tournament today?"

It went without saying that my suggestion was met with unanimous agreement.

Surprisingly, even Miss Karina voted yes. I guess her brother's rudeness didn't stop her from being interested in the tournament herself. I asked Sebaf to arrange for a carriage and our seats at the stadium, and we returned to our rooms to change clothes for the outing.

◆

"These seats are pretty good," I commented to Miss Karina as I settled into the soft sofa.

The other kids had gone to buy snacks at the nearby stands, so the only ones left in the luxury seats were Miss Karina, her maid Pina, and myself.

The seats were open to the stadium grounds but walled in on the other three sides, with refined decor in muted hues. Given that it was for the use of nobles only, it was no surprise that the furniture was proportionately luxurious.

Miss Karina was looking out at the stadium from the balcony. She turned to me and responded.

"I-indeed. The lower seats are terribly crowded."

Just as she said, the general seating was jam-packed.

The areas closest to the grounds were especially full of people, to the point where the onlookers seemed liable to spill onto the field.

The area where the combatants would be fighting was an elliptical shape, around the same size as an average running track. The pamphlets in the premium seats explained that the stadium was ordinarily used for jousting.

"Lady Karina, please be careful not to lean over the balcony too far."

The drop from our seats to the general seating was about ten feet, so Karina's maid Pina looked worried.

Just then, the door slammed open, and Mia and Nana returned from their shopping.

"Satou, 'aah.'"

Mia put one of the candies she held in both hands into my open mouth.

…Syrup candy.

Taking the stick from Mia's hand, I saw that this confection was colorless, unlike the light-brown malt syrup candy I'd eaten with Zena in Seiryuu City. It was probably a starch syrup made from rice and sugar.

"Master, I have taken custody of these apple larvae, I report."

Nana had bought a basket of candy-size apples called "dwarf apples."

"Could I have one?"

"Affirmative."

Nana held out the basket, and I brought one of the fresh dwarf apples to my lips.

As soon as I bit into it, juice flowed into my mouth, along with the tart sweetness characteristic of the fruit. A moment later, the scent of apples filled my nose.

"Very tasty."

"Yes, master."

It did seem a little lacking in sweetness, but that was probably because I ate the syrup candy right before it.

"Mrrr?"

Mia, who was also tasting the apple right after the candy, furrowed her brow in a similar reaction.

Next, Lulu came back with Pochi and Tama in tow.

"Octopus skewerrrs!"

"And squid skewers, sir."

An appealing smell wafted over me from the large bag the two beastfolk girls were carrying.

"I thought most people didn't eat octopus and squid here?" I asked, vaguely remembering something I'd heard.

"Really?" Lulu answered. "There were commoners buying them at the stands."

I guess it's mostly nobles and people from other territories who don't like them.

As she spoke, Lulu set up the folding table that was in the corner of the luxury box and expertly arranged the skewers on top.

"We're baaack!"

"Master, we have returned."

Last to arrive were Arisa, Liza, and Karina's maid Erina.

"Man, that was rough," Arisa grumbled. "The chicken and meat skewer stands were really crowded."

"Right? Not to mention all the fistfights and pickpockets about." Erina nodded.

With help from Lulu, Liza added the chicken and various kinds of meat skewers to the table.

Aside from the meat, there was also a modest stack of baguette-shaped bread loaves decorating one end of the table.

"Look, look! I got boiled edamame and peanuts for Mia, too!"

"Arisa. Thanks."

"Huh, that looks pretty good."

Snacking on the edamame and peanuts made me crave a nice cold beer.

While we were sampling the various snacks, the time came for the matches to begin.

The copper gong rang out, and an announcer's voice echoed through the stadium.

"Match one: Magic Swordsman Tan, the Bloodiron Explorer, versus Zi-Gain Master Kajiro, the Samurai of the Saga Empire."

Most of the group turned to watch the two combatants enter the grounds, but Arisa and Mia seemed more interested in something else.

"That announcer sounded a little muffled. Are they using Wind Magic with a speaking tube, perhaps?"

"Mm. Those."

Mia pointed to several huge tubes sprouting up among the audience seats.

According to the AR display, they were magic tools called **wind speaker towers**. Arisa's guess was right, but she'd already moved on.

"Ooh, Tan might be a weird name, but he sure is handsome. And this Kajiro fellow is wild and unshaven—like a real warrior!"

Peering through one of the luxury box's longscopes, Arisa relayed some utterly useless information.

I used my "Telescopic Sight" skill to take a look at the competitors myself.

The tall and muscular Kajiro was shouldering a longsword that was more than six feet long, waiting quietly for the match to begin. He was barely wearing any armor, so maybe his style was "victory to whoever makes the first move." Befitting his introduction as a samurai, the man was wearing a kimono and *hakama*. Since he was blond with Italian facial features, it called to mind a foreign Japanophile. As a native of the Saga Empire, famous for its hero summoning, he was probably influenced by Japanese culture in his upbringing.

Meanwhile, Tan was equipped with a one-handed mithril sword and a buckler and clad in glossy armor made from the shell of some kind of beetle monster.

Tan was level 42, while Kajiro was level 39.

Both exceptionally high levels, which was probably to be expected in the semifinals—too high, in fact. Both were in the top five of the tournament competitors.

So they're matched up so they can crush each another before reaching the finals... No, maybe that was overthinking it.

"Hmm, I can't see their stats from this distance." Arisa grumbled discontentedly, then offered her predictions aloud. "From what I hear, Tan's probably going to win, since he can use magic."

"Arisa, that is quite premature. In addition to Sir Kajiro's large frame, one must not underestimate the range and power of that enormous longsword. No doubt the match will be decided by whether Sir Tan is able to use magic before he is struck down."

Ooh, that's an unusual amount of talking for Liza.

Tan seemed to have a few levels on his side, but Kajiro was more of a pure fighter, so he could probably make up the difference easily in a swordfight.

"Whoa, tacky."

"Yes, his garments rather lack refinement."

The subject of Arisa's and Liza's appraisal was the referee, who'd just walked into the arena in brightly colored clothes, holding large red and white flags as well as a horn.

The combatants entered two circles outlined on the ground, about a hundred feet apart.

This appeared to be the starting position. At this distance, a magic user probably wouldn't be able to finish a lengthy chant before their opponent attacked.

The referee blew a horn and shouted that the match had begun.

"The warrior man charged, sir!"

Before the sound of the horn had faded, Kajiro sprang forward. His white blade flashed down toward Tan.

"...██ *Instant Shield Hirameki Tate!*"

A defensive barrier spread from Tan's shield like a ripple of light, repelling the longsword's attack. It reminded me of the reactive armor you'd see on a tank.

Before Kajiro could swing his lengthy sword back around, Tan's one-handed blade lashed out toward Kajiro's face.

Kajiro contorted to dodge the strike, only to face a triple lunge from Tan.

"Oh, he's moving away, sir!" Pochi flailed her now-empty skewer stick.

"Mmph! Mmph mmph?"

"Tama, try to finish eating before you speak, okay?"

Tama tried to join in on the commentary with a mouthful of food and was met with a light scolding from Lulu.

Gaining some distance, Kajiro slid his feet to adjust the space between them, while Tan used a short Body Strengthening chant to power himself up.

"Strengthening?"

"I guess he's using some kind of buff spell."

Mia and Arisa listened keenly to the chant, trying to predict its effects.

"But why doesn't Kajiro attack while he's invoking the chant?"

"Arisa, that is precisely what Sir Tan wants him to do. If he fell for it, he would likely be met with a severe counterattack." Liza knew her stuff.

"Master, the samurai unit's movements are strange, I inform."

"Yes, that's a slide step…"

As I started to explain the move to Nana, the fighters went back into action.

No one was listening to my explanation, so I returned my attention to the match as well.

Unlike the previous bout, this time they were exchanging blows in rapid succession, their blades creating noticeable sparks.

"Wow. He hasn't stopped chanting for a second, even while he's deflecting all those sword blows."

"Very calm."

Arisa and Mia crunched away on their snacks as they provided a magic user's perspective on the match.

Then, whether it was thanks to the level difference or the Body Strengthening, Tan slowly began to take the lead.

The battle was so intense that the cheering audience lapsed into silence, watching with bated breath.

"Ah!"

A loud clang resounded through the stadium as Kajiro's enormous weapon snapped in half.

"Kajiro!"

I heard a woman cry out from the passage leading to the stadium's waiting room.

She must be a member of his family.

Even with his sword broken, Kajiro refused to give up the fight, swinging toward his opponent in a last-ditch attempt at a comeback.

But Tan was ready for him and blocked with his own sword wrapped in purple lightning.

A static-like *ZAP!* boomed through the stadium, and Kajiro fell to the ground.

Tan must have paralyzed him with an electric shock.

Tan held his sword point to Kajiro's neck, then looked to the referee to pronounce him victorious.

Bloodthirsty voices rang out from the audience.

"Kill hiiiiim!"

"Death to the loserrr!"

Uh, no, this isn't a Colosseum death match.

It was only a few dozen men, not the whole stadium by any means, but the scattered jeers calling for Kajiro's death were painful to hear.

But Tan simply shrugged as if to dismiss the demands, refusing to rise to the bait from the ill-mannered spectators.

This gesture appeared to go over favorably with the ladies; shrieks of admiration rose from the crowd.

"Winner: Magic Swordsman Tan!"

When the referee finally declared Tan's victory, an uproar rose from the crowd that drowned out the unpleasant jeers.

Naturally, we joined in to applaud the excellent bout.

While we waited for the next match to start, we munched on snacks and discussed the previous battle.

"Was that a *hakama*? What a wonderful piece of equipment. I did not expect it to hide his footwork so well." Liza seemed impressed with Kajiro's Japanese-style outfit.

Tama and Pochi were both attempting to mimic his footwork, but they couldn't quite get the hang of it.

"This is haaard."

"I can't help lifting my feet, sir."

"Here, try it like this."

Taking off my shoes, I demonstrated the slide step for them. Of course, since it was mostly based on what I'd seen in manga, I had no idea whether I was doing it right.

Explaining the basic move was easy enough, but showing them how to fine-tune it with their toes was harder.

Tama and Pochi crouched on the floor, squinting at my toes.

"Wiggle, wiggle?"

"Like a slug, sir."

Taking a liking to the movement, Pochi sprawled out on the floor and began shunting herself around like an inchworm.

Should I tell her that's not how a slug moves?

Just as Tama was about to start doing the same, Lulu cut in, "Pochi! Good girls don't roll around on the floor in their best clothes, you know!"

"N-nooo, this is different, ma'am. Lulu, I didn't mean to, ma'am."

"How is it different, exactly? Now, what do we say when we do bad things?"

"I'm sorry, ma'am."

Shoot. I guess I should've scolded her.

Pochi knelt down in a suitably apologetic pose.

"Pochi baaad."

Tama shrewdly scurried over to Lulu's side, putting on a reproachful look.

You were about to worm around, too, weren't you?

I gave Tama a pointed look, and she hurriedly switched to the same "apologetic" pose.

Okay, that's better.

The next match was a fierce swordfight between two beastfolk.

This time, both combatants ended up bleeding. It wasn't very pleasant to watch. In fact, the way they were slashing at each other with fierce grins on their bloodied faces was terrifying.

"Master, they're whacking each other, sir."

"Liza could wiiin."

"While I would by no means go down without a fight, I somehow doubt that I could defeat either of them."

Both beastfolk were level 30, so from a numerical standpoint, Liza would probably lose.

"Oh! What a move!"

"Twiiirl?"

"My head is spinning, sir."

"Mm. Wow."

The younger group raised a chorus of admiration for the acrobatic fighters.

Getting overexcited, Tama and Pochi started dangling themselves a little dangerously over the railing to cheer them on.

"You mustn't lean over the railing, you two," Liza warned.

The two backed away immediately, but each time one of the beast-folk landed a blow or executed an acrobatic dodge, they leaped right back on.

Finally, tired of telling them off, Liza picked up Tama and Pochi and held them like a pair of stuffed animals.

The foxfolk man swung his broadsword around like a shot put, using the momentum to let loose a spinning slash like something out of a manga.

Not to be outdone, the raccoonfolk man separated his sword vertically into two thinner swords and began whirling himself around as well.

"Three tuuurns?"

"My head is really spinning, sir."

Tama and Pochi, still secure in Liza's arms, whipped their heads back and forth dizzyingly as they watched the fighters. Between their flailing arms and tails, I was afraid something was going to go flying off.

Still, this is a martial arts tournament, right? Not, like, a circus?

It was definitely interesting, but something was off. All I could do was assume that as one's level rose, the stat inflation allowed for moves that would normally be impossible.

"Master, can I move like that, too? I inquire."

"If you use Body Strengthening well enough, I'm sure you can."

Unfortunately, this comment also caught the attention of Miss Karina, who had been watching the match quietly.

"Why, in that case, perhaps I could do it, too."

"Indeed, Lady Karina, it is possible."

The intelligent item Raka blinked on Miss Karina's chest.

The heated battle between the two beastfolk had the crowd worked up into a fervor, but shockingly, it ended in a draw when the fighters knocked each other out simultaneously. The rematch would be held the next day.

*   *   *

The final round of the morning was between a beastfolk spearman and a female samurai who appeared to be around twenty years old.

Apparently, she was a relative of Kajiro, the longsword-wielding samurai from the first match. She wielded both a polearm and a short sword.

Both combatants' levels were in the mid-twenties, significantly lower than the fighters we'd seen so far.

"Just you wait, Golao. Papa's going to win this tournament and get a government job."

"I vow to restore Lord Kajiro's pride."

My "Keen Hearing" skill was now able to pick up the mutters of the combatants under the cheering of the crowd. It must have adapted to the loud environment.

I guess even after maxing out a skill, I can still improve its performance by using it well.

When the allotted time for evaluating the opponent was up and the match began, the spearman immediately went on the offensive.

""""Yaaaah! Kill herrr!""""

The audience was getting a little vicious. They must have been worked up after the previous fight's anticlimax.

The edge of the spear's cross-shaped tip sliced through the woman's sleeve, and the other end bit into her arm. Blood sprayed into the air, agitating the audience.

""""Bloooood! Woooo!""""

I didn't exactly love where this was going.

In the gamelike system of this world, blood loss seemed to result in continuous damage. The samurai's HP and stamina bars steadily decreased as time passed.

""""Yeaaaah! Kiiiill!""""

The blood loss sent the woman staggering, and the crowd roared madly.

"Mrrr…"

"Weh…"

Tama and Pochi, still in Liza's arms, curled up fearfully with their ears flattened and tails hiding between their legs. Even Liza, normally so stoic, had turned pale.

Something was most likely frightening them— *Oh, no. Of course.*

"Arisa, could you cast Calm Field on Liza, Tama, and Pochi, please?"

"Okeydoke!"

Arisa obeyed my quiet request without making a scene. The magic quickly took effect, easing the beastfolk girls' panic. I caught them before they collapsed, bringing them over to rest on a sofa.

"What's the matter?" Miss Karina asked.

"The intensity of the crowd seems to have gotten to them."

But that wasn't quite what had happened.

In all likelihood, the real cause of their distress was that the jeers of the crowd reminded them of the riot back in Seiryuu City. If the magic soldier Zena hadn't stepped in to help, the three of them might have been killed. It made sense that the experience would have traumatized them.

"It's all right," I murmured, laying my hands over theirs. "We're here for you."

"You've got me, too!"

"And me."

"I will defend you, I declare."

"Mm. Safe."

Everyone else was just as worried about the beastfolk girls, and they all gathered around to put their hands on top of mine encouragingly.

I think Miss Karina wanted to join, too, but she hesitated too long and missed her chance, so instead she just stood outside the circle looking left out.

"Master, I apologize for worrying you."

"We're okaaay."

"P-Pochi is just fine, sirs."

The beastfolk girls smiled with a little difficulty and returned to their seats.

And yet, the cries of "Kill her!" were still roaring through the stadium.

Come on, people—read the room a little.

But my snide mental commentary stopped dead in its tracks when I saw the man standing over the bloodied samurai woman with his spear raised.

However reluctantly, he appeared to be trying to stab her in response to the audience's demands.

"Why isn't the ref—?"

Before I finished my question, I realized the woman was still holding her broken short sword.

From a refereeing standpoint, that probably meant the fight was technically still on.

The woman rolled to avoid the spear a few times, but finally the spearman trapped the arm holding the short sword under his foot, rendering her powerless.

"That's it! Kill her! If you do well, the house of Count Bobino will gladly employ you!"

An arrogant voice called out from another section of the luxury seats.

At this, the spearman muttered as if he'd lost his mind. "Golao... Papa's going to do it..."

Shoot, this doesn't look good.

"Stop! Golao is watching!" I used my "Amplification" skill to try and bring the man back to his senses.

"Golao..."

Shaken by my cry, the man shifted his spear to the side, the cross-shaped tip stopping just short of the woman's neck.

"Winner! Spearman Jirau!"

As soon as his victory was announced, the man dropped to his knees. The medical staff came in to help up the samurai woman and carry her off the field.

"Well, I know I'm bored of this now. Should we go back?"

"I agree. This bloodthirsty atmosphere doesn't suit my delicate senses."

I wasn't really bored, but I didn't like how cruel this was getting.

Besides, the yells of the crowd were probably stressing out the beast-folk girls.

"If Sa—Sir Pendragon is going back, I suppose we shall as well."

With that, we all headed to the carriages.

Along the way, my "Keen Hearing" skill picked up an interesting conversation.

"Hey! What do you think you're doing?! I'm a direct descendant of the esteemed Bobino family, I'll have you know! Foolish knights!"

"Quiet down, please. We are detaining all members of the Bobino family by order of His Grace the duke. Any resistance will be considered mutiny against him."

The first voice was that awful, arrogant noble from before.

On the map, I confirmed that the duke's men had surrounded the Bobino estate, where the Wings of Freedom members had been hiding out, and an elite force of imperial guards were facing down the count's private army.

The duke had made good on his word from the night before, dispatching his troops the very next day.

I'm glad to see he's so quick to action.

◆

When we returned to Count Worgoch's manor, I decided to try to comfort the beastfolk girls by preparing hamburg steaks at their request.

The maid of the house was able to get some tofu for me, so I made a test run of a tofu version for Mia as well.

"Pochi!"

"Tamaaa!"

Seeing the steaks, the two squealed and clung to each other joyously. I was glad they weren't just pretending to be cheerful anymore. Hamburg steaks had been the right choice.

"Satou?"

Mia looked at me doubtfully when I placed the steak in front of her.

"This is a tofu hamburg steak. It may look like a normal one, but it's made with soy and wheat flour, so I think you should be able to eat it."

It included eggs as well, but she regularly ate pastries that contained eggs. It shouldn't be a problem.

"Just try a bite, okay? If you don't like it, I'll make you something else."

"Mm." Mia hesitantly reached her chopsticks toward the tofu hamburg steak. "Yummy," she mumbled.

Then, after thoroughly chewing up and swallowing the single bite, her eyes sparkled.

"Delicious! It falls apart in your mouth, and the mysterious flavor is nothing like bread or vegetables. It's so good—it's amazing!"

This time, she spoke Elvish to declare her approval at length.

Good, guess she liked it.

For a while now, I'd wanted to make a hamburg steak that Mia could eat, since she always looked disappointed watching the others eat theirs.

"Hamburg steak... I never knew that such a thing existed...!"

Miss Karina trembled with emotion at her first taste of the dish.

"Yummy-yummy!"

"Master, the hamburg steak is delicious, I commend."

Tama and Nana had limited vocabularies, but they still expressed their enjoyment of the food clearly.

"Oh man, hamburg steak is the best! ...Sir."

"Makes you want to jump up and shout, 'Aww, yeah!' right?"

Pochi and Arisa, on the other hand, were a little hard to understand. Arisa seemed to be having a major influence on Pochi's vocabulary; I might have to do something about that soon.

At any rate, after I enjoyed everyone's reactions for a while, I soon gave in to their demands for seconds.

"Satou, more."

"Sorry, Mia. I don't have enough tofu to make another helping."

"...Whomp-whomp."

Mia almost never said sound effects aloud like that. Guess she was really disappointed.

I managed to earn her forgiveness by promising to make her hamburg steak again for dinner.

In the end, everyone but Mia ate too much and went down for the count. They were all flopped out on the floor groaning. Once I got them to take some stomach medicine and lie down properly, I decided to leave them to recover for a while.

I called out to Mia, who was cleansing her palate with fruit water.

"Seems like we have some time to kill. Want to go check out the aristocratic quarter's magic shop?"

"Mm, let's."

The magic shop was within walking distance, but the Bobino mansion roundup was still going on, so I decided it would be smoother and safer to take one of the Worgoch mansion's carriages.

The magic shop was on the outer edge of the aristocratic quarter, near the lesser nobles' estates.

There was a magic shop for commoners in the downtown area, too, but I decided on this one because it was the only place that carried intermediate attack magic.

As I entered the store in high spirits, I suddenly ran into an acquaintance.

"Ooh, if it isn't Sir Satou!"

"Hmm? Is this an acquaintance of yours, Tolma?"

"Yeah, I told you about him before, remember? When that army of monsters attacked Muno City, he…"

Tolma was inside the magic shop, chatting with someone who appeared to be the manager.

He spun the tale of the defense of Muno City as if he had witnessed it with his own two eyes.

The store manager was a large, muscular man with a grim face, hardly the sort you'd expect to run a magic shop. An ax or a broadsword would be more fitting in his hands.

The manager grinned as he listened to Tolma's excited tale. If his expression was anything to go by, he probably figured that Tolma was exaggerating as usual. He certainly didn't seem seriously convinced.

"The name's Kikinu. I was born in a small kingdom in the east, so forgive me if my name seems strange. If it's too hard to pronounce, feel free to call me Meathead or Manager or Old Man or something."

"Not at all. My name is Satou."

"Tsk, tsk, tsk." Not liking to be ignored, Tolma shook his finger. What was it about him that made me want to punch him so much?

"You really should give your full name, you know."

I hadn't given my surname because I wanted the man to speak freely with me, but as usual, Tolma couldn't read between the lines.

"My apologies. I am Satou Pendragon, an honorary hereditary knight."

"Oh-ho? You must be fond of heroic legends, eh?" The manager noticed that my name was taken from a fictitious hero.

"This guy's master is Baron Muno, who used to be called Baronet Donano."

"I see… That explains that, then."

Guess Baron Muno was famous for his love of hero stories, even in the old capital.

"Ultimately, I chose the name Pendragon myself."

"Well, that's all right. Only fellow die-hards would recognize it anyway."

So Mr. Kikinu was a fan just like Baron Muno.

"Anyway, what's a swordsman like you doing in a place like this? Collecting more scrolls, I suppose?"

"Well, yes, but I also wanted to see the spell books."

"Spell books? Why?"

"Some of my traveling companions use magic, like this one here."

I gestured to Mia, who was hiding behind my back.

Briefly raising her downcast eyes to peer at Kikinu from under her hood, the elf briefly mumbled "Mia" by way of introduction.

"A beginner's book for the little lady, then? I might have a few that would work."

"No, no need for that. Could you show me any intermediate or higher books, please?"

Mr. Kikinu raised his eyebrows. "I think those would be too difficult for a child…"

"Mrrr."

Mia didn't like being treated like a kid. She shifted her hood slightly, showing the man her pointed ears.

"A-an elf?!"

"Mm."

"Mia is an elf of the Bolenan Forest," I explained on her behalf.

"I-I'm terribly sorry for my rudeness!"

Kikinu ducked his head with such vigor that it almost smashed into the counter.

"Okay." Mia was apparently moved by his sincerity, and her dour expression quickly vanished.

"I didn't know you were a fan of elves, too, Kikinu," Tolma said.

"I don't know about 'fan,' but… Did I ever tell you that I'm from the Black Dragon Mountains?"

"Oh yeah."

"The monsters from the mountains often carried plagues into our villages."

Kikinu began explaining his background.

"Black Dragon Mountains" sure sounds like an exciting name.

"Every year, villagers fall ill to these plagues, but thanks to the Tree of Healing Rest that the elves planted long ago, people rarely die."

"Mm. Good tree." Mia nodded wisely.

"Huh. I bet you could profit off a tree like that if you cut some roots from it."

"Impossible. One fellow did try to plant it somewhere else to make money, but it withers if planted anywhere but where the elves put it."

Kikinu shook his head.

"Not enough spirits," Mia whispered to me, explaining the real reason for the replanting failure.

I guess you needed spirits for a Tree of Healing Rest to grow. Come to think of it, the land around the dwarves' home of Bolehart City was withering because of a lack of spirits or mana, too.

"Regardless, that's why I feel indebted to the elves."

After chatting amiably with Mr. Kikinu for a while, I had him show me his lineup of scrolls and spell books.

Naturally, the variety of a major city's magic shop turned out to be extensive.

"This one looks good."

"Really? These books here are old staples, but that one's practically a joke..."

The volume I was holding was called *Rotation and Romance*. It was by the same author as the magic-tool-creation book I'd found in Sedum City in Kuhanou County.

"Oh, I don't know about that. Some of Professor Jahado's inventions are pretty remarkable."

Until now, I only knew the author's name from the cover of the magic item book, but the author bio in this one revealed that he was an old professor living in the royal capital. I would love to meet him once we got there.

There were other books by the same author, who seemed to be fixated on a certain theme: *Where Rotation and Reciprocating Motion Meet* and *New Magic Born of Rotation*.

The "old staples" the manager recommended were *Foundations of Staffs and Catalysts*, *Gems and Cores*, *Thirty Circuits for Use in Magic Tools*, *Magic Tools and Carving Magic*, *How to Engrave Runes*, and *From Seals to Magic Circles*.

Every one of these titles grabbed my attention, so I decided to purchase all of them.

Unfortunately, there was nothing about how to make scrolls.

"I'll take all of these, and one of each kind of intermediate spell book, please."

There were also manuals for Explosion Magic and Destruction

Magic, the two that Miss Ringrande was said to have revived. Unfortunately, I didn't see any on Space Magic, Gravity Magic, or anything that might be considered taboo.

"Th-that many?! ...Oh, right. I almost forgot, since you're a friend of Tolma's and all, but would you mind showing me your noble identification papers, please? And you need a certain license to purchase any books containing spells that could be used for military purposes..."

"Will this do?"

I showed him the silver plate denoting my nobility and the permit I'd received from the duke the day before.

"An unlimited permit? And with the duke's official seal?! H-how on earth did you...?"

I couldn't bring myself to tell the speechless Mr. Kikinu that I got it as payment for some tasty tempura, so instead I flashed him a trademark Japanese smile.

Next, I had him show me his scroll collection.

"You could just buy these directly from our workshop, you know."

"Hey, Tolma. Don't try to steal my customers." Mr. Kikinu smiled drily, evidently accustomed to Tolma's oblivious remarks.

"Don't worry, Lord Tolma. I have all kinds of strange scrolls to order there when I visit."

In fact, I was planning to try to get custom scrolls of my self-designed spells, so I figured I'd buy the ones that were available in-store first.

The general scrolls Mr. Kikinu showed me were no different from the ones I'd bought in Gururian City, but I bought quite a few military magic scrolls.

They were all lesser or intermediate level only, but I got attack spells like Fire Storm, Laser, and Explosion, two communication spells called Whisper Wind and Telephone, and a magical interference spell called Break Magic, to name a few.

Ah, if I'd had all these spells before, it would've been so much easier to defeat the demon lord.

Unfortunately, though, there weren't any scrolls of a few other spells I wanted, like Aqua Heal, Remove Poison, Cure Disease, and so on.

According to Mr. Kikinu, the scroll versions weren't very effective, so potions were considered much more reliable.

"What about spells like Magic Hand, Lock, and Unlock?"

"I'm sorry, but—"

"Sir Satou," Tolma interrupted, "making scrolls like Lock and Unlock that could be used for crimes is strictly prohibited."

So military spells are all right, but not those...

Other spells like See Through and Clairaudience were also forbidden, since they could be used for spying. I was told that nobles often had special constructions on their grounds to prevent that kind of magic.

Mr. Kikinu added that some of the books I'd just bought, like *Magic Tools and Carving Magic* and *From Seals to Magic Circles*, contained spells that could be used for spying, too.

Incidentally, the Magic Hand spell I asked about was supposed to be similar to telekinesis. As it turned out, though, when it was used from a scroll, you couldn't do much more than lift a pen for less than a minute, so it wasn't exactly in high demand.

Tolma added that Viscount Siemmen's warehouse had a Magic Hand scroll, though, so I'd have to see if I could get it from him.

Once I'd collected a good number of things I wanted, I decided to wrap up my shopping here.

I paid a rather substantial amount using gold coins from my Garage Bag and put away all of my many purchases.

"Oh-ho? Is that an Item Bag? How fitting for a noble."

"Do you carry these here, too?"

"Sometimes, but we don't have any in stock at the moment. They're high-class made-to-order items. It can take years to get one in."

Oh-ho-ho?

I had assumed that it was the kind of relic you could find only in a labyrinth or an ancient empire, but from what Mr. Kikinu said, they were still being made in magic tool workshops.

Come to think of it, I guess Miss Karina did mention back at Muno Castle that she had a Magic Bag, too.

I asked Mr. Kikinu a little more about their functionality and learned that even the highest-quality Item Bags held about the same amount as the Garage Bag I'd found in the haunted fortress in Muno Barony.

So the one I first picked up from the Valley of Dragons was unique after all.

◆

Once we finished our business at the magic shop, Tolma showed us around the bookstores and trading firms of the nobles' quarter, then guided us to the other magic shop downtown.

The reason I wanted to visit the trading firms was to buy a cask of wine to send to Elder Dohal and the dwarves. I also sent a special high-grade sake set to Mr. Garohal, who had sold me the Forge scroll that helped me defeat the demon lord.

At first, I smiled blandly when Tolma commented, "The old capital is like my personal garden!" but it turned out to be truer than I expected.

Tolma led us all over the old capital, showing us the hidden sights. We went down strange back alleys, cut through other people's gardens, and generally followed a path that was more like a naughty child's favorite obstacle course than a shortcut.

Tama or Pochi would probably have loved it, but Mia started falling behind pretty quickly, and I ended up carrying her on my shoulders.

Eventually, this sketchy course led us to a strange patch of land between two buildings, almost like an empty lot.

Because it was actually surrounded by a grove of trees, not buildings, it was more like a natural park, but it still struck me with that impression.

"Fresh," Mia murmured.

True enough, the scent of greenery was strong here.

Suddenly, I got a strange feeling and glanced at the radar in the corner of my vision. As it turned out, this place was treated like a different map area.

It was a tiny space, but just to be safe, I used my "Search Entire Map" skill. Fortunately, it didn't alert me to any hostile presences.

"Sir Satou! Over here."

Tolma had already pushed his way forward through the weeds and was waving us over.

Looking in his direction, I saw a single house buried among all the greenery.

"This is one of the best shops in town. They've always got tons of good finds."

Cheerfully ignoring the CLOSED sign on the door, Tolma walked on in as if he himself owned the place. Maybe I could learn a thing or two from his boldness.

The entrance of the ivy-covered brick building was too small to enter with Mia on my shoulders. Even at my height, I was a little worried I'd hit my head going in. I lowered her to the ground, then took her hand and entered the store.

"Hey, Gramps!" I heard Tolma yelling farther inside. "You alive in here?"

After a moment, there was a crashing noise and a yelp of pain from Tolma, followed by an angry retort from an old man.

"Am I alive, my arse! If anything, it's been so long since I saw ye that I thought ye might be dead yerself." The old shop owner was too short to see behind Tolma. "Anyway, Tolma. Who d'ye think yer bringing into my store?"

"Oh, these are some friends of mine..."

Tolma turned to introduce us, finally giving us a glimpse of the shop owner.

He had a green hat like a nightcap, a wrinkled face, pointed ears, and grayish skin with silver eyes. According to the information on the AR display that popped up next to him, this man was a kind of fairy-folk called a **spriggan**.

If I remembered correctly from video games and such, spriggans were treasure-hoarding sprites. Perhaps that was why the shelves behind him were full of magic items, scrolls, and so on.

"It's too bright... I cain't see."

The old shop owner shaded his eyes with his hands for a moment. When he lowered his arm, his silver eyes were now jet-black.

"Looks like a little humanfolk boy... Hmm? Isn't that the Silent Bell of Bolenan? I see, I see."

Noticing the bell hanging from my belt, the spriggan shopkeeper folded his arms and nodded wisely.

Then he noticed Mia hiding behind me.

"Oh-ho-ho? Is that young lady an elf? Yer the spitting image of Cyriltoa, though ye mustn't be."

"Mm. Mia."

A little sullen, Mia lowered her hood as she offered a terse introduction.

"...I'm sorry if I offended ye."

The old shop owner took off his cap and stood behind the counter.

"My name is Eucham Bolesven. As you can see, I'm but an old spriggan."

"I am the youngest elf of Bolenan Forest, Misanaria Bolenan, daughter of Lamisauya and Lilinatoa."

The spriggan introduced himself in Elvish, and Mia did the same.

Her expression returned to normal as smoothly as if her pout had been wiped away with a cloth. *I guess there are certain rules and customs that only fairyfolk know.*

Oblivious to the quiet change in the mood, Tolma began pestering the shop owner.

"Got a few minutes, old man? I want you to show these two that special item you were telling me about, the one you called a book of treasures."

"Hmm, that one, eh…? Very well. Just a moment."

The old fellow disappeared into the back of the shop, and Tolma set about making tea and rearranging the chairs in the room as if it were the most natural thing in the world.

"I come here to buy adult books all the time."

"Erm, then this 'book of treasures' you mentioned…?"

"Ha-ha-ha! Of course not. At my age, I wouldn't come here to buy those."

Tolma laughed off my concerns easily.

It wasn't that I wasn't interested in the adult books of this world, but I didn't exactly want to go through a whole song and dance of introductions just to get my hands on them. Fortunately, Mia didn't seem to know what "adult books" meant; she didn't declare me "guilty" this time.

"Satou, tea snacks."

"Is something like cake or cookies all right?"

"Honey nut cookies."

I took out the sweets from my Garage Bag as requested, placing them on a handkerchief in lieu of a plate.

"Something smells sweet in here, eh?"

"Please, help yourself."

I offered the cookies to the old shopkeeper as he returned with string-bound books and scrolls.

"Delicious. Bring these next time, too." The old spriggan must have been a fan of sweets. This was probably also a roundabout way of granting me permission to come back.

While the shopkeeper ate with relish, I turned my attention to the books he'd brought.

Could it be...?

I read through the scrolls stacked along with the books. These weren't magic scrolls like the ones I bought at Mr. Kikinu's place but rather rolled-up notes of some sort.

The books bound with strings listed the chants for various spells.

There wasn't a single line of explanation in the Shigan language, either. Instead, the rolled-up papers contained guides and notes for reading the scrolls, so I used those to try to read them.

It brought me back to my time as a student, when I would try to reverse-engineer the source programs for games from the binary code. I'd always enjoyed stuff like that.

It wasn't encrypted like the guide to making Holy Swords, making it relatively easy for me to read.

"Is this Space Magic?"

"That's right. I'm impressed ye could decipher it so quickly, boy!" The spriggan raised his eyebrows in surprise, then smacked my shoulders admiringly. "No wonder ye were entrusted with the Silent Bell. A traveling sorcerer left these with me and asked me to give them to the first person who could read them," he explained, telling me the origin of the spell book.

I never would have expected to get this handy volume here, and I was extremely pleased. It would make a good souvenir for Arisa, who was back watching the mansion.

"Incidentally, Sir Eucham... Are the scrolls on the shelf behind you for sale, by any chance?"

I pointed to the shelf that had caught my attention a little while ago.

"Hmm, ye have a sharp eye. I normally dinnae sell them, but they were left to me by the same sorcerer. Perhaps ye ought to have them, if ye like."

"Yes, please!"

Thanks to my enthusiasm, the old shopkeeper agreed to sell me four scrolls.

They included the Space Magic spells Clairvoyance and Clairaudience, the Practical Magic spell See Through, and the light magic spell Illusion.

The spriggan man warned me not to peep too much, but I had no intention of using it that way.

Tolma seemed to want to chat with the old shopkeeper for a while, so we decided to go on ahead.

Following the shopkeeper's instructions, we proceeded straight from the door and came out an alley near the main street.

"Huh. So this is where it's connected to?"

I looked over my shoulder, only to find nothing but fences.

A glance at my map told me there were several empty lots full of trees.

When I searched for Tolma and Mr. Eucham, I found that the store was actually located some ways away.

"Wandering Forest."

I put together the information from Mia's short explanation in my head and filed it away.

From what I gathered, Wandering Forest was a Spirit Magic spell that formed a barrier to protect the shop. If one were to proceed in any direction but the correct path, they would come out in a different area like we just did.

So there was a reason for Tolma's meandering route after all.

Feeling rather satisfied, I found a street carriage to take us back to the mansion.

"Lady Cyriltoa does not meet with anyone without an appointment, I am afraid."

On the way home, we'd passed by the concert hall where Miss Cyriltoa the Songstress was performing, so I'd stopped in to see if Mia could meet her. Unfortunately, the older lady at the reception counter sharply refused.

"Then, if I could make an appointment, please—"

"Even if you were the son of a noble or a royal from another kingdom, I could not accept your request. If you would like to make an arrangement in the future, you will have to acquire a 'songstress meeting license' from His Grace the duke."

What is this, a side quest?

I managed to keep my irritation from showing with my "Poker Face" skill.

"Call Ciya."

"Excuse me? Who do you think you are? Calling the great Lady Cyriltoa the Songstress by a nickname!"

The old lady's eyebrows practically shot through the ceiling. She had to be a devoted fan of Miss Cyriltoa—more like a worshipper, really.

But her attitude quickly changed when Mia lowered her hood.

"Call her."

"…Those ears! You look like…! Could you by any chance be a relative of Lady Cyriltoa?!"

"Mm. Mia."

Unmoved by the woman's shock, Mia replied with her usual shortness.

After that, we were able to meet Cyriltoa the Songstress without any further trouble.

"Welcome! If it isn't Laya and Lia's daughter Misanaria. How long has it been? A century? Why, you've grown so much! How lovely."

"Uh-huh."

To my surprise, Miss Cyriltoa spoke normally for an elf. The ones I'd met so far, Mia and the store manager in Seiryuu City, both spoke mostly in one- or two-word sentences; I'd assumed she would be the same way.

Miss Cyriltoa was a young elf girl who bore a striking resemblance to Mia.

Her hair was closer to light blue in color, long and straight, but other than that you could barely tell the difference. Her age was several times more than Mia's, making her older even than the store manager.

Elves must age physically very slowly, no matter how old they are. A lolicon would probably be thrilled.

"My, it's been so long since I had fresh fruit from the Mountain-Tree."

"Mm, good."

The slice I offered Miss Cyriltoa put a smile on her face.

She had declined the baked goods and dried fruit I offered, saying they would be bad for her throat, which was why I'd brought out the fruit instead. I took it from Storage through the Garage Bag, of course.

"The Bolenan Senate contacted me to say that you were missing, Mia. Did you run away with this human boy, then?"

"Mm. Lovers."

As usual, Mia was deadpanning, so I explained in her stead.

She didn't seem too happy to be corrected, but I thought it was best to cut off rumors like that before they started.

"How wonderful. So you rescued our princess from an evil sorcerer."

"Romantic."

When I finished summing things up, each elf commented on the story.

I guess Miss Cyriltoa is preoccupied with love, too.

"Lady Cyriltoa, it's almost time for your next performance..."

As the three of us were chatting, the receptionist from before came to call Miss Cyriltoa away. We must have been talking for longer than I thought.

"Oh my, what a shame. Will you be staying in the old capital awhile?"

"Mm. Will come back."

When Mia noticed Cyriltoa seemed reluctant to part ways, she nodded reassuringly.

"Oh, I know! Mia, you can have this."

Miss Cyriltoa took an instrument case off a shelf and handed it to Mia.

"Ciya!"

"I don't use it anymore. It'll be happier with you."

Lady Cyriltoa stroked the case lovingly. Her hand, encased in a glove up to the elbow, was labeled **artificial hand** in my AR display.

Its movements were so natural that it was impossible to tell it apart from an ordinary hand, but it must have been inadequate for a master musician.

"...Mm. Okay."

After hesitating a little, Mia accepted the musical instrument in its case.

As the receptionist panicked further, Cyriltoa took her sweet time saying good-bye.

"I would love to chat again."

"I'll make some sweets that are easy on the throat for next time."

She giggled. "I can't wait."

Waving her gloved hand, Miss Cyriltoa left the room.

In the carriage on the way home, Mia hugged the instrument case to her chest as she relayed stories about the elfin songstress in short, halting sentences. As it turned out, she'd lost her arm in a tragic accident while exploring in the Labyrinth City Celivera.

Mia remembered her singing abilities as being average, so she must have devoted herself to training her voice after losing her arm.

I had a lot of respect for her ability to persevere in the face of adversity.

While I was discussing this with Mia, the carriage arrived back at the mansion, and I decided to take everyone to see her perform sometime.

◆

Late that night, I returned into the labyrinth ruins under the old capital.

Naturally, I wanted to test out the scrolls I'd acquired.

The reason it ended up being so late was that I had to explain to Arisa and Mia the Space Magic spell book I'd only just gotten.

As soon as I explained, Arisa wanted to learn it right away, but she didn't have enough skill points to reach the level that allowed her to use Teleportation; she ended up rolling around on the floor in despair.

Anyway, it was time to start experimenting.

"Hmm. This one's more powerful than I expected…"

When I used Fire Storm from the magic menu, it utterly destroyed everything I set up to test out my spells' effectiveness: rocks, armor, and more. The temperature itself was lower than that of Forge, but its overall power was much higher.

Spells created specially for combat really were destructive.

I didn't feel like going too far, so I started my experiments in a relatively high level of the labyrinth, but at this rate, the spells might actually cause noises or tremors aboveground.

Just to be safe, I moved closer to the middle tier of the labyrinth to experiment with the other scrolls.

The attack spells all packed a punch, but the Light Magic spell Laser did relatively little area damage.

Since it was possible to reduce its power by adjusting the number of beams fired, it might be handy in a variety of ways.

If used in conjunction with Condense, a spell I'd acquired previously, I discovered I could focus all the beams together to raise its power, alter its trajectory, and things like that. *Glad Condense has its uses after all.*

I didn't get to test Break Magic very much, but it seemed decent, too. However, if I used it to cancel out an intermediate spell like Fire Storm, the excess magic would end up surging in all directions. I'd have to find a way to protect against that.

According to one book, Mana Section was the best way to prevent this magic "surge." There was another one for the list of scrolls I needed.

The communication spells were all very handy. Clairvoyance, which could be used to check in on faraway companions, and Telephone, which could communicate with them, seemed especially useful.

Hopefully, Arisa or Mia could at least learn how to use Telephone from the Space Magic book. Maybe Lulu could, too, since she had the Chant skill.

Sightseeing in the Old Capital

Satou here. Prince Shotoku is said to have been able to listen to eight people talk at once and understand what each of them was saying. Whenever I hear that story, though, I always wonder why he didn't just ask them to speak one at a time.

"Master, please look at the sky!"

The normally calm Liza was pointing up excitedly.

Following her finger upward, I saw an airship drifting through the morning mist. According to my AR display, it was a **Shiga Kingdom Large Rigid Airship**.

"Monsterrr?"

"Watch out, sir! It's a giant peanut, sir!"

Tama and Pochi hopped up and down as they tugged on my sleeves.

The other kids, too, all stood outside the Worgoch mansion to peer up at the sky in surprise.

The airship was indeed peanut-shaped, with jumbo jet–esque wings protruding from the indented area in the middle. It could be said that the globe-shaped turrets attached to the ends of each wing made it even more fantasy-like.

According to the book I bought from Mr. Kikinu's magic shop, it flew using a magic apparatus called a "skypower engine."

"Whoa! Now that's some fantasy RPG stuff right there. How cool is that?"

"How does it stay in the air?"

Arisa and Lulu seemed curious, too. I guess there weren't any airships in their hometown.

"Airship," Mia muttered.

Mia didn't look as surprised as the others. Maybe she had seen one before.

"Airshiiip?" Tama tilted her head.

"It's a flying ship," I explained.

"Are there people on board?" Miss Karina asked.

I nodded.

"Amazing, sir! I want to ride one, sir!"

Yeah, me too, Pochi.

Thinking about it logically, though, they were probably for military use only, so I wasn't sure if we'd have the opportunity to do so.

I might be able to work out a reward with the duke if the upcoming evening party was a success, but even then, I doubted I could negotiate for everyone to be able to join me. And I'd rather ride with my whole group if possible. Perhaps I could see if Tolma had any suggestions when I went to visit him and Viscount Siemmen.

"Master, I would like one, I entreat."

"Hee-hee, it is cute, isn't it?"

Nana was reaching out toward the airship, making what could only be described as "grabby hands."

I wasn't sure if it was really as cute as Lulu said, though. Maybe we just didn't have the same aesthetic sense.

"Perhaps master could make you an airship plushie?" Lulu suggested. "It would be cute *and* soft."

Nana clapped her hands together once, then turned toward me.

"Master, I would like an airship plushie, I entreat."

"Sure. Why don't I show you how to make it, too?"

It wouldn't hurt for Nana to have a hobby besides combat.

"How to make it? I inquire."

"Yeah. Then you could make as many plushies as you want, right?"

"I see! That is an excellent idea, master, I commend!"

Nana nodded excitedly, although her expression remained blank as always.

After I made a pinkie promise with Nana, we watched the airship start to come in for a landing on the other side of the duke's castle.

"I know we were planning to go to the town marketplace, but would everyone like to go see the airship first?"

My question was met with a chorus of enthusiastic yeses.

I'd also like to add that the first person to answer was none other than Miss Karina.

◆

We were riding in one of Count Worgoch's carriages, so that was probably why we were able to reach the landing site without a problem.

Because beastfolk tended to be frowned upon in the nobles' quarters, the girls were wearing long hooded cloaks to hide their ears and tails.

"There will be lots of grumpy noblemen around. Try to stay quiet when we get out, okay?"

"Aye-aye, siiir."

"Our lips are sealed, sir."

Tama and Pochi nodded and mimed zipping their lips shut. Arisa must have taught them that particular gesture.

When we got out of the carriage, we had a clear view of the huge airship.

I had wanted to watch the landing process, but it was already firmly on the ground with a ramp stretching from the middle of the ship.

"It's huge!" Arisa exclaimed. "I wonder how long it is?"

"About three hundred feet."

I calculated the size from the information on my map.

"Seriously?! Why, that's only about half the size of a zeppelin."

"I'm impressed you knew that…"

As I admired Arisa's knowledge of various trivia, we walked up to the rope near the airship. It must have been to prevent entry past that point.

"Don't go past this rope, okay?"

"'kay."

"Yes, sir."

Tama and Pochi responded in small voices without lowering their hoods. I guess they took my warning to heart.

There were more spectators than I'd expected gathered around the rope. Most of them were nobles, but there were a few young ladies in servants' clothing. Somehow, it was like a crowd of fans eagerly waiting for a celebrity to appear.

"Why, it's Sir Pendragon! Did you come to greet a friend or something?"

I turned to see Imperial Knight Sir Ipasa Lloyd addressing me from the back of his horse. Apparently, he was patrolling the perimeter of the airship.

"No, I just came out of curiosity. This is my first time seeing an airship. Should I have gotten permission first?"

"No, nobles are allowed to come here without special permission. As well as their companions, of course."

Sir Ipasa nodded cordially to the beastfolk girls as he added the second half of his response.

I was glad he wasn't averse to them.

"This is quite a crowd," I remarked.

"Yeah, that's because—"

But just as he was about to tell me the reason, a chorus of shrieks drowned him out.

The girls and women in the crowd were screaming things like "Your Highness!" and "Sir Knight!"

The source of their excitement seemed to be the handsome young man in white armor who had just started descending the ramp. According to his AR label, his name was **Sharorik Shiga**. The detailed description informed me he was the third prince of the Shiga Kingdom.

Two knights who appeared to be his attendants, then an entourage of ten or more—including robed sorcerers, maids, and other servants—followed him.

"Do you know of His Highness Sharorik, Sir Pendragon?"

"No, I'm not familiar," I answered honestly.

I could find out more with the detailed information in the AR display to a certain extent, but it wouldn't include any public opinions or rumors.

"He is an associate of the Eight Swordsmen of Shiga, and he was granted His Majesty's permission to wield the Holy Sword Claidheamh Soluis."

"He can use a Holy Sword without the Hero title?"

Noticing that the prince didn't have the Hero title, I asked the question without thinking.

I was remembering the incident in the Seiryuu City labyrinth. Until I'd gotten the Hero title, I'd taken damage just by holding a Holy Sword.

"Yes, His Majesty can appoint someone as the wielder of Claid-heamh Soluis."

His Majesty means the king, right? There must be some special way to change the master of the sword by using the City Core, then.

The rest of Sir Ipasa's report detailed a colorful romantic history you might expect to read in a celebrity gossip magazine. He had caused all kinds of problems in the past, so I'd have to make sure he didn't get near the likes of Nana or Miss Karina.

By the way, the Eight Swordsmen of Shiga were holders of a title granted to the strongest Holy Knights in the Shiga Kingdom.

Thanking Sir Ipasa for the explanation, I turned my gaze back toward the prince. He wore an irritable expression and didn't so much as wave to the crowd of young women fawning over him. I guess he wasn't the sociable type.

As soon as the prince stepped down from the ramp onto the carpet leading to his carriage, his maids rushed forward to scatter flower petals at his feet, like you'd see at a wedding.

Suddenly, he lifted his eyes and focused on a flying wooden horse that was taking off from the duke's castle.

Maybe he knew Miss Ringrande?

"Ah!"

The short cry drew my attention to one of the flower girls, who had tripped and fallen in a most unladylike manner. Fortunately, her skirt landed in a way that wasn't too revealing, but that was the least of her problems.

She had flung her flower basket into the air as she fell, and now, it was directly on the prince's head. Evidently, it had hit him in the face while his attention was elsewhere.

The basket perched over his handsome features was like something out of a romantic comedy.

"Wh-why, you…" His voice seemed far sharper than it needed to be.

"I-I-I'm so sorry!"

The prince was trembling with embarrassment and rage.

The apologetic maidservant looked familiar. It was the girl who had helped me at the banquet the night before.

"How insolent. Off with her head!" the prince ordered in a voice that was shaking with anger.

…Huh? Seriously? Feudalism is terrifying.

Stunned by the sudden development, I nonetheless took a penny coin out of Storage, intending to stealthily intervene.

"Yes, sir. Sorry, missy, I have to obey His Highness's orders!"

With a sadistic smile, the prince's young knight attendant raised his sword.

I bent the edges of the coin to make it curve in the air as I waited for the right moment. This way, I should be able to prevent the boy's act of brutality without revealing my identity.

However, as it turned out, the bent coin never came into play.

"...That's enough."

The other knight, a much older man, stood in front of the girl, stopping the blow with his large shield.

"What's this? Swordsman of Shiga or no, Sir Reilus, should you really be defying His Highness's orders?"

"By the Holy Shield bequeathed on me by His Majesty, I cannot let this injustice pass before my eyes."

It looked like the old knight was charged with keeping an eye on the short-tempered prince.

"Hmph! Stubborn old fool. Very well, I shall overlook it this once. See that the duke metes out a suitable punishment."

The sullen prince snapped at the old knight and the butler who came rushing over from the carriage.

"Tch. And here I was all excited to cut down a girl...," the young knight grumbled as he followed after the prince.

What a dangerous pair. I would have to avoid them both when I went to the duke's castle.

"Thank goodness Sir Reilus jumped in."

Sir Ipasa returned from the other side of the rope. In all likelihood, he had been rushing in to save the maidservant, too.

The prince's behavior made me want to write off feudal societies entirely, but at least there were nobles like the old knight and Sir Ipasa. I guess I shouldn't make such sweeping generalizations.

◆

After our visit to the airship, we piled back into the carriage to visit the old capital marketplace, which extended from the largest gate to the port.

We climbed out of the carriage in a parking area near the gate and walked from there.

"Crowded." Mia's eyes widened.

"Yes, it must be because of the tournament. It's like a melting pot of all kinds of people!"

Arisa offered her own impressions with much less surprise.

There were dark-skinned humans (which I hadn't yet seen in this world), humans with Asian-like features, and many kinds of beastfolk.

Of course, I also noticed plenty of people with Shigan features, as well as people from other kingdoms, including some dressed in sari-like outfits or nomad attire.

Unlike the quiet nobles' quarter, the harbor ward was crowded even by the standards of modern-day Japan.

Not only that, but a strange excitement filled the air, like the liveliness of a market in Southeast Asia. Swept up in the mood, the rest of our group was in even higher spirits than usual.

"Melting pooot?"

"Is that tasty, sir?"

"Pochi, you're always thinking about food." Lulu giggled at the pair.

"Hey, look at that!"

"Oh? I've never seen these here before."

Arisa pulled me by my sleeve to point out a particular table, stocked with an incredible variety of items. The large river must make for prosperous trade.

"They're a little sour but still tasty! Oh, I know! Let's eat them with sugar and condensed milk when we get back!"

The source of Arisa's excitement was a batch of fresh strawberries.

She always has a taste for the classics.

"Yummy?"

Mia indicated her interest, too.

"Condemned miiilk?"

"I'm sure the sugar will make it sweet and yummy, sir."

Tama tilted her head curiously, while Pochi nodded with baseless confidence.

"All right, I'll make some when we get home."

"Hooray!"

The younger kids were overjoyed at my rash promise.

Mixing the milk and sugar would be a bit of a pain, but I did have a Water Magic spell for whipping cream and such, so it should be fine.

Once we passed the section of fresh fruits and vegetables, we emerged into an area full of preserved food.

Of course, I had already stored our spoils so far in the Garage Bag. Recognizing the magic item, a few thieves made a pass at it, but the beastfolk girls and Miss Karina's maids dispatched them without any difficulty.

"Ooh, dried grapes, huh? That would be great in a cheese soufflé."

"Mm. Dried figs."

Evidently, dried fruit was a popular dessert for ordinary folk. It seemed expensive, though; the ability to eat it frequently would probably depend on one's economic status.

We stocked up on smoked fish and meat, as well as any dried bonito and shellfish I could get my hands on.

Everyone was quite pleased by the time we left that area, and then we arrived in a section full of daily necessities and fashionable supplies.

"They've got lipstick and face powder!"

"You're too young for that stuff, Arisa. This lipstick might suit Nana or Lady Karina, though, don't you think?"

"Master, please apply it, I request."

"I—I suppose I wouldn't mind if you put it on for me as well."

Miss Karina did her best to piggyback on Nana's supplication. Unfortunately, unlike modern Japan, there weren't any samples for testing, so I had to buy it before we could try it out.

I did get to see Miss Karina sheepishly closing her eyes and puckering her lips, though. I felt like I got a pretty good deal.

"Master, could we purchase this soap and a pumice stone?"

"Sure. How about this sachet, too? It smells nice and sweet. Would you like me to buy you one?"

When I saw Liza demurely picking out everyday necessities, I wanted to treat her to something, too.

"B-but sir, to buy something so expensive for a mere slave would be—"

She started to refuse, but not quite as swiftly as usual. The scent of the sachet seemed to appeal to her.

"You always take such good care of everyone, Liza. You deserve to be rewarded from time to time."

After some additional persuading on my part, Liza meekly accepted the sachet.

*   *   *

As I was enjoying shopping with everyone, an alarming conversation suddenly reached my ears.

"...You say you're going to assassinate him, but how are you going to defeat the Holy Swordsman prince and one of the Eight Swordsmen of Shiga?"

"What, you think I'm gonna fight 'em head-on? Yeah, right. I'll use poison."

"Hmm. Hydra poison would certainly do the trick, but it's not easy to get that stuff here..."

It was great that my "Keen Hearing" skill picked up on an assassination plot and all, but I couldn't tell where in the crowd it was coming from.

I listened closer, trying to pinpoint the source.

But this time, I heard a different voice.

"I made a deal with that criminal guild. They're going to cause a disturbance while we sneak into the duke's dungeon and rescue our brethren."

"Now we'll definitely get promoted!"

...Another sinister plot. So there were several groups of criminals around.

The former men were members of a criminal guild, while the latter seemed to be leftover members of the Wings of Freedom.

I checked on the map, but there were so many members of the lawless guild around that I couldn't tell who was talking. The conversation had ceased, too, so I was out of luck there.

On the other hand, I found the Wings of Freedom dregs pretty quickly.

As it turned out, they were already in trouble: The scheming pair was completely encircled by old capital guards.

It didn't look like I'd be needed this time. This place had pretty good guards, as far as I could tell.

"Master, they're selling something unusual there."

When Lulu called out to me, I closed my map search for now and looked where she was pointing.

"Is that meat jelly?"

"I'm surprised you know such a humble food for common people, sir," the shopkeeper said, eyebrows raised. "Are you really a nobleman?"

So it's only popular with commoners here? But it's so good.

"I am, albeit a newly minted one," I replied with a smile.

I ordered enough for everyone to try it.

The wobbly texture of the jellied broth was a big hit with the kids. With better ingredients and presentation, it could be popular with nobles as well.

While I was musing on this, the younger kids had already moved on to a new target.

"Something smells good, sir."

"Ooh, I'd know that smell anywhere! Someone's cooking with soy sauce." Arisa searched the area eagerly. "There it is. Squid teriyaki! Private Pochi, Private Tama, secure the suspects at once!"

"Secuuure."

"You're under arrest, sir."

Tama, Pochi, and Arisa went running up to the stall. Mia followed after them, drawn in by their enthusiasm, but she probably wouldn't be able to eat it. Liza and Lulu followed the younger girls at a calmer pace.

…That really does smell good.

I decided to put any extraneous thoughts aside to enjoy our tour of the old capital in peace.

"Master!"

Nana pulled on my arm. She tugged me in the opposite direction of the others, where she had found something else that caught her interest.

"…Master?" Liza noticed my absence at once.

"Watch the kids, please. We'll be back in just a minute."

With my map, it wouldn't take long to meet up again.

Besides, Nana was pressing my arm into her chest in a decidedly pleasant way.

She ended up leading me toward two ratfolk children. They were right across the main street.

As it turned out, they weren't ratfolk at all—the way their heads bobbed as they walked and the slickness of their skin said differently. My AR display revealed that they were **sealfolk sisters**.

"The movement of those larvae does not compute. It is inefficient, yet I cannot look away, I report."

So the kids were what Nana wanted to see. Their unusual gait certainly was cute.

After watching for a moment, we turned back to rejoin the others. My arm was very happy, but I didn't want to worry everyone by staying away too long.

Just then, a single shout brought an abrupt end to the tranquility.

"Runaway horse! Get out of the way!"

Not far away, I heard screams, neighing, and the sounds of people and things being knocked over willy-nilly.

Since we had just stepped back into the main street, I carried Nana over to the side of the road.

"Master! The larvae are in danger, I declare!"

There was a rare note of distress in Nana's monotone voice. Looking back into the crowd, I saw the two sealfolk children crouching underfoot in terror.

A moment later, a large tigerfolk man accidentally tripped into the pair, kicking them both into the air.

"Larvae!" Nana cried.

Before I knew it, she had jumped out of my arms. Somersaulting through the air, she landed clear on the other side of the crowd in a matter of moments.

She seemed to have used the Foundation ability Body Strengthening, though I'd never seen it invoked so quickly.

At the same moment, the tigerfolk man looked over his shoulder at the children he'd kicked.

In a moment of poetic justice, the rampaging horse came bolting down the street straight toward him. The horse collided with the tigerfolk man, sending him flying into the air like a scene out of a gag manga.

I was concerned for both the man and the horse, but first I ran over to Nana, who was holding the two sealfolk kids in her arms.

"Master, master! The larvae are leaking liquid from their mouths. Emergency treatment is required, I request. Please hurry quickly and with utmost urgency, I entreat!"

I took a few potions out of Storage through my pocket and had the two sealfolk children drink them.

Their HP gauges quickly returned to normal in the AR display.

Just in time.

I wasn't sure why, but the crowd of onlookers who'd gathered around us all cheered.

Sealfolk must be pretty popular. No wonder Nana found them so charming.

The rampaging horse turned out to have a Wings of Freedom member as its rider, so the guards were quick to tie him up and take him away.

The tigerfolk man was bloodstained and unconscious, but I didn't see any serious threat to his life, so I stood by as other tigerfolk carried him away. However, I didn't feel like offering him a potion, because he never apologized to the children.

Deciding not to deal with any more leftover cult stragglers, I searched the old capital on the map again.

Aside from the ones who had just been arrested, the only remaining members were all imprisoned, either in jail or at the duke's castle. Expanding the search range a little, I found several more members aboard a boat entering the harbor.

I could hardly just leave dangerous terrorists alone, but going to arrest them myself would be a pain—I mean, outside my authority. Better to leave these things to the professionals.

"I have a message from His Grace the duke."

"What? Where are you?"

I slipped down a back alley and used my "Ventriloquism" skill to whisper to the guard captain standing on the main street.

I thought this was more than ventriloquism, but I wasn't going to look a gift horse in the mouth.

"There are surviving members of the Wings of Freedom aboard a ship currently entering the harbor, the SS *Liberation*. You are to raid the ship and capture them."

The captain looked more dubious than convinced, so I added, "You must act quickly." At that, he seemed to decide it was best not to ignore it and gathered a few men to head over to the harbor.

Since the guards here had some skill, I figured I should be able to leave the rest to them.

"…Yummy."

When I went back to Nana, I found the sealfolk kids still licking the insides of the vials from the potions. They must have liked the sweetener I added.

Watching them, I remembered little Ine, the witch's apprentice who

I'd met in Kuhanou County. No doubt she was still studying away under the old witch's guidance.

"Master, I would like us to adopt these children, I propose."

Nana held up the two sealfolk kids pleadingly. The sisters made no move to protest, still absorbed in licking the last drops from their vials.

"No."

"Master, please reconsider."

"Sorry, Nana."

Nana pleadingly came closer, but I couldn't just give in to her this time.

Before long, the distant ringing of bells sent the children into a panic in Nana's arms.

Of course, I instructed her to let them go. She hesitated a little, but seeing how frantic the children were, she relented and put them down.

For some reason, the two were heading toward the rest of our group, so we ended up following behind them.

The sealfolk kids led us to a plaza lined by seven temples, where various priests and volunteers were currently feeding the hungry.

Which was great and all, but...

"Line uuup, line uuup?"

"Please get in line, sir! Cutting is a no-no, sir."

For reasons unknown, Tama and Pochi were supervising the line.

Mia was there, too, not helping them but playing a leaf flute while staring at the crowd curiously. Evidently she wasn't used to seeing lines like this.

"The line ends here. Please have your bowls ready and line up in three columns."

"You there! Don't fight, or we'll send you to the back!"

Liza and Arisa were in charge of the end of the queue.

The sealfolk kids joined the throng per their instructions. Nana moved to line up with them, and I put my hand lightly on her shoulder to stop her.

"Oh, master, there you are. What were you and Nana doing?"

"She wanted to protect those kids."

I briefly explained to Arisa about the runaway horse situation.

"Is that right? Here I thought you went off to mess around together somewhere."

Even if that was true, I was sure Mia would have found us right away.

Last time I asked her how she was able to track me down, she'd simply answered, "Spirits," so maybe they helped her find me or something. It certainly struck me as the kind of thing an elf would do in a fantasy world.

"So how did you all end up helping with this soup kitchen line, anyway?"

"It just sort of happened, I guess? A bunch of beastfolk men were pushing through the line and causing a ruckus, so Pochi scolded them. When they tried to attack her, Liza and the others had to take them down a notch. Next thing you know, we were volunteering to help with crowd control."

I see. I could certainly picture all that unfolding.

"That's good, I guess. Then why is Lulu helping out in the booth?"

"There was an older lady doing the serving, but she got injured while those jerks were causing trouble."

Mia was able to heal the old woman's wounds, but she was still in shock from the violence, so she ended up going home. As a result, they were short-staffed, and Lulu offered to help.

"There's only about an hour left. Do you mind if we stay and help? I'd hate to ditch them halfway through."

"Of course."

Interacting with the locals was an important part of sightseeing. Besides, I saw someone I knew standing next to Lulu.

I wanted to bring Nana to help them as well, but she refused to leave the sealfolk kids, so I let her have her way.

"Master!"

Lulu noticed me and smiled brightly, a bandanna tied around her black hair. If she had a tail like Pochi's, I guarantee it would have been wagging like crazy.

"Satou!"

Then, stepping out from behind Lulu, wearing a pure-white shrine maiden–like outfit, Sara smiled at me, too.

It was hard to believe that just yesterday she'd been bedridden with the status condition **Weakened: Mild**. Must be nice to be so young.

"Good to see you again, Lady Sara..." I managed to catch myself right before adding, *How are you feeling?*

"So we meet again."

Sara's voice was full of emotions, and her eyes caught mine and refused to let go.

…Like a maiden in love.

"Well, I did promise you at the castle in Gururian City."

"……Of course."

Caught up in the moment, I spoke with more charm in my voice than I'd intended.

I suspect that was the cause of the strange silence hovering in the air.

It was broken by little growls from Arisa and Mia, who had approached without my noticing.

Sorry, Sara, but it looks like the romantic mood ends here.

I bopped the two younger girls on the head to reset the tone of the conversation.

"By the way, you came here on an emergency summons from the temple, right? Has the issue been resolved already?"

"Y-yes… It was a false alarm, it seems."

"A false alarm?"

"Indeed."

Sara bit her lip and nodded.

The men who'd plotted to resurrect the demon lord with Sara as a sacrifice must have sent the summons.

Putting that in the back of my mind, I tried to lighten the mood with a friendly chat.

Suddenly, I felt eyes boring into me from behind, so I turned around.

Miss Karina was watching me intently, but behind her, I saw a group of temple knights in the shade of a grove near the food stall.

They must be watching over Miss Sara. Among them, I saw the young man and woman I'd met in Muno Barony. Sir Keon Bobino was nowhere to be seen—unsurprising, considering his family's current situation.

Having just recovered after losing her life in a sacrificial ceremony to summon a demon lord, Sara naturally had increased security. Aside from the temple knights, there were several imperial knights disguised as citizens hovering nearby.

I wondered why they hadn't intervened earlier when my kids had to stop the ruckus, but it was probably either because Sara herself wasn't in danger or because the beastfolk girls simply moved faster.

"Lady Sara, the people in line are waiting."

"Oh no, I'm sorry."

"My apologies for interrupting. I'll go and help with the cooking while you get back to serving, if that's all right."

I felt bad for making the people wait, so I decided to move out of the way.

Seeing Sara and Lulu handing out food together was truly a sight for sore eyes. I felt like a staff member keeping an eye on an idol duo's meet-and-greet event.

The food they were distributing looked to be a seaweed-based soup with dumplings inside. As far as I could tell, there weren't enough hands making the dumplings; I went to offer my assistance.

"Here, let me help."

"No, it's all right, erm…sire. I couldn't have a noble help us, sire."

One of the older ladies who was cooking politely refused. Her manner of addressing me was a little strange.

"It's all right. Sir Knight here is a friendly fellow. Back home, he even made sweets for the children in town."

"W-well, if you say so, Pina."

Miss Karina's maid escort Pina was kind enough to vouch for me as she helped with the cooking herself.

The other maid, Erina, was watching the work from beside the booth. At some point, Mia wandered over to sit with them, still playing her leaf flute.

After exchanging brief greetings, I started helping the other cooks.

"Please wear this, young master."

A young lady offered me an apron, commenting that it would be a shame for my clothes to get dirty.

Her task of grinding fish paste looked like the hardest, so I took over for her.

Bored of hanging around, Mia came over to peer at what I was doing.

"Little miss, would you come and make dumplings with me?"

"Mm, sure."

Mia shuffled over to help the older lady.

"Lady Karina, would you like to join Mia as well?"

"I–I…erm…n-no, thank you!"

Miss Karina had made it clear she wanted to join in, but she turned down my invitation. She was probably too nervous about interacting with strangers.

Well, I don't want to force her to do anything.

"You're rather strong for a noble."

One of the old ladies came over to praise me.

"If you like, why don't you come work at our shop? You can marry my daughter."

What is it with old ladies and their matchmaking schemes?

"No."

""""N-no!"""""

Mia and Lulu were quick to decline on my behalf. Oddly enough, Sara and Mia spoke in perfect unison with Lulu.

""""...Huh?"""""

All three of them looked at one another in surprise.

It was cute to see Lulu and Sara clap their hands to their mouths and all, but the people waiting for food were glaring at me. I prompted them to return to their work.

Miss Karina wasn't bothering anyone, though, so I left her alone with her obvious surprise.

Sara and Lulu were too young to be romantic interests for me, but they were certainly cute to look at. Maybe in five years or so, they could form a duo.

Or wait, maybe Miss Karina could join them, too, and make an idol group?

In that case, though, we'd have to do something about Miss Karina's shyness first.

Before long, the soup kitchen closed up for the day without too much difficulty.

There were a few people exclaiming about how the meat dumplings suddenly turned into gourmet cuisine partway through, but a glare from Liza silenced them before it turned into a riot.

I guess my maxed-out "Cooking" skill was probably to blame for that, huh?

"Helping out is great and all, but keep it in check next time!" Arisa chided me in a whisper.

Well, excuse me for not realizing I had to restrain myself when all I was doing was grinding fish paste with a mortar.

Even if I turned off certain skills, it didn't change much at this point. After using "Formulation" and "Transmutation" enough times, I was able to deliberately make items of lower quality, so maybe the same would prove true with enough "Cooking" experience.

I don't really want to make gross food on purpose, though. If I'm going to cook, it might as well be tasty.

Chatting as I cooked with the older ladies, who were mostly local housewives and temple peons, I learned a lot about the soup kitchen and downtown life.

The five local temples took turns running the soup kitchen, which was held once every other day. The temples, as well as contributions from local nobles and celebrities, covered the costs.

Because the priest in charge of collecting donations happened to be around while we were discussing this, I gave ten gold coins, much to his shock. As it turned out, a lesser noble like myself would usually just donate a few silvers.

As I was reflecting on all this, we finished cleaning up after the cooking, so everyone helped carry the equipment to the nearby Tenion Temple in the plaza.

By the way, the temple where I visited the head priestess was in the nobles' quarter. This one was evidently for commoners.

"Cleaniiing!"

"Sir!"

Tama and Pochi made for an adorable sign as they hoisted a long table in the air together.

"One-two, hup!" Arisa was directing them by waving a stick in the air.

"I'm sorry you wound up helping us clean, too."

"It's no trouble at all; don't worry."

I was just having a normal conversation with Sara, Mia. You didn't need to kick me in the butt.

Lulu walked by carrying a heavy-looking stockpot as if it weighed next to nothing. Thanks to the benefits of leveling up, even Lulu was stronger than the average adult male now.

"Look up there!"

"It's Lady Ringrande!"

The pair of young temple knights exclaimed and pointed at the sky.

Ah, this feels like déjà vu.

I looked up to see a familiar flying wooden horse with a lovely woman aboard descending toward us.

"Sister Rin…"

Sara scrunched up her face in a childish pout, an unusual expression for her.

As the cheers of "Ringrande!" started up around us, Sara frowned and pulled me by the hand into the temple storehouse. The other kids panicked and followed behind us, still holding the cooking equipment.

"Lady Sara, don't you want to greet your elder sister?"

"N-not really. I left the house of Duke Ougoch, after all…"

I wanted to try to mediate between the sisters, but Sara wasn't having any of it. I guess she really wasn't too fond of her older sister.

"Sara! There you are!"

Bursting through the door of the temple and into the storehouse, Miss Ringrande called out to Sara with a huge smile.

Miss Ringrande, on the other hand, seemed to love her little sister.

"You've gotten so big since I last saw you! You used to be so small— Oh? Is that Satou?"

Miss Ringrande stopped in the middle of her attempt at friendly conversation with her sister and stared at me. Then her eyes flicked over my hand, still joined with Sara's.

Arisa's and Mia's intense, reproachful stares had probably drawn her attention.

The rest of the group had already gone back to helping with the equipment, but Arisa and Mia had stayed behind as chaperones.

"Satou, you're awfully close with my sister, aren't you?"

"Satou… Have you and Sister Rin met before?"

Miss Ringrande and Sara were both gazing at me intently.

…*Huh? What is this, a soap opera?*

I couldn't keep my heart from pounding at being interrogated by two beautiful sisters, but I forced myself to calmly answer them in turn.

"I became acquainted with Lady Ringrande when she briefly landed on the ship we took to the old capital."

"Come now, why be so reserved after the exciting encounter we had on that ship?"

Miss Ringrande's response to my simple explanation was just begging to be misinterpreted.

"……E-exciting encounter…?" Sara repeated.

She was starting to glare at her sister like a mortal enemy, so I hastily intervened.

"Yes, we had a practice duel on the deck."

"Yes, and then you treated me to some of your delicious cooking, remember? It was on par with the cuisine of the royal castle or the Saga Empire's imperial court."

Sara had started to look relieved until her sister added more superfluous details.

"W-was it, by any chance, that transparent soup…?"

"No, that takes much too long to make."

"I see…"

Sara's expression softened again, and her grip on my hand relaxed a little.

"Transparent soup? Is that the consommé soup that Father asked you to make for the next evening party?"

Come on—can't we move on from this topic already?

Unfortunately, I couldn't simply ignore the words of a member of the duke's family; I nodded reluctantly.

"An evening party, you say…?"

Sara furrowed her brow, conflicted.

She probably wanted to eat it, but since she'd relinquished her status as a noble, she might have a hard time participating in the party.

As a friend, I decided to throw her a line.

"I was thinking of bringing consommé soup next time I visit the Tenion Temple, too. Do you think the head priestess and everyone would like it?"

"Yes, of course! I'm sure they'll all be thrilled!"

She accepted my suggestion with high enthusiasm.

I didn't think the head priestess could eat much, but she should be able to handle some soup.

This time, it was Miss Ringrande who was acting a little sullen at being left out.

"Satou, are you after my sister? Sara left home to join the temple because she didn't like living as a noble, you know. If you're trying to use her to get ahead in society, you'll have to fight me first!"

"Sister Rin!"

Sara's lovely eyes widened at her sister's challenge.

It didn't seem like she really harbored any ill will toward Ringrande, so I smiled at her before answering the accusation.

"Lady Ringrande, there is no need to worry about any such thing. I consider Lady Sara a dear friend, but I would never harbor such high aspirations." For good measure, I added, "And I don't want to get ahead in society, either."

"I see... Very well, then."

Ringrande didn't seem entirely convinced. She was probably still sorting out her emotions.

Sara, meanwhile, smiled bashfully when she heard the words *dear friend*. As the granddaughter of a duke and a chosen Oracle priestess, she most likely found friendships only rarely.

"I'll believe you, at least for now. So, how did you get so close to Sara, anyway?"

"I was appointed to be Lady Sara's guide during her visit to the Muno Barony, and we eventually became close after that."

"Close..." Both Ringrande and Sara muttered.

Though they were repeating the same word, their expressions were very different.

Sara cracked a small smile, while Miss Ringrande had the wariness of a mother bear protecting its young.

Hmm. Maybe I should have phrased that a little more carefully?

"Lady Sara! Come quickly! The prince! His Highness Prince Sharorik draws near!"

The priestess burst into the room, dispelling any minor regrets on my part.

What could that dangerous prince possibly want with Sara?

Considering his general attitude toward women, I was a little worried.

The Old Capital in Turmoil

Satou here. In a psychological manga I once read, there was a line that went something like, "Absolute power corrupts absolutely." I suppose this mantra might apply in parallel worlds, too.

"You wait here, Sara. I'll take care of His Highness."

"No, I'll go with you."

Miss Ringrande wanted to protect Sara, but she was too stubborn to hide away and let someone else take care of it.

She had no apparent intention of letting go of my hand, either. She led me toward the door to the temple, too.

I told Arisa and Mia to go join Liza and the rest.

Unfortunately, we ended up running into the prince and his attendants on the way to the temple's drawing room.

The only attendants with the prince this time were the boy knight and one of the chamberlains. There was no sign of the shield-bearing knight who had kept him in line before.

"How unusual to see you set foot inside a temple, Your Highness."

"Rin! So it was you riding that wooden Pegasus!"

The prince was all smiles, in stark contrast with Ringrande's displeased expression.

"Please do not call me by a nickname, Your Highness."

"Why not? What's wrong with using a nickname for my fiancée?"

"Your *former* fiancée. I obtained permission from His Majesty before leaving the kingdom."

So she'd had enough of his philandering, basically.

The prince, on the other hand, didn't seem to know when to give up.

"Those are your words, not mine. I don't recall approving of any such thing. I've dealt with all my illegitimate children, and Yureen and Demetina have both agreed to welcome you. What's the problem?"

What, indeed? Even I can tell that there are plenty of problems here. For one thing, his use of the phrase *dealt with* was definitely alarming. I had no desire to become any more acquainted with his dark side.

"Have you forgotten what you did to a bride the night before her marriage into another family? It nearly caused a county to defect from the kingdom."

"Razena? That's already taken care of. And that churlish duke has been replaced."

The prince's smile couldn't have been any scarier if he tried. For lack of a better word, it made him look soulless.

"…So, what business might you have at the temple today?"

Glowering at the prince, Sara stepped in to interrupt.

"Why, you insolent—"

The back of the prince's hand flew toward Sara's face.

"Ah!"

A heavy thud overlapped with Sara's scream.

There was no way I was just going to stand by without protecting her, of course.

The prince's hand, clad in a metal gauntlet, was stopped dead by my own palm.

Clearly, he had planned to backhand her with all his strength.

If he hit an ordinary girl like that, her neck would probably snap, killing her instantly. Even Sara, who was level 30, would've undoubtedly sustained a severe injury.

"Your Highness!"

Miss Ringrande stepped toward the prince menacingly, but he held her off with one arm and glared at me.

"Interrupting my conversation with Rin was bad enough, but making physical contact with royalty? That's a guaranteed death sentence, plebian."

Wow. I've never been called a "plebian" in real life before.

"Do it."

"Yes, sir! It's okay if I take both of them out, riiight?"

The young knight drew his sword.

How could anyone want to cause bloodshed at a temple in a world where gods were real, tangible beings?

"Stop!" Ringrande shouted.

"Sorry! Prince's orders, I'm afraid."

Ignoring her, the boy pointed his sword toward me.

In reality, it would be easy for me to defeat him in combat, but I could get in big trouble if the action was construed as drawing my sword on royalty. Instead, I decided to take the classic Japanese strategy of nonaggressive defense.

Stepping in front of Sara to protect her, I pulled out a wet towel from Storage by way of the Garage Bag and used it to intercept the young knight's sword. I'd forgotten to put it in the laundry after bathing yesterday.

"What in the world is that? Some kind of magic item?"

"It's just a towel."

"A towel?! Don't you dare mock me!"

Oddly enough, the boy didn't like my honest answer to his question. Flying into a rage, he came at me like a berserker. *All right, then.*

"I thought I told you to stop."

Just then, Miss Ringrande's sword came up and stopped his.

Thank goodness. I didn't want my favorite towel to get ripped.

"Tch! It's impolite to interrupt a battle, you know. But if it means I can fight the Witch of Heavenly Destruction, I'll be happy to take care of those nobodies later."

The boy knight licked his lips eagerly, but I was pretty sure he was thoroughly outclassed.

Sure enough, the young man was on the temple floor with a broken sword in a matter of seconds.

"What is the meaning of this?!" the prince demanded.

"I'd like to ask you the same question. First you try to kill my little sister, then my apprentice who protected her? Are you perhaps trying to get the Ougoch Duchy to withdraw from the Shiga Kingdom this time?"

Miss Ringrande's tone was dripping with sarcasm.

"This brat is your younger sister? What a terribly plain child. To think that I should have to marry such a girl..."

"Excuse me? Are you out of your mind?"

The prince's remark was a bombshell, but Miss Ringrande could get herself accused of treason with a reply like that.

Sara, unable to process the sudden turn of events, clung to my sleeve and listened nervously.

"I'm quite sane, thank you. I must wed the daughters of three dukes to attain the rank of emperor."

"Are you trying to usurp the throne? Everyone knows that Prince Sortorik is an excellent heir, skilled with both the pen and the sword."

"Usurp, you say? Hmph, so you support that so-called prodigy, too…" The prince scoffed at Ringrande's anger. "Don't you know why the 'Oracle' was split between temples?"

Hmm? Does the prince know why?

Miss Ringrande looked shaken by the prince's confidence.

"What do you…?"

"The time of great upheaval is upon us. An era of drastic change will come, just as when the ancestral king and the first hero of the Saga Empire founded the kingdom."

It was as if the prince was delivering a monologue onstage.

Miss Ringrande was too entranced by his words to move.

As for myself, I wished he'd refrain from using loaded phrases like *great upheaval* and *era of change*. That was sure to trigger some dangerous flags.

"And it is I, Sharorik Shiga, who will defeat the demon lord, overcome the trials of the era, and create a new kingdom—no, a new empire of all humanfolk!"

Since there were no middle names in this kingdom, his dramatic declaration of his name felt a bit lacking.

"Rin! Abandon the hero of the Saga Empire and return to me! If you do so now, I shall forgive the past and welcome you with open arms!"

The prince had decided to shelve their former issues as he tried to win back Ringrande.

Miss Ringrande's eyes, on the other hand, were so cold they could've frozen a bonfire.

Just as she opened her mouth to give a sharp response, though, more red dots appeared on my radar.

In addition to the two representing the prince and the boy knight, there were now ten others.

Seven were in the plaza in front of the Tenion Temple, while three more were behind it.

According to my map search, the three in front were remaining Wings of Freedom members, while the rest belonged to the assassins' guild Hog's Hoof.

The former group must have been the ones who came on that ship. Wondering what happened to the guards I sent, I checked the ship to see that they were locked in a fierce battle with the other Wings of Freedom members.

Come on, you're not supposed to trigger events in two different places at once.

"Lady Sara! There is danger afoot! You—"

Charging in, the temple knight stopped short when he saw the chaos.

Outside, temple knights were fighting the Wings of Freedom group, while the assassins were coming in through the back door of the temple.

Instead of joining the battle, my kids were heading toward the warehouse to find me.

Given the high levels of Miss Ringrande and the prince, I decided to leave fending off the enemies to them and take Sara with me to meet up with the others.

"Lady Ringrande! I'll take care of Lady Sara. Please defeat the attackers!"

"All right, I suppose."

Miss Ringrande filled an amulet-like object under her cloak with magic power, and it activated Anti-Arrow Defense and Body Strengthening buffs.

What a useful magic item.

Just then, the temple knight standing near the entrance of the shrine went flying, as if he'd been hit by a dump truck.

GROOROROWN.

With a bizarre roar, a giant monster appeared at the entrance with dark-gray tentacles sprouting from his head.

It was a lesser hell demon, only level 30, but he had three unusual race-specific abilities: Stretch, Steel Body, and Regeneration. It would be tough to fight him in close quarters with ordinary weapons, but the prince's Holy Sword or Miss Ringrande's magic should make quick work of him.

From behind the demon, a number of mechanical-looking silver flying insects were zipping into the temple.

Behind them, I saw another lesser hell demon outside spewing the insects from his nest-like head.

He seemed to have the race abilities Production and Defense Wall and the skills "Lightning Magic" and "Direction."

"There she is! That's the girl, Sara! If we capture her, we can still rescue our brethren and resurrect His Majesty the demon lord! Our comrade will take care of the fools around her, now that he's a demon."

An intellectual-looking fellow in a purple robe appeared behind the demon and kindly explained their entire plan.

That was nice of him. I guess I'll go easy on that one.

"Master! Instructions, please!"

Liza poked her head out from the door to the storehouse.

I was proud of her for not just jumping into action.

"Help me protect Lady Sara. Lady Sara, my apologies."

I lifted her up bridal-style and headed to the storehouse.

"They're getting away! After them!"

"Do you really think I'll let you do that?"

"Out of the way!"

One of the remnants of the cult tried to chase after us and was immediately reduced to a corpse by a slash of Miss Ringrande's sword.

"…A lightning broadsword? Is that the Heavenly Witch of Destruction?! What is one of the hero's followers doing here?!"

The intellectual turned pale when he saw the purple lightning crackling along Ringrande's sword.

A streak of lightning shot toward the man, but a gorilla-like lug jumped out to take the hit instead.

The men who charged the prince and his young knight were already lying in a pool of blood.

People here really have no problem with killing…

I felt a little sick, but I pushed it down and rushed into the storehouse with Sara in my arms.

My radar let me know that some silver insects were flying after us. They were about level 15—low enough that my friends should be enough to handle them.

"Liza! Defeat those bugs, please."

"Understood!"

There were a total of five of them behind us, a bit too many to leave to Liza alone.

"Tama and Pochi, you two take on one of the insects together. Nana, protect the others."

"Okaaay."

"Of course, sir!"

"Yes, master."

The beastfolk girls rushed toward the insects with their weapons at the ready.

"I...I can fight, too!"

"Then please take care of one, too, Lady Karina."

I quickly gave Miss Karina an assignment. At her level, she probably wouldn't be able to beat it, but with Raka's barrier, she should be able to at least hold her own.

As I lowered Sara to the floor, I used my free hand to take out the remaining two with pebbles from Storage. The insects burst on the impact, their remains scattering everywhere.

That would be tough to clean up after.

"Sara, stay near Nana, please."

"O-of course."

Nana equipped a Kite Shield from Storage. Her usual shield was too big to fit inside.

"Arisa, take this!"

"Okeydoke!"

Miss Karina produced the demon-sealing bell from her chest and tossed it to Arisa.

As soon as she caught it, Arisa filled it with magic until it glowed blue, then rang it to slow the silver pests immediately.

"Satou."

"Master, more insects!"

Hearing Mia and Lulu call out, I looked back to the entrance to see a man guarded by two of the bugs. It was the beefy guy who took the lightning strike for the academic one earlier.

"What?! It's not working!"

Arisa suddenly cried out in surprise. She must have tried to use chant-less Psychic Magic on the bulky cultist.

"Arisa, hide behind Nana with Mia..." I stepped in front of Nana as I spoke, my eyes on the muscular man. "He's a demon."

As if on cue, the man's body swelled up immensely. As it grew, it smashed through the wall between the temple and the storehouse, scattering stones and dust.

According to my AR, he was a level-45 intermediate hell demon. He looked like a bipedal bull with purple skin.

I walked toward him steadily, holding in my hand the fairy sword I'd taken out of the Garage Bag.

Trying to intimidate me, the demon snorted and breathed red flames from his half-open mouth.

GELWBAOOOWN.

As he roared, a multitude of fireballs formed around him.

Sorry, but those aren't coming anywhere near me. I used Break Magic from the magic menu to dispel the fireballs.

Then, with a casual swipe, I sliced the demon's head off, along with the arm he tried to use to defend himself.

Almost too easily, the demon turned to black dust and scattered into nothingness. All that was left was the used long horn and a large, low-grade core.

"Huh? How did you defeat a demon so easily?"

"I've fought that type before. He's usually just a diversion. He looks scary, but he's actually quite weak."

Sara nodded, apparently convinced.

"Master, we're finished over here," Liza reported. The group had already defeated the silver insects.

"My dress got a bit torn, I'm afraid."

"My apologies, Lady Karina. I must have made the barrier a bit too small."

There was a two- or three-inch cut on the end of Miss Karina's skirt.

"I shall sew it for you when we return to the mansion."

Pina consoled the disappointed Karina.

"Pochi, you okaaay?"

"This is nothing, sir."

"Heal."

I noticed Mia treating Pochi's injured arm.

Walking over, I peered into her face. "Are you all right, Pochi?"

"Yes, sir. It's my fault for letting my guard down, sir. When we get back to the house, I'll train more, sir!"

"Tama toooo."

"Very good, you two."

I patted Pochi and Tama on their heads, then straightened up.

I hadn't expected Pochi to get injured by the silver fliers. Better take care of the rest myself.

"Master, are we going to assist the others?"

"No, stay here. We'd only hold them back."

I put my fairy sword away in Storage, taking out a short bow and some cheap arrows instead. It was a set I mostly used for hunting small birds.

With the bow in hand, I instructed Liza and the others to keep an eye on the alternate entrance and went to see how the rest of the temple was doing.

As my radar had already told me, Miss Ringrande and company were still fighting the lesser hell demons. Not surprising, since it had barely been a minute since I left.

They were having trouble concentrating on the fight with the demons because the silver creatures buzzing around near the ceiling kept swooping down to attack. On top of that, since Miss Ringrande wasn't wearing armor, she was fending off attacks from the demon's tentacles with her sword while she quickly chanted spells to defeat the bugs.

Two assassins hidden in a corner of the ceiling were aiming their crossbows at the prince, so I quickly fired at them with my short bow. The arrows sent them tumbling to the floor, where they vanished in the cloud of dust.

My "Keen Hearing" skill picked up two dry cracks—breaking bones. Judging by the slow rate of their declining HP, though, they shouldn't be in any immediate danger.

When one of them stubbornly pulled out a blowgun to aim at the prince, I knocked them both down with a piece of scrap wood I found on the floor.

I didn't particularly care to protect the prince, but if he was killed inside the Tenion Temple, it might cause trouble for Sara and the other priestesses.

Noticing that I'd saved him, the prince grimaced as he fended off the nest-headed demon.

I'm not going to say you owe me or anything. Just hurry up and beat this guy already.

I had plenty of arrows. I supposed I could help a little.

It wouldn't be too hard to beat the silver insects, but I decided to strategize a little by just shooting their wings.

The huge bugs jerked this way and that in a manner reminiscent of Brownian motion. They stayed still for a fraction of a second while changing direction; I attacked at that moment.

Firing arrows one after the other, I dropped the insects easily.

The young male knight, who had staggered back onto the battle-field, started dispatching the wriggling insects with the remains of his mithril sword.

The pests would occasionally slash back at him with the ends of their bladelike wings, so he was starting to get a little bloody. I was planning to have my kids finish them off after to raise their levels, but I guess it was better not to put them through that.

"Well done, boy!" the prince called. "Without these small fry to hinder us, we'll win in no time. Prepare to witness the power of a Holy Sword!"

With this last shout, Sharorik began to fill his Holy Sword, Claid-heamh Soluis, with magic power.

Cut the speeches and just beat him already, would you?

Emitting a pale-blue light, the sword destroyed the nest-head demon's magic barrier in a single blow.

"I'm impressed, demon! Few can withstand a strike from a Holy Sword!"

With more gratuitous shouting, the prince swung his sword back the other way.

The demon crossed his branch-like arms to catch the Holy Sword.

The sword shredded the demon's limbs, but it wasn't able to cut through them completely and got tangled up instead.

Maybe Claidheamh Soluis isn't as strong as the other Holy Swords? Or perhaps he couldn't bring out its full power without the Hero title.

Miss Ringrande, on the other hand, created small magic explosions to blow away the tentacles that shot toward her, then slipped through the opening to cut the demon's head off with her Spellbladed Magic Sword.

"Rin! Don't let your guard down! It's not over yet!"

I shouted a warning at Miss Ringrande as she turned to assist the prince.

There wasn't enough time to call out her lengthy name, hence the nickname. Hopefully she'd forgive me.

With my short bow, I shot down the severed gray tentacle that was reaching to cut off Ringrande's leg.

Miss Ringrande hurriedly sliced up the headless demon as he lurched toward her, then slashed his head in half on the floor, finally turning him to black dust.

"Thank you, Satou." Miss Ringrande glanced toward the prince. "Looks like he's done, too."

"Yes, so it would seem."

As I responded, I fired one last shot. The arrow grazed the prince's cheek as it flew past him.

"How dare you, you—"

The prince's insult was cut short when the assassin behind him shrieked in pain.

That was the third and final assassin. A nearby temple knight hastily ran to arrest him.

"My apologies, Your Highness. I'm afraid there wasn't a moment to spare to call out first."

"Hmph. I suppose I see why Rin took you on as a pupil. The reward for your assistance shall cancel out the punishment you would have earned for this scratch."

"I appreciate your generosity."

I responded as blandly as I could. I wasn't exactly expecting a reward from him, anyway.

"Here, I'll give you this, too."

The prince picked up the core that had fallen at his feet and tossed it to me.

I was just gonna assume it was an accident that it came right at my face.

"Rin, we'll continue our conversation in the duke's castle. Come to my room when you get back," the prince commented toward Ringrande before he left, looking a bit disappointed that I'd easily snatched the core from the air.

...Did you forget about Sara already, Prince?

"What an idiot. Why would I ever do that?"

Miss Ringrande glowered at the door after the prince left, muttering under her breath.

I picked up the short horns scattered on the floor, added the one I already had on hand, and gave them to Ringrande.

This was a calculated move to hide the long horn dropped by the intermediate hell demon. There could be trouble if people found out what kind of demon I'd defeated so easily.

"Lady Ringrande, please give these to His Grace the duke."

"Oh? You're not going to keep calling me Rin, then?"

Miss Ringrande winked and lightly touched a finger to my chin.

So she did remember that.

"I'm terribly sorry about that. It was an emergency. I felt I had no choice."

"Yes, I appreciate that. And I suppose I shouldn't tease someone who saved my life. But you really can call me Rin…" She grinned mischievously. "Once you're strong enough to beat Hayato the Hero, of course."

"Then it may be a long time yet," I responded.

Turning toward the storehouse entrance, I beckoned to the others. The temple was safe, and that dodgy prince was gone, so I figured we should leave before we got in the way too much.

If possible, I'd been hoping to get my group baptized by the Tenion Temple so they'd meet the conditions of the Treasure of Resurrection; now didn't seem like the moment to bring it up, though. It could wait until next time.

Sara thanked us and saw us off as we left the downtown Tenion Temple behind.

◆

Many of the vendors on the main street had closed early, probably because of the whole mess with the demons, so we decided to go elsewhere, too.

First, I had to persuade a reluctant Nana to let the sealfolk kids go home. As thanks for going along with her, I gave them some tasty baked snacks. Then we took the carriage past the large wall to the museum that was between the nobles' and the trade districts.

The music hall across from the museum was an option, too, but the latter won out in the popular vote.

This was technically part of the nobles' quarter as well, but commoners could enter as long as they were reasonably well dressed. There were no rules against demi-humans, either, of course.

Still, it was probably better to play it safe so nobody would bother us on our sightseeing trip.

"Yamatooo?"

"King, sir."

Tama and Pochi, clad in hooded coats that covered their ears and tails, read the sign above the museum entrance.

The museum consisted of three areas, connected by a main hall. The largest area was currently home to a limited-time exhibition called the "Ancestral King Yamato" exhibit.

"Looks pretty crowded over there," Arisa remarked with some surprise.

The limited-time exhibit was as crowded as a popular attraction at a theme park.

"You're right. It doesn't seem like we can get a fast pass or anything. Let's check out the other areas first."

"Agreeeed."

"Yes, sir."

There was a recommended viewing order anyway, so we decided to follow that route.

The first area was mainly taxidermy specimens and skeletons. A glass wall protected the more valuable ones, while a sign stated that the open displays were mostly local specimens and could be freely touched.

"Watch out, sirs! Go on without me; I'll hold them off, sirs!"

"It's all cup to youuu."

"Pochi, we'll defeat the demon lord! Come find us!"

Guys, please, don't put on a whole performance. Just look around normally. And Tama, you mean "it's all up to you." What would "cup to you" even mean?

"Master, can it not move? I inquire."

Nana pointed at a taxidermic animal that resembled a cross between a kingfisher and a squirrel.

"No, because it's stuffed."

Maybe a necromancer could make it move.

"Oh, master, look at this! It's so cute."

Personally, I thought Lulu was much cuter.

"An unusual animal, is it not? It has very small wings for a bird."

"Penguin."

Lulu, Liza, and Mia were all examining a stuffed penguin.

So penguins existed in this world, too. Hopefully, there weren't any stuffed penguinfolk or anything.

Still, though, why weren't there any other people around but us? This area was strangely unpopular.

The atmosphere was pretty similar to the museums back in Japan, but with monster specimens among the exhibits, it definitely packed an extra punch.

"It looks like it could jump out and bite you at any second."

"Scaryyy?"

"I'm not scared. It's just a taxiderry, sir."

Abandoning their little drama, the beastfolk girls gathered around a large stuffed creature called a "fortress tiger."

Oh, hey.

"Pochi, come here for a second."

"Coming, sir."

Pochi tottered over, and I picked her up, moving her hand toward a ferocious-looking beast.

"That doesn't scare me, sir."

Pochi rolled her eyes at me.

"I'M...GOING TO...EAT YOU UP!"

I used "Ventriloquism" to tease her in a weird voice. Her unimpressed expression vanished immediately, and she flailed around in my arms.

"D-don't eat me, sir. I wouldn't taste good, sir."

"MEAT...TASTY."

"Meat is yummy, but I'm not meat, sir. So you can't eat me, sir."

Pochi was starting to look genuinely scared, so I put her down and showed her how I'd done my little trick.

"Sorry, Pochi."

"That was mean, master, sir. I was scared, sir."

I guess I took it a little too far.

Arisa came over and whispered into Pochi's ear, clearly giving her some kind of suggestion.

"I demand a 'pology and reprations, sir."

"Will having meat for dinner do as reparations, then?"

At that, Pochi's eyes sparkled, all traces of tears gone.

Naturally, Tama and Liza quickly swiveled their heads to listen intently.

"Hooray, sir! I want hamburg steaks, sir!"

"Are you sure? We just had the same thing yesterday."

"I have a separate stomach for hamburg steaks, sir."

That sounded pretty strange to me, but I decided it would be rude to question her.

Because no one else seemed to mind, we decided to have hamburg steaks for dinner. Mia's would be tofu, of course.

With that settled, we proceeded to the next room, a traditional costume display.

Among the clothing from various regions, I spotted what looked like nurse costumes and ao dai. There was even a bunny suit for some reason. I wouldn't mind seeing Nana or Miss Karina try that on. Sadly, other staples like maid outfits and gothic lolita were nowhere to be found.

I guess whatever Japanese person popularized certain fashions here must have had a personal bias.

"Master! Over here!"

While I stood musing in front of the ao dai, Arisa called me over from farther down the hall.

Coming to look, I found my friends dressed in traditional Japanese clothing, or something like it.

"Sa— Sir Pendragon. H-how do I look?"

"It's quite lovely on you."

Miss Karina was striking an awkward pose in a *Shinsengumi*-style haori, so I paid her some obligatory compliments.

"Have at theee."

"Have at thee, sir!"

Tama and Pochi were wearing similar outfits to Miss Karina's, brandishing wooden swords made to look like katana. They even put on Japanese-style kerchiefs to cover their ears.

"You sound more like Arthurian knights than *Shinsengumi* to me."

Sorry, Arisa. Nobody here's going to get that joke, including me.

I put on a vague smile and brushed off Arisa's remark.

"Aren't those items for display only, though?"

"No, not these ones. We bought them over there in the souvenir corner."

When I went to check it out, I found all kinds of things for sale. I decided to make some purchases, too, mostly small objects like folding fans. They would be good souvenirs to send to Zena in Seiryuu City with my next letter.

"Look, look! There are hairpins, too! Maybe I'll buy one…"

"Arisa, it isn't wise to squander away money."

Liza rebuked Arisa as she gazed at the hairpins.

"Don't worry—I still have plenty left from the wages I got from Miss Nina!"

"A slave's possessions belong to her master. You mustn't spend it without permission."

This idea that "a slave's possessions belong to the slave's master" was the general consensus in the Shiga Kingdom, but with my Japanese sensibilities, I just couldn't get used to it.

"Liza, all of you can use your spending money however you like."

"Very well. If that is your wish, master…"

Liza was perplexed, but she accepted my decree without further comment.

Spending your pocket money on things you wanted was the best way to learn its value, if you asked me.

Past the souvenir shop, there was an exhibit of weapons resembling Japanese swords, but they were simply referred to as "ancient weapons." The elegant refinement of a katana hadn't caught on as a weapon to be used against monsters.

"…They're beautiful."

A voice made me turn my head, and I saw a familiar-looking man and woman gazing at the swords.

It was the samurai pair from the Saga Empire we'd seen in the martial arts competition: Kajiro and the woman who used the polearm.

"Ah! The samurai, sir!"

The two turned to look when they heard Pochi's inadvertent exclamation.

"Oh? What do we have here but two little samurai."

"You both look very heroic."

Seeing Pochi and Tama in their cosplay, Kajiro and the woman smiled.

"I apologize if my companions bothered you," I said.

"No, not at all. But I'm surprised you recognized us as samurai without our swords."

Kajiro gave a grin that didn't seem to match his gruff features.

"We saw you fiiight?"

"You were very strong, sir."

"Ah, I see."

The samurai seemed fond of children. His smile lit up at Pochi's and Tama's praise.

"I want to be that strong, too, sir!"

"Me tooooo!"

Tama jumped up and down so eagerly that her kerchief slipped off her head.

She quickly caught it and held it in place, but Kajiro, standing directly in front of her, got a clear glimpse of her ears.

"Cat ears? Are you by chance one of the catfolk?"

"…Uh-huh."

Tama looked ready to cry.

"Oh dear, forgive me. I did not mean any harm. I was simply surprised, as I've never seen any outside of the beastfolk sanctuary in the Saga Empire…"

Oh? There's a sanctuary for them? After we train in Labyrinth City, maybe we should go look for Tama's and Pochi's kin there.

"Incidentally, young nobleman, I have a proposal for you…"

After I introduced myself, I listened to his proposal.

"…Martial arts instruction?"

"Yes, that's right. Judging from the way they were swinging around those heavy wooden swords with one hand, these kids must be about the right level for it. From the look of their footwork, they haven't had any formal training. The animal-eared folk are known as a warrior race, so I'd be more than happy to teach them our style. And we have to pay for travel somehow," he added with a chuckle.

The samurai pair explained that they were on a journey to Labyrinth City to increase their combat skills.

And their weapons were currently being repaired from the damage they took in the tournament. As a result, they couldn't earn money by exterminating monsters or taking escort missions.

I had just been seeking out a teacher for the beastfolk girls, so this was perfect timing. I accepted Kajiro's proposal and drew up a contract of employment for the duration of our stay in the old capital.

He would come to the mansion each day until I received permission from the former count, who would hopefully agree to let him stay in an empty room of the guest mansion.

When the bells rang to sound the time in the museum, Kajiro excused himself and the woman.

"The main battles of the tournament are today, so we must take our leave."

I had no qualms with that. We were planning to start training the next day anyway.

Evidently, a lot of the other guests were just killing time until the tournament, too; the crowd at the Ancestral King Yamato exhibit soon all but vanished.

"So the royal capital used to be here." Lulu was reading the Shiga Kingdom chronology written on the wall.

"Relocatiooon?"

"I'm confused, sir."

I explained the meaning of "relocating the capital" to Pochi and Tama.

The Shiga Kingdom was founded in this city. When the royal capital was moved to its current location, this became the old capital, beginning the reign of King Sharorik the Second. He sounded a lot different from the current third prince, despite sharing the same name.

We proceeded along the preset route, where the items were arranged in chronological order.

"Ah! I know this one. It's a painting of the crazed king Gartapht's demi-human war."

Arisa pointed at a painting that depicted various kinds of demi-humans and humanfolk murdering one another. Apparently, a copy of the same painting had been in the castle where she used to live.

Four hundred years ago, there was a massive amount of persecution against demi-humans, which led to a great war with the demi-human countries to the east and northwest of the Shiga Kingdom. This war had the most casualties of any non-demon-related war in the past millennium. In the end, even the elves and a summoned hero from the Saga Empire got involved to stop the bloodshed.

This painting was made in the era of the wise king Zara, who succeeded the crazed king and restored a dynasty. It was meant to serve as a reminder for future generations that extreme persecution could only lead to tragedy.

As far as I could tell, persecution and discrimination still had a hold on this kingdom, but perhaps it was better than when a demi-human would get killed on sight.

After a few more similarly bloody images, a painting that was leaning against the wall caught my eye.

It was a simple scene of a single door on top of a hill. Curious, I examined it more closely.

Oh?

After a few moments, the door in the painting swung open, and a tiny girl peeked out and waved at me. A moving oil painting? Now, that was classic fantasy stuff.

I waved back, and the girl reacted with delight. Very interactive.

The girl beckoned me over from inside the door.

Instinctively, I took a step forward, but...

"It's huuuge!"

"Sir!"

...Tama and Pochi chose that moment to tackle me from the side.

The suddenness of it surprised me, but they were too light to make me stagger or anything.

"What is it, you two?"

"Come heeere?"

"There's something amazing over here, sir!"

The excited pair grabbed my hands and dragged me toward the next room.

Casually glancing over my shoulder as we left the room, I saw that the painting I'd been looking at was gone.

Since it had been on the floor, it was probably just being moved. If there were any others like it, I'd love to show everyone.

"Looook?"

"It's amazingly amazing, sir!"

Tama and Pochi pulled me into a hall with an enormous tapestry on display.

It was huge, about fifteen feet tall and one hundred and fifty feet long. According to the museum label, it was made over the course of more than forty years.

"Master, the demon lord is very large and dangerous, I report."

Nana pointed at one section of the tapestry with a grave expression. It depicted an enormous monster with the head of a boar that dwarfed the castle beneath it.

"The giant demon lord appeared before the great ancestral king Yamato, trampling a castle under his feet…"

A clear voice rang out behind us. I turned around to find a stage set up at the far end of the hall. An orchestra was providing background music as a minstrel stood center stage and described the scenes on the tapestry.

I listened to the voice as I gazed at the tapestry.

"The demon lord's chief henchmen, the six-colored veteran demons, caused much trouble for the humanfolk armies…"

Standing in front of the demon lord was a green snake, a pink mochi-like slime, and the familiar blue and red greater hell demons, all led by a four-armed yellow demon.

He said "six-colored"; maybe the last one was the black shape that looked like the yellow one's shadow?

The minstrel intoned the details of each demon's special powers. The green one could shape-shift, the pink one specialized in defense, the black one appeared and disappeared unexpectedly, and the yellow one, as the de facto leader, was much stronger than ordinary demons.

The minstrel's tale went on for quite a while.

"The demon lord manipulated the orcs, turning them into *boushi mouhei* to fight against the knights."

I'd never heard of *boushi mouhei*. Was this some made-up Japanese-style word from this world?

The little humanoid shapes at the yellow demon's feet were probably the orcs.

When it occurred to me that I'd never met an orc, I ran a map search on a whim and found two living downtown in the old capital.

Like the kobolds I'd met in the giants' village, they were considered fairyfolk, not monsters.

These two orcs managed an alchemy store in a corner of the slums. They didn't seem to have any offenses in the **Bounty** section of their information, so I decided to go check them out at some point during our stay.

"The cryptid knights of the Flue Kingdom joined the battle mounted on griffins. Then the demon lord summoned his sky fortress, Tovkezerra, and countless monstrous fish swam through the skies."

Where's this part?

I tried to find this "Tovkezerra" thing, but I couldn't figure out what it was. Maybe it was the giant shape at the top left corner of the tapestry, which looked like either an airship or a sperm whale?

A swarm of sharklike monsters was emerging from the magic circle in front of the airship, crushing buildings and soldiers like a tidal wave.

The griffins were depicted as well, but clearly, there weren't enough of them to stand a chance.

"Just as the kingdoms were on the verge of destruction, our savior appeared on the back of a sky dragon: the ancestral king Yamato himself."

On the right side of the tapestry was the silver head of a dragon, with a knight in blue armor standing between its horns. *This must be Yamato, then.*

The knight held a large shield and a staff, and several glowing blue swords were floating around him.

Okay, the part about the swords floating in the air has got to be artistic license. It was like a scene out of an anime or something. For one thing, the Holy Sword Claidheamh Soluis didn't fly around when the prince had used it against those demons earlier.

"So this brave figure must be the ancestral king Yamato."

"A great king though he may have been, I do not believe that a dragon would allow anyone to ride on its head."

Miss Karina seemed impressed, but Liza not so much. Maybe her race viewed dragons as sacred creatures.

"A dragon knight? Now that's hot!"

I had a strong suspicion that Arisa wasn't referring to the temperature. Next to her, Mia nodded sagely; I decided I didn't want to know why.

Arisa, please don't corrupt this world's culture too much.

"Master, there is a replica of the Holy Sword over there, I report."

Turning to look where Nana pointed, I saw a ten-foot-tall bronze statue of the ancestral king Yamato, as well as an equally giant replica of Claidheamh Soluis.

If my memory of the real one was anything to go by, this size must be an exaggeration to emphasize the king's greatness.

Thinking back, the ancestral king statue I saw in Sedum City in Kuhanou County was similarly grandiose. I guess that was the default size for statues of Yamato.

As we admired the statue of the ancestral king, a carriage arrived to pick us up. Evidently, it was just about time for us to visit the home of Tolma and Viscount Siemmen.

We stopped by the house to drop everyone else off, except for Arisa and Nana, who wanted to come along. Then, the carriage took us to the viscount's estate.

The man had a hooked nose, a furrowed brow, a carefully groomed mustache, and swept-back golden-blond hair. His eyes were intense, full of strength and determination.

The man was so serious, it was hard to believe he was Tolma's brother.

If anything, from his somewhat aged features, he could pass for Tolma's father. He certainly looked older than thirty-four years old.

"I thank you for saving Tolma's life."

How strange. For some reason, his thanks sounded more like a scolding from my boss.

This was Tolma's older brother, Hosarris Siemmen.

The only people in the room were the two brothers, Arisa, and me.

As soon as we arrived, Nana wanted to go to the adjacent house where Tolma's family was staying, and I let her do as she liked. By this time, she was probably doting on baby Mayuna.

"Sorry, Sir Satou. My brother always talks like this."

"How rude, Tolma. What's wrong with the way I talk, pray tell?"

His words were normal enough on their own, but something about Hosarris's tone made him sound like a straitlaced teacher addressing a particularly disappointing student.

Inexplicably, Arisa was about to start drooling. I couldn't help but be concerned by the gleam in her eyes. *Whatever you're fantasizing about, please keep it to yourself.*

As the conversation continued, it felt more like a job interview than a friendly welcome in the parlor.

Tolma had already told the viscount about my top priorities, namely purchasing scrolls from the warehouse and ordering more, so the arrangements were made easily enough. It helped that I showed my permit from the duke, of course.

"If collecting scrolls is your hobby, would you like to tour our workshop?"

"Could I really?"

I was so excited about this unexpected turn of events that I instinctively leaned forward on the table.

"I don't see why not. Miss Nina the Iron-Blooded even called you 'trustworthy' in her letter of introduction. Besides, Tolma is an excellent judge of character."

What a gentleman. I could even see him being a charismatic company president in modern Japan.

My "Keen Hearing" skill picked up a conversation in the hallway.

"...Which is why we simply must use ink made from the dew of a firefly lily."

"That ink certainly would allow for very precise work, but think of the cost."

"But Mr. Djang, I could say the same of the dragon powder and drill powder you insist upon using. How are we to profit?"

These must be the scroll craftsmen that Mr. Hosarris called for.

"You have need of us, my lord?"

"At your service, Lord Hosarris."

The pair that entered was a middle-aged man who gave obesity a whole new meaning and a young woman with freckles and glasses.

The girl was a fairly average-looking gnome, neither beautiful nor ugly. As you might expect from a member of her race, she was even shorter than Arisa.

"This is Djang, the workshop manager. He may not look it, but he is the greatest scroll master in all the Shiga Kingdom. And the young lady is Natalina, the most ingenious artisan in our workshop. I have no doubt that they will be able to meet your expectations, Sir Pendragon."

I sensed a certain implication behind Hosarris's use of the word *ingenious*. Maybe she was the type who liked making strange scrolls that wouldn't sell or burned up budgets for her experiments.

Once he'd introduced the duo, Mr. Hosarris took his leave along with Tolma.

That was all right. I was told when I first arrived that he might not have much time to spare. I was just glad he introduced me to the artisans first.

I showed the list of scrolls I wanted to Mr. Djang, and we began to make arrangements.

Sadly, it turned out that greater magic couldn't be fashioned into scrolls.

He also wasn't able to make scrolls of spells that could be used for criminal purposes, like Fake Patch and Unlock. I'd been told the same thing at Kikinu's magic shop, so this wasn't that surprising.

As it turned out, finishing scrolls required someone who had the skill for the adapted spell. Gravity, Shadow, Psychic, Ghost, and other such types of magic couldn't be produced, either.

Because the resident Space Magic user was currently away in the royal capital, I wouldn't be able to order scrolls of that sort for another month. However, the warehouse already had a scroll of the only intermediate teleportation spell, Return, so that wasn't a problem.

I hesitated a little but eventually agreed to buy the Return scroll for one hundred gold coins.

My "Estimation" skill gave the price as about thirty coins, but one hundred coins was nothing if it meant I'd be able to teleport. Besides, if you included all the different currencies I had in Storage, I had upward of ten million gold coins.

Additionally, while it was technically possible, creating Holy Magic scrolls was forbidden for religious reasons.

"Say, Mister Knight… I get that you're a collector and all, but the scroll versions of the spells on this list are all fairly ineffective. You sure you're okay with that?"

"Natalina, you ought to address him more respectfully."

"Whaaat? I was being respectful. Wasn't I, Mister Knight?"

"I only recently became a noble anyway, so I don't mind if you speak to me normally, if that's what you would prefer."

"Really? Whoo-hoo!" Natalina struck a triumphant pose, prompting Mr. Djang to bop her on the head. I understood all too well the pain of playing the straight man to a goofy young girl.

"As for your concerns, Miss Natalina, the aim is to collect them. As long as they can be used, I have no problem if the effect is weak," I promised.

We completed a sales contract for the scrolls in the warehouse, then moved on to my creation requests in order of priority.

"These are some weird spells, huh? They're easy to read but real inefficient. They probably count as lesser magic, but the long chants make 'em pretty hard to use."

Natalina tilted her head as she observed my handmade spells.

My spells were considerably different from the standard spells here, since I took a structured programming approach.

They were very readable and effective, but their magic efficiency and spell length were much worse than traditional spells.

There wasn't much I could do about that trade-off. For me personally, the disadvantages were all but irrelevant.

"Will you be able to make them into scrolls?"

"Yeah, no prob. They're a little weird, but they still follow the normal rules of magic, so I think I can figure it out...sir."

Noticing Mr. Djang's glare, Natalina hastily added an honorific with an apologetic tone.

"Well then, Sir Knight. It will take some time to gather the inventory for your order. Would you like to see the workshop while you wait?"

"Oh yes, please."

We headed over for a tour. I brought Arisa along to alleviate her obvious boredom.

The workshop was underground below the viscount's property, with powerful security provided by both people and magic equipment.

The security guards were all level 20 or higher, with espionage-related skills like "Detect" and "Observation." There were also magic items for surveillance and alarms, including small guard golems that patrolled around the vents.

While they couldn't tell me the details, the workshop was clearly very thoroughly protected against any kind of spying magic.

The workshop was also divided into several small rooms, each of which was used only for specific parts of the process.

This way, very few people actually knew the entire process. It might be inefficient, but keeping their techniques secret seemed to be of utmost importance. They were extremely thorough.

The paper for the scrolls was made in a different place; when I appraised it, the results said things like **scroll paper: B**.

From the artisans' conversations, I gathered that core powder was needed to make the ink. It turned out Mr. Hosarris had been in the royal capital for the express purpose of stocking up on high-quality cores. The ones needed to make an intermediate magic scroll could be obtained only from powerful monsters of level 30 or higher.

The unprocessed core they showed me as an example was an even deeper red than the ones I got from the hard newts a while back.

"This room is where the ink is made."

Mr. Djang cracked the door open and let me peek inside, but I wasn't allowed to enter. They were currently making **scroll ink: A** in this room. I was able to identify most of the ingredients, one of which was **scroll ink: B**. The whole process seemed very involved.

It was more than just writing the spells out on special paper with special ink, too. There were a number of other necessary steps.

As a result, even standard scrolls took two to four days to make, and custom orders took several days more than that.

After the tour of the workshop, we returned to the parlor to find a small mountain of scrolls waiting.

There were a lot of interesting spells in the warehouse besides the Return spell I mentioned before.

I acquired three intermediate attack magic spells, Ice Storm, Thunder Storm, and Implosion; five or so lesser attack spells, including Toss Stone and Air Cannon; four defense magic spells, Flexible Shield, Canopy, Air Cushion, and Mana Section; two more magic interference spells, Mana Transfer and Mana Drain; three operation spells, Magic Hand, Magic String, and Float Walk; two healing spells, Water Heal and Aqua Heal; the anti-espionage spell Secret Field; and four support spells, Enchant: Magic Protection, Enchant: Physical Protection, Enchant: Sparking Blade, and Enchant: Shield.

If I could master all these spells, the rest of my journey should be a lot easier.

The custom spells I ordered were as follows.

From the existing spell books, I chose three Everyday Magic spells,

Soft Wash, Dry, and Bandage; two healing spells, Remove Poison and Cure Disease; and two smelting spells, Sampling Metal and Melt Metal.

As for original spells, I ordered the interpersonal combat spells Light Stun and Remote Stun; three spells for making magic items, Liquid Control, Air Control, and Electronic Control; two spells just for fun, the Fire Magic spell Fireworks and the Light Magic spell Fireworks Illusion; and three experimental spells, Shooter, Standard Out, and Graphic View.

Standard Out was simply designed to display the text **Hello World** in my menu log, while Graphic View should open a rectangular window with the same text on my menu screen.

Both spells would only have meaning for me, but if they worked, I was planning to start developing spells like Sound Recorder and Photo.

Meanwhile, Shooter was a spell that combined Explosion Magic and Practical Magic, designed to shoot bullets ranging from the size of a small pebble to a baseball.

It could theoretically be used as a gun, but it was both less efficient and less powerful than lesser attack magic.

My main objective with this was to be able to fire sacred arrows already stocked with magic power in case I had to fight anything like another demon lord.

In my previous battle, I had realized I needed both hands to use a bow, so switching between that and a sword ended up being a pain.

I had considered using a crossbow, too, but because I was concerned that the bolts would fall out if I was moving around at full speed, I decided to try developing a new spell for it.

Once we finished the contract, with Mr. Djang overseeing, I requested some help with testing out my original spells in the courtyard. During the tests, I found some careless mistakes, so I had them revised on the spot.

"Wowie, mister! This is amazing!"

"It's beautiful. Reminds me of the big fireworks festival in Tokyo Bay."

Natalina jumped around in excitement at the sight of my Fireworks spells, and Arisa was a big fan, too. Once the scrolls were completed, we could all get dressed up and have a fireworks festival of our own.

"Mister Knight! You gotta sell this magic to me! Please!"

"Natalina! Don't accost our guest without permission."

Mr. Djang's scolding wasn't enough to calm Natalina's excitement, it seemed; she insisted that we could continue the conversation when Mr. Hosarris returned.

Since I'd made the spell in my spare time, I would've had no reservations about giving it away for free, but Arisa cleverly suggested that we would consider it if they would allocate more workers to my scroll order.

The price of my order ended up being quite high, but I had no problem paying it on the spot.

Then, I stored the premade scrolls I'd purchased in my Garage Bag and went to pick up Nana from Tolma's house.

Tearing her away from baby Mayuna was no easy feat.

"Whew, I thought my dinner was going to come back up for a second there."

"Maybe if you didn't eat so much…"

"But it was sooo good!"

After dinner, I brought Arisa along to the labyrinth ruins under the old capital for my magic experiments.

I was planning on coming alone, but she insisted on going with me.

"Why did you want to come to the labyrinth with me, anyway? There aren't any monsters here for you to level grind."

"Nah, that's not why." Arisa shook her head.

"I thought you wanted to raise your level so you could learn Space Magic?"

"But of course! That's the whole point!"

Now she was striking a bizarre pose. *What's going on?*

I thought she said last night that she didn't have enough skill points to raise Space Magic to the necessary level.

"Could you explain it in a way I can understand?"

In response, Arisa climbed on top of some nearby rubble and regarded me smugly. "Bwa-ha-ha! If you think skill points are set in stone, you're making a big mistake!"

Her grin widened as she took an imperious pose.

"What do you mean? You can't reassign skill points that have already been allocated to something, can you?"

"Sure you can. Didn't I tell you?"

No, this is the first I've heard of it.

I had a huge amount of skill points left, but until I came anywhere near leveling up, I might need to reassign some eventually.

"How do you do it?"

"You just have to pick 'Reset' from the skill list. It'll return the points from all your skills, aside from Unique Skills, gifts, and things like that."

How convenient...

And frustrating.

I couldn't choose skills from a list, which made this information useless to me.

"But it's not like it's a totally unlimited reset, of course."

If it was unlimited, you could change your skills around for every battle. *Come to think of it, there was an anime sort of like that, wasn't there? Sano the ESPer or something.*

Oblivious to my distraction, Arisa continued her explanation.

"Each time you use it, you lose five to ten percent of your skill points. And there's no way to get those back."

So even if I could use it, I'd lose anywhere from 155 to 620 skill points... That was definitely not worth it. Now I understood why Arisa had never used it before.

"There's another reason I don't wanna use it, too..."

"What is it?"

"Well, it really hurts."

So she wanted to come here so that the others wouldn't hear her cries of pain and worry about her. In that case, I could've just used my new spell Secret Field.

"All right, here goes nothing."

"Wait, at least drink something for the pain first."

That should make it a little better.

"Thanks, but I've heard that using medicine can increase the amount of points lost."

Grimly, Arisa pressed the medicine back into my hand.

Evidently, it was Hayato, the hero of the Saga Empire, who taught her about Reset back in her hometown. Which must mean Hayato knew Arisa was a reincarnation...

"A girl's gotta have guts! Reeeeeset!"

Arisa plunked down on my lap and bellowed a war cry.

...*Ow.*

I'd agreed to hold her through the process at her request, but her shrieks coupled with her nails clawing into my back was actually really painful. I discreetly turned on "Pain Resistance."

For a minute, I was worried her lilac hair would fade to white, but that seemed to be a needless concern.

As soon as the Reset was finished, she fainted away, so I let her rest her head in my lap, but...

"Arisa, if this is just a ploy to harass me, you're going on the ground."

She was tough—I had to give her that. Despite all the pain she'd just endured, she still pretended to roll over in her sleep to put herself in a creepy position.

"So, did it work?"

"More or less! I didn't quite have enough points, but I managed to get Space Magic to level six at the cost of some Psychic Magic."

She looked proud of herself, but I had to nip something in the bud right away.

"Arisa, this is an order. I forbid you from intruding on baths or watching anyone change clothes except in case of emergencies."

"What?! C-come on! You could at least wait until you catch me in the act. Don't deprive a pure maiden of her tiny little rewaaaard!"

So she really was planning on it, then... *I knew it.*

Because Arisa wanted to go somewhere where she could use magic to her heart's content, we ventured down toward the middle level of the labyrinth.

"Hmm, so this is where you fought the demon lord?"

"No, that was deeper."

"I wanna see!"

I tried telling her there was nothing there, but she still insisted, and I took her to the bottom level.

"I...I thought I was gonna die..."

She was really exaggerating. I'd made sure to slow down before I made sharp turns and everything.

Wobbling a little as I set her on her feet, Arisa stumbled over to the altar where the ceremony had taken place and surveyed the cave.

"Say, master, did you get the True Hero title for defeating the demon lord?"

Nodding, I changed my title to True Hero to prove it.

"Wow, you really did…"

Arisa entwined her hands behind her back, turning away from me.

"Then…does that mean…?"

Arisa trailed off.

Somehow, she didn't quite seem like her usual self.

"Does that mean, y'know…you're going back to Japan?"

Arisa steadied herself and gazed back at me.

Huh?

"What do you mean? We still have to take Mia home, and then we're training in Labyrinth City, remember? Plus, once everyone gets stronger, I want to travel the world together and go on more adventures. Even if I do go back to Japan, it won't be for a long time."

When I spotted tears in Arisa's eyes, I answered as lightly as I could.

Of course, I didn't even know if I could get back to Japan.

"Where's this coming from, anyway?" I gently asked her after I wiped away her tears and waited for her to calm down.

"'Cause…'cause…! Hayato told me that when heroes defeat demon lords and become true heroes, they get an offer from the gods to send them back home."

So that was why she was worried.

As she explained, if you said yes, you'd be sent back to your original world, leaving your Holy Sword behind.

The tricky part was that the question would be asked only once, and if you didn't answer right away, it'd be taken as a "no."

Come on, you could at least let people choose when they go back.

Besides, even if I did get an offer like that, I wouldn't feel right leaving until everyone was strong enough to at least defeat demons. And since I didn't come here like a normal summoned hero, that might not be an option for me in the first place.

If I did get an offer to go home before I was ready, maybe I could get them to send my family a letter instead.

My parents were a lot more happy-go-lucky than I was, so as long as I wrote "I'm safe and satisfied" or something, they'd probably accept it.

"Anyway, master, is your hero outfit really just that blond wig and silver mask from before? If you wear your usual robes, you're gonna get found out sooner or later, don't you think?"

Putting on a brave face, Arisa changed the subject.

"No, my silver mask broke, so now it's a purple wig and a white mask. And I wear these high-class priest robes with it."

I used "Quick Change" to demonstrate.

"Whoa, that was fast! What the heck was that?! It's like you transformed or something!"

"Pretty handy, right?"

Trying to cheer Arisa up, I struck a silly pose of my own.

"I guess a *shota* priest could w… I mean, shouldn't it be more different from your usual outfit?"

"I suppose. Like a ninja or a samurai, maybe?"

"Let's see… Oh, I know! A diviner! That'd be a great concept!"

I could almost see the light bulb going off over Arisa's head as she folded her arms in thought.

"You mean like an *onmyoji*? With Edo-style clothes and all that?"

"Exactly! A white base, classy black headgear, a circlet with a veil that hides your mask, and maybe some gold embroidery to give it a little flair…"

I tried to picture the outfit. "Won't that still be kind of plain?"

Using the Light Magic spell Illusion, I conjured up an image of the clothes Arisa was describing.

"Ooh! That's lovely. I suppose it is rather plain, though. You should add some flair with magic or a magic item! Like angel wings or a ring of light behind you like a Buddha!"

I wasn't sure how well angel wings would go with the whole ancient occultist theme. Instead, I tried adding a circle of light on the back of the image.

"That's still kinda boring. You should triple it and add more light radiating from the center. Oh, and since you can basically fly, maybe some rocket flames on your feet!"

I bopped Arisa lightly as her earnest suggestions got sillier and sillier.

Rocket feet? What am I, a mecha?

Somehow, I ended up with flame wheels on my feet that spun to match my speed and left an afterimage as I moved around.

I was only trying it out for fun, but controlling it ended up being more trouble than it was worth. The illusion moved autonomously as I directed it, but details like the number of turns and the amount of light had to be manually changed.

At any rate, with my alter ego's outer appearance decided, we started to discuss his interior.

"Are you changing your voice or speech patterns at all?"

"When I spoke to Baron Muno or the head priestess, I used another voice and acted all haughty. With the duke, I tried to sound androgynous and speak as little as possible," I explained.

"So you switched it up, huh?"

"Yeah. I changed my voice for the arrogant persona, but it wasn't so unlike mine that you couldn't trace it back to me, so I tried something somewhat different with the duke."

Because I said so little, I figured the latter method might be better for misleading people.

"Then maybe you should be a hero with multiple personalities or pretend there are several of you?"

"I feel like it'd be hard to keep things straight that way."

"Then just make sure your default hero character is different enough from your main self, and the arrogant one and the one who doesn't talk much can be like sub-characters. Like the main character and supporting characters in a game," she added.

Well, she seemed to be the expert; I asked her to elaborate on how to differentiate them from my "main" self.

"Well, your defining personae are 'mature *shota*,' 'oblivious harem protagonist,' and 'OP cheater,' which means—"

"Arisa. Would you mind not bringing your creepy opinions of me into this?"

Arisa grinned mischievously; I pinched her nose in response. From there, I got her to give an actual list of my defining traits and come up with ways to distance myself from them.

"So, to be the opposite of yourself, the points you want to hit are 'childish,' 'overly familiar,' 'no respect for anyone,' and 'can't take a hint,' I'd say."

Then Professor Arisa spent an hour or so giving me pointers on how to play Nanashi Version III.

For some reason, her teaching style involved hiding half her face behind her hair and using an odd speech pattern. I didn't know what she was basing this on, but I had no doubt she was acting out a scene from some anime or manga.

"Voilà! You're like a love interest from an *otome* game now!"

Applauding wildly, Arisa finally gave my performance the seal of approval.

Hopefully, I wouldn't have to put on this particular act too often.

"Hey, did you get any rare drops from the demon lord? Like a demon lord core?"

It sounded probable, but there was no such item in my loot from the battle. Maybe that was the purple sphere that had hit the ground and shattered after I defeated him.

"I guess I got his sabers and a spear he made from his own bones, stuff like that? But they're all too big, and most of them are broken anyway."

I also got a cornucopia from the Wings of Freedom cult.

Happily, this included a large amount of goods and materials, including rare substances like ice stones and dark stones. They must have been making a hideout down there or something.

There were also a few unused long horns like the one the intermediate hell demon had dropped earlier in the day, but I planned to let them rot in Storage so they wouldn't fall into the wrong hands.

"There were some spell books and such, too."

I showed Arisa the lineup.

There were all kinds of spell books in my loot from the demon lord battle, including one called *Demon Summoning* and ingredients to make a magic circle for summoning short horns.

Among the materials was a boost item for summoning called "hair of Yuriko," a braided purple plait. I didn't want to get cursed, so I pretended not to have seen it and sent it away deep into Storage. The last thing I wanted was to pull it out again and find that the hair had grown or something.

"This *Demon Summoning* book doesn't use a cell phone or a laptop or whatever, right?"

"Of course not."

However, the book contained dangerous information like demon lord resurrection ceremonies and methods for summoning different kinds of demons. I planned to keep it stored away like the long horns.

I could probably burn it, but I was hanging onto it in case its contents came in handy for making other spells.

While Arisa practiced to get the hang of Space Magic, I used each of my scrolls to register them in the magic menu, then tested out the power of the menu version.

Practical Magic spell Magic Hand—basically telekinesis—proved particularly difficult to operate.

It was easy enough when I tried picturing a single hand, but when I tried to do it with two and control separate objects at the same time, things got way more difficult. Mastering it would take some training.

Interestingly, when I touched objects with Magic Hand, it was possible to put them in Storage. The spell had a much farther reach than any stick or spear, so it might come in handy in unexpected ways.

I planned to wait until after I brought Arisa back to the mansion before testing the intermediate attack magic spells Ice Storm, Thunder Storm, and Implosion.

With how much power they had behind them, they could do some serious damage.

"These Mana Transfer and Mana Drain spells are totally cheating."

Arisa had agreed to help with my experiments, and she was shocked when they were over.

I couldn't blame her, since my Mana Drain had robbed her of most of her magical power, then Mana Transfer completely restored it.

Sure, the large difference between our levels was part of it, but using Mana Drain against a magic user might be downright unfair.

We also tested out the Space Magic spells for communication and spying.

When we experimented with Clairaudience and Clairvoyance on each other, Arisa didn't detect anything amiss when she was the subject, but I felt a slight sense of discomfort. It would probably be best to avoid using it on anyone overly perceptive.

"Arisa, I was planning to carve a seal slate and leave it here. You can use it, too, right?"

"Seal slates are landmarks for the Return spell, aren't they? I think it'd be better to do it closer to the surface, then. This place is so deep, it might be hard to teleport here from aboveground."

I see. That makes sense.

"Then I guess I'll set them up in several places, not just here."

"Can you really make a seal slate so easily?"

"Yeah, it's not too complicated."

Arisa seemed worried, but I had plenty of the liquid I needed, and it would take only a few minutes to make the magic circuit for the seal. It was reasonably cost-effective, too, only about two silvers per slate.

While I was at it, I made a few extras for Arisa to keep in her Item Box.

"I bet a Space Magic expert could make a killing as a trader."

"You're the only person OP enough to do that, master. I can only do a little over half a mile at a time." Arisa shrugged with a small sigh.

At her current skill level, she could teleport only herself and one other person at most.

"But if it was a serious emergency, I could probably use Over Boost to escape with everyone at once!"

"That's good to know, but don't use it unless you absolutely have to, all right?"

I didn't want to burst her bubble, but I wanted to make sure she didn't abuse that power too much. I had a good reason for that, too: the advice that the Undead King Zen had given me before he died.

Abusing Unique Skills would only lead to ruin.

"Yes, sir!"

Arisa saluted. I hoped she was taking me seriously.

…Wait, huh?

Come to think of it, my "Menu" was supposedly a Unique Skill, too, but nothing had happened to me even though I'd been using it regularly for months now, as far as I could tell.

Maybe it was different because it was a passive skill?

I racked my brain as we went back to the mansion.

Oh, and the next morning, I used Magic Hand to help the kids swim through the air, which was a big hit with the younger girls.

Cooking and Dancing

Satou here. I'm not particularly interested in fossils in general, but for some reason, whenever I go to a hotel or department store made with marble, I end up looking for them. Maybe it's just another way of killing time?

"Wow! Master, look at that! The ceiling is amazing!"

"How fitting for a ball hosted by a duke of the great Shiga Kingdom."

Lulu and Arisa pointed excitedly at the ceiling. Not long before, they'd also pointed out the fluffy carpets and mythical engraving on the marble wall with equal enthusiasm.

The pair was attending the ball as my cooking assistants, not guests, which was why they were wearing black dresses with lace-trimmed white aprons. The other children were at home watching the house.

The venue was as large as the Nippon Budokan in Tokyo, with mirrors on its domed ceiling sparkling brilliantly in the light of the chandelier.

According to the AR display, a mithril alloy frame supported the ceiling's enormous weight.

On the outer edge of the venue were spaces for resting and light conversation, as well as the booth where we were preparing the food.

It seemed that evening parties were generally buffet-style; between each booth and rest area was a large space with a few small, elegant tables.

Much of the food consisted of light hors d'oeuvres so that the nobles could snack easily during their casual conversations.

In a way, it wasn't much different from a contemporary buffet-style party.

"Sir Knight, are these arrangements satisfactory?"

The maids had gone all out with the presentation, even decorating the buffet with flowers to make the food especially pleasing to the eye.

Furthermore, they'd treated the flowers so the fragrance wouldn't affect the dishes.

"Yes, it's perfect. You've made my food look much more appealing."

"It's an honor to assist your cooking in any way, Sir Knight."

I thanked the maids, who appeared pleased as they moved on to prepare the next booth.

Before long, the guests began to arrive.

I had expected gourmets like Marquis Lloyd and Count Hohen to come running in first, but it turned out that they were still working with the duke in a conference room at the castle.

Considering how much they were looking forward to this, I made a note to save some food for them just in case.

I prepared four dishes for the occasion.

The first, of course, was the consommé soup the duke had specially requested.

Since it took a long time to prepare, I cooked it beforehand at the mansion and brought it to the site of the party. Putting out all five pots at once wouldn't leave much room in our booth, so I brought out only two.

I had really put Mia to work fixing the special soup. Consequently, she was down for the count back at the mansion.

Earlier that morning, we brought some of the finished soup to Tenion Temple. There was no time for me to see Sara, but hopefully she'd try it along with the head priestess.

"Ooh! So this is the soup that the young master Lloyd praised so highly!"

"But it looks like water…"

"You can't call yourself a gourmet if you let appearances fool you."

"Indeed. It smells deliciously rich."

As soon as I took the lid off one of the consommé soup pots, people started crowding around.

Apparently, Imperial Knight Ipasa, aka "the young master Lloyd," had been spreading the word about the dish.

Since the oil for the tempura wasn't hot enough yet, I decided to dish out the consommé soup first. I served it in heat-resistant glass containers from the duke's castle.

"Delicious! What in the world is it?"

"How heavenly."

"Wonderful. It tastes even better than it smells."

"Ahh... I must have been born to eat this soup."

A little embarrassed by the nobles' extravagant praise, I started preparing the tempura.

Before long, I ran into a problem that wasn't entirely unexpected: Many of the guests were eating several bowls of soup each.

I didn't want to get stuck making it again if we ran out, so I limited it to three bowls per person. A few of them got childishly whiny about it, but I managed to distract them with the second dish.

The demand for the tempura wasn't quite as high as the soup, but plenty of people still wanted to try every kind.

I was on the verge of falling behind the demand, but luckily, I was able to borrow a few of the kitchen's sous chefs to help with the prep work. In fact, they were all quite happy to oblige. Maybe I'd won them over with those vegetable fritters before.

"I dunno about this one. It looks nice and all, but..."

Arisa's face clouded at the sight of the third dish.

This was my take on the "meat jelly" that we'd found in the city market.

I'd heard it was a commoner's dish that nobles would never have at their table, so I had tried making a more elegant version of the sort you might find at a traditional Kyoto restaurant.

At Arisa's suggestion, I also used colorful ingredients to avoid an unappetizing brown color.

And it was "colorful" in another way, too.

"Oh-ho, how clever! You've crafted our duke's coat of arms in edible form."

This compliment came from a gentleman with an impressive beard.

I had indeed arranged the jelly into the duke's coat of arms. Unfortunately, this meant none of the nobles wanted to be the first to take a piece and thus destroy the crest. Maybe I should have thought that through a little more...

"It looks like the jelly spoken of in the legends of Ancestral King Yamato."

"Is this a new dish, Satou? I can't wait to try it. Everything you make is always tasty."

Behind the gentleman was Miss Ringrande, wearing makeup and a dress for the occasion.

"Oh, so this is the fellow you mentioned, Rin?"

"It's a pleasure to meet you, sir. I am Satou Pendragon, an honorary hereditary knight."

According to his AR label, this man was Ringrande's father, the next duke.

"Pendragon, eh? So you're the savior of Muno City who Tolma mentioned, too? You're much younger and more diminutive than I imagined."

Damn that Tolma. Gossip or not, I had to get him to stop talking me up as "the savior of Muno City." For one thing, the "savior" label was honestly kind of embarrassing.

"That Tolma would be a great lobbyist," Arisa muttered.

She was crouching behind the booth, snatching up food on a small plate.

I didn't mind her slacking off a little, since her main role was to coordinate with the kitchen and supply power for Lulu's magic item.

"Tolma bragged about your deeds as if they were his own. Why, you even defeated a demon in Gururian City, did you not?"

Politely dodging the future duke's compliments, I tried to redirect him toward the food.

"I hate to destroy this work of art, but I am quite interested in your cooking. I'll take a serving."

I gave Miss Ringrande and her father each a plate with two of the best kinds: jellied mackerel and jellied vegetable broth made with edamame and carrots.

"Hmm, I've never had the likes of this before. It's very flavorful."

"It really is. The fish is delicious, but so are the vegetables…but… Argh! No matter how good your cooking is, I'm not letting you marry Sara."

I think her love for her sister almost lost to her appetite for a second there…

It appeared many of the nobles from the old capital had a powerful weakness for food.

"Sara is a kind girl, too kind for the life of a noble. Besides, she has left the house of the duke for the sanctuary. If you wish her to return to secular life, you would first need to convince the holy woman of Tenion Temple."

"Rest assured, I am not trying to court Lady Sara. It is only a misunderstanding on Lady Ringrande's part, you see..."

The next duke was quick to understand and accept my explanation. If only Miss Ringrande would do the same.

Now that the ducal pair had broken up the crest, the rest of the nobles ventured to try the jellies as well.

Between the people clamoring for food and the ambitious ones trying to cozy up to the duke's heir and Miss Ringrande, the booth was getting crowded.

"Hmph. Have you changed roles from a so-called savior to a servant, then?"

Of course, this rude comment came from the third prince, dressed to the nines in royal garb. This time, he was attended by only the old knight, not that deranged young one.

I wish he hadn't gone out of his way to approach me.

Where did he even hear about the whole "savior" thing, anyway? *How am I going to deal with him...?*

But before I racked my brain for too long, the future duke came to my rescue.

"He is an honored guest of the duke, Prince Sharorik. My father heard of his fame as a miracle chef and requested that he make some of his famous dishes tonight."

The prince, who hadn't noticed the next duke amid the flock of nobles, looked startled.

Please don't start calling me "miracle chef." Isn't "savior" embarrassing enough?

"He is also Rin's friend and my youngest daughter's benefactor. I shall not look kindly on insults toward him, not even from a prince."

The duke's heir stepped forward as if to protect me from the prince. Even I could tell Sharorik was out of his league here.

Then, to add to the confusion...

"Sir Satou! I hope there's still some of that incredible shrimp tempura left for me!"

"Or the superior pickled ginger tempura!"

The pair of epicurean nobles, Marquis Lloyd and Count Hohen, raced each other to the front of the crowd.

"...Hmm? If it isn't Prince Sharorik."

"As if bringing dishonor on Lady Ringrande's name wasn't enough, now the fool dares to insult Lord Satou?"

"Quite so, quite so! An upstart who fails to appreciate Lady Rin's swordsmanship or Sir Satou's cooking has no place at Lady Sara's side."

Rein it in, you two! I wanted to exclaim. I appreciated their eagerness to defend me, but picking a fight with royalty seemed like a bad idea.

His temper sparked, the prince reached for the Holy Sword at his waist, but luckily someone else came to the rescue.

"Why, there you are, Your Highness. Won't you come and regale us with tales of the royal capital?"

Cutting through the crowd, a small army of women in slightly heavy makeup came to lure the prince away. Mercifully, he deigned to join them and brusquely took his leave.

Miss Ringrande's father sighed as he watched the prince go.

"If only he would mature a little, perhaps—"

"I doubt that'll ever happen. He hasn't changed a bit from ten years ago."

"But he is one of the finest swordsmen in the kingdom..."

"Father, physical strength has no bearing on strength of character. Otherwise, even Hayato would be more—"

Ringrande was evidently about to slander the hero, but she clapped a hand to her mouth at the last moment with a guilty look.

Because it would be improper for me to comfort her, I simply waited for the duke to arrive and recommend the consommé soup to everyone. Before too long, the atmosphere was back to normal.

Food tasted better when you were having fun, after all.

Once the older and higher-ranking nobles, like the duke and his family, drifted away from our booth, the younger ones who'd been watching from a distance scrambled to grab some food.

Several of them inquired into my relationship with Miss Ringrande, but I assured them that she was only teaching me swordsmanship occasionally.

I thought I had brought plenty of food, but somehow I ran out of everything in less than thirty minutes. I guess the combination of novelty and the smell of freshly fried food won out.

"Sir Pendragon, might I speak with you?"

Miss Karina approached me with a young man on her arm—although not in an amorous way. The young man was Orion, Baron Muno's eldest son and Miss Karina's younger brother.

Despite his apparent fondness for the martial arts tournament, he couldn't get out of attending the duke's evening party.

"Hello, Lady Karina. And this must be the brother you spoke so highly of? I am Satou Pendragon, a hereditary knight. Pleased to make your acquaintance."

"Indeed. I'm Orion Muno. Nice to meet you, Sir Pendragon."

Orion nodded importantly as he introduced himself. He appeared to have reached the age where a young boy tries to puff himself up as much as possible.

He did mumble his first name, though, probably because his hero-loving father had given it to him. From what I understood, he was named after Orion Pendragon, a fictional hero from the legends.

After a short chat, the two went off to the main hall. I discreetly advised them to steer clear of the prince.

At the center of the hall, the dance was picking up as young noblemen invited beautiful young ladies to join them at the edge of the floor. It was a pretty good place to meet people.

If a new noble like me tried to join in, I'd probably just get burned, so I had no intention of inviting anyone to dance. Besides, the unmarried young ladies were far too young for me, as their ages ranged from thirteen to eighteen.

After watching over the youthful attempts at romance for a while, I decided it was time to bring out the last course.

My fourth and final dish was dessert.

Originally, I wanted to make strawberry shortcakes or cheesecakes, but I couldn't perfect my sponge batter in time. I decided to settle for crepes.

Despite the buffet-style service, the nobles seemed averse to eating with their hands, so I came up with a creative solution.

Instead of the large crepes that were a popular street food in modern Japan, I decided to make mini crepes and cut them into quarters.

The reason I went with such small slices was so that even the young women could eat them in a single bite. I also added a sauce made from strawberry jam to keep them from looking so lonely on the plates by themselves.

"My, that smells delicious."

"They'll be ready soon, ma'am."

I placed fresh cream and sliced strawberries in the hot crepes. Then I cut them up quickly, put them on a plate Lulu was holding, and presented them to the waiting young woman.

As soon as she tasted the bite-size crepe, the girl's face melted.

Even the makeup that she'd worked so hard to apply couldn't disguise her innocent glee in that moment. Charmed by her reaction, a gaggle of young male nobles gathered around as soon as she finished eating and asked her to dance.

Good luck, you crazy kids.

"You realize you're making a total old-man face, right?"

Arisa munched on a crepe as she sniped at me from the floor.

Oh, come on. What's wrong with cheering on young love?

With no time to answer her out loud, I simply kept making crepes at the demand of the young women.

Interestingly, no one mistook me for a servant. Maybe it was because of my fancy clothes. Thanks to that, though, I had to exchange introductions every time I took an order for a crepe, meaning I ended up learning the names of over a hundred girls.

I ran out of ingredients partway through, so Lulu and Arisa had to run and grab more cream and strawberries from the kitchen.

Phew, at least I can rest for a minute now...

"S-Sir Knight! Would you like to share a dance with me, please, maybe?"

Perhaps I looked bored or friendly, because a girl in her early teens who was just making her societal debut came over to me almost immediately.

Thanks to my "Dancing" and "Sociability" skills, I should be able to handle it.

"Certainly, if you'd like."

Besides, the fear of rejection was written all over her face. I felt I should at least oblige her for one song.

"Please, there's no need to be so tense. Just pretend the people around us are trees or statues. And you can think of me as a father or older brother–like figure, if it puts you at ease," I whispered, and the tension seemed to leave the girl's shoulders ever so slightly. "Don't worry, just relax. Try to go with the flow, like a princess."

Taking the lead, I tried to make sure she enjoyed the dance, reassuring her each time she made a misstep.

Eventually, the song ended, and I walked my partner off the dance floor, only to find a whole line of girls waiting for their turn.

As far as I could tell, it wasn't so much that they liked me personally, just that they'd deemed me an ideal practice partner for a societal debut.

Lulu and Arisa still weren't back with the cream, so I obliged their requests.

Before long, several of them invited me over to their homes.

I wasn't exactly looking to marry into money, but I did my best to politely acquiesce to these invitations.

Sure, one or two of their parents owned workshops that I'd been hoping to tour, but more importantly, I figured it'd be best to have a lot of noble allies in case I ever made an enemy of someone powerful like the prince.

Dealing with problems was a lot less stressful when you had people you could rely on.

Eventually, the next round of supplies ran out as well, so we decided to head home, leaving the cleanup of the booth to the castle staff. Before we left, I naturally checked in with the duke's butler, who was in charge of orchestrating the party.

Because Lulu had to run back to the kitchen to get something she'd forgotten, Arisa and I waited in the courtyard, gazing up at the stars in the cool evening breeze.

"Even out here, you can still hear the music from the ball."

"Yeah."

The lilting strains of a waltz were still faintly audible.

"You were pretty popular with the lolis in there, huh?" Arisa was rather peeved.

"You think so? I figured they just needed a practice partner to get used to dancing with men."

I stood up with a shrug.

"…Are you mad?"

"Of course not." I smiled at her. "More importantly, madam, may I have this dance?"

"Huh? Oh, umm… Yes! It'd be my pleasure!"

Arisa was briefly puzzled by my playfully theatrical invitation, then broke into a big smile.

We danced lightly around the courtyard. Arisa was surprisingly good; perhaps she'd had lessons back when she was a princess.

After we'd danced to three songs, Lulu reappeared.

"Sorry to keep you waiting, master, Arisa."

She'd taken longer than expected because the head chef had stopped her and told her she could work there anytime she wanted. Of course the old man would try to recruit her as soon as my back was turned.

"Even from a distance, it's still beautiful."

Lulu gave a little sigh as she gazed past the hedges at the lit-up ballroom. *Might as well see if she wants to dance, too.*

"Miss, would you care for a dance?"

"O-of course! I'd love to."

We twirled in the faint light from the ballroom, and Lulu's long black hair swayed gently to the rhythm.

"Ah, it's just like a dream…"

"Glad to hear it."

Lulu and I danced on and on, a faraway expression on her face.

"H-hey, come on! Don't I get another turn?"

Lulu giggled. "Hee-hee. Oh, Arisa, you're so cute."

I was planning to stop whenever Lulu got bored, but I started to suspect she never would. Instead, I traded places with the ever-jealous Arisa.

With the occasional warm looks from passing maids and servants, the three of us took turns dancing the night away.

It was nice to spend an evening like this every once in a while.

After the ball, my days only got busier.

It was still way easier than the weeks of nonstop work back when

I was a programmer, of course. The endless tea parties hosted by nobles or their daughters were a far cry from how I'd spent my days in Japan.

It felt strange by modern standards to bring a gift to a tea party, but the custom among nobles here was to give something to the hosts when you were invited over for tea for the first time.

If the butler hadn't told me about it beforehand, I could've been in big trouble.

The token couldn't be just any old gift, either. If you gave something too expensive, the host would assume that you were trying to curry favor for marriage, civil service, or something of the sort. But of course, something cheap would be an insult to the recipient.

And the ideal gift differed depending on the faction and influence of the family, too.

I wasn't thrilled about tackling such an impossibly difficult game without a reset button, but an unexpected savior came to my rescue.

Tolma, of all people.

"Good evening, Sir Satou. I heard you were invited to the homes of some young ladies for tea, so I thought I'd come over to give you the rundown on the families and their preferences and such."

Showing up on my doorstep with a bottle of high-class wine in hand, Tolma gave me unusually detailed information on all the noble families in the old capital.

He inhaled the mountain of snacks I had prepared as he listed the likes, dislikes, and personalities of each and every member of the aristocracy. He even warned me about which topics never to mention around certain people.

I filled a thick notebook with information until he was finally too drunk to continue.

I decided to call this treasured new object the "Tolma Memo."

Which was great and all, but...

"Well, you might not need that much info anyway, since you managed to mediate between Sir Lloyd and Count Hohen. Those two fight like cats and dogs."

...I wasn't expecting that comment.

"Those two, like cats and dogs? But they seem like such good friends."

And I didn't remember doing any mediating.

All I'd done was have some nice chats with them about cooking and spell books.

"Good friends, eh? You're a pretty weird kid, Sir Satou."

Maybe my "Negotiation" and "Mediation" skills just acted of their own accord.

The tea parties were going smoothly, thanks in no small part to Tolma's help.

I brought cheese soufflés and other baked goods, and for hosts who didn't have a sweet tooth, I took soufflés baked with brandy and raisins.

At Arisa's suggestion, I also brought some plainer baked snacks for the maids of each home.

For the gifts, I tried making jewelry like earrings and necklaces on thin silver chains.

With my own personal twist, of course.

"Mother, do look at this."

"Why, isn't that lovely!"

A rune appeared in the center of the small pendant as it glowed in the young lady's hands. I had carved the symbol into a light stone scarcely bigger than a grain of rice, a simple design that would glow if charged with magical power.

I'd used information from the Carving Magic book I bought at Mr. Kikinu's magic shop.

A single rune wouldn't have any special effects, but there were some with meanings similar to Japanese *omamori* charms, like "peace and prosperity" or "luck in love," so I used one of those.

"How wonderful. It's a good-luck rune."

"This one is a rune for bravery! Let's have Father carry it when he goes out to lead the highway patrol."

I smiled at the host family, glad to see them so enamored with my gift.

When I was first asked who made the glowing pendant, I randomly made up a name, so now a fictional magic tool engineer called Trismegistus was gaining fame throughout the city. Of course, I didn't inscribe any name on the pendants.

It was technically a magic tool, but such an insubstantial effect shouldn't pose any problems.

However, the pendants ended up going over a little too well…

"S-Sir Satou, would you like to come for tea at my home, too?"

"No, no, you should come to my house! My father is a baron, not a baronet like Ferna's."

…So all the other girls wanted one, too.

Before I knew it, I went from having tea parties every other day to every day, and in the end, I wound up with three per day.

Making new friends was good and all, but I was having a hard time keeping track of all these different faces. Luckily, thanks to my high INT stat, I was able to memorize names and faces right away as long as I made a conscious effort to do so.

Incidentally, since I made the light stone pendants myself, they cost me less than one gold coin each. However, as demand grew, the price displayed by my "Appraisal" skill rose until its value reached twenty gold coins.

Because of my high "Metalworking" skill, the slender chains I made had a delicacy rarely seen in accessories in this world. Making them was a very finicky process. If I hadn't been able to practice Magic Hand at the same time, I probably would've switched to a different gift right away.

All that training paid off big-time, though. By the end, I was able to use one hundred and twenty Magic Hands at once to create the chains assembly line–style.

Not that this was my aim, but befriending all these nobles did get me permission to tour the workshops they owned.

I was too busy at present, but once the tea party marathon was over, I figured I could take everyone along.

As an added bonus, I was able to convince several of the nobles who had old or inferior stocks of rice, preserved food, and so on to contribute them to the Muno Barony for little to no money.

The retired Count Worgoch helped organize transportation for these supplies to the barony. Hopefully, by the time I came back, I'd be able to buy plenty of *sasakama* there.

However, making new friends among the upper crust wasn't always a good thing.

"Master, you've received letters and photographs for marriage interviews."

"Again…?"

When I came home from the latest tea party, a disgruntled Arisa greeted me.

I'd been receiving these with increasing frequency over the past few days.

"Karina, you okaaay?"

"Pull it together, ma'am! It's only a flesh wound, ma'am!"

"Tama, Pochi…"

Tama and Pochi comforted Miss Karina on the couch where she'd collapsed as soon as she entered the living room.

I'd been taking her along to some of the tea parties to help her expand her circle of friends, but so far it wasn't going very well.

"Sorry, Lulu, but could you bring my blue-green tea to the study?"

"Of course, master!"

I took the letters along to the study, leaving the photos behind.

"You're going to turn them down without even looking at the pictures?"

"It'd be more insulting to reject them after seeing them, wouldn't it?"

I shrugged at Arisa and headed into the study.

As I wrote my letters of polite refusal, I noted the names of the girls and their families who had proposed in my memo tab.

They were all lower-class nobles, and a handful even included requests for loans at the same time.

Some of them must have seen me as a member of the nouveau riche who bought expensive magic items as tea party gifts.

I asked Lulu to deliver the finished letters to the butler to be sent.

"Satou?"

"Master, are you going out again? I inquire."

The sharp eyes of Mia and Nana noticed right away that my coat was in my hand.

"Yes, sorry. I've been invited to Marquis Lloyd's dinner party."

"C'mooon, another one? Weren't you just at Count Hohen's yesterday?"

In addition to the tea parties, Marquis Lloyd and Count Hohen had been inviting me over for dinner almost every day.

I'd given both of their head chefs the recipe for tempura, so this time I was being invited as a proper guest, not a chef. By the way, I gave the tempura recipe to the chefs of Count Worgoch and the duke, too.

Then, at the dinner parties…

"Sir Knight, what did you think of that dish?"

"Delicious. The duck was cooked perfectly."

"I appreciate that, but what needed to be improved?"

…the chefs kept accosting me for advice. Still, I got to eat some exquisite fare and learn new cooking techniques. It was a win-win.

"Sir Satou, will you be working again tonight?"

"Certainly, if you'll allow me the honor."

"I admire your passion. But be careful not to neglect your health. Your body is not yours alone, after all."

Out of context, Marquis Lloyd's choice of words could easily be misinterpreted.

"Many of us often find ourselves eagerly anticipating your next dish," he added.

With that, I gained permission to head back into Marquis Lloyd's library.

I took a chained spell book down from the shelf and started reading. Because of all the valuable texts, there was a librarian on duty to guard them, but I didn't mind.

I gained permission to peruse this collection in exchange for sharing the original Water Magic spell I used to make consommé soup.

Since the permission was granted on the condition that I couldn't write anything down, I didn't copy any of the books into my memo tab, either.

However, thanks to my extremely high INT skill, I was able to memorize the pages with amazing accuracy, and our contract said nothing about writing things down from memory once I got back to the mansion.

Besides, each house seemed to have several libraries, which meant they would probably keep anything truly secret in a different room.

I made similar contracts with other important nobles like Count Hohen and Duke Ougoch, so I was able to read a great deal of valuable books. This included the former Count Worgoch, too, of course.

Thanks to that, my knowledge of greater magic increased exponentially. I still couldn't use the spells myself, though.

And so, I spent my time blissfully grappling with esoteric texts and acquiring new knowledge.

> Title Acquired: Library Master
> Title Acquired: Scholar of the Written Word

It was six days after the evening party, our tenth morning in the old capital.

I had a little time to spare before I headed out, so I decided to watch my kids train for a bit.

"Masterrr?"

"Master! Sir! Come see how hard we've been practicing, sir!"

Once I was prepared for my outing, I went into the courtyard and was promptly greeted by Tama and Pochi.

"Tama, Pochi, you mustn't touch master's clothes with dirty hands."

"Master, I would like you to praise the results of my training, I entreat."

Liza and Nana were there, too. As usual, Nana couldn't hide her true motives.

They'd all been working hard, though. I had no trouble giving them generous commendations.

"Why, the young master is here! Why don't you spar two-on-two and show him the fruits of your training?"

Mr. Kajiro, the Saga Kingdom samurai who was drilling the vanguard team, gave the signal for the mock battle to begin.

"Remember, Ayaume will ambush you if you let your guard down! Watch yourselves!"

Miss Ayaume, the female samurai, was hiding behind a nearby bush with a short bow in hand. Instead of arrowheads, the tips of the arrows were wrapped in cloth to prevent any injury.

This training must be to prepare them in case of bandit attacks.

I stood next to Mr. Kajiro and watched the battle play out. They certainly seemed to have fewer openings than before. Pochi, in particular, who was normally focused solely on attacking, was paying closer attention to her surroundings.

Whenever one of them let their guard down for a moment, Ayaume would shoot an arrow at them or surprise attack them from a tree with a twig.

Mr. Kajiro explained that they had to do extra training for each time they fell victim to one of these surprise attacks.

Liza and Tama ended up winning the sparring match, but Nana and Pochi performed well, too.

As I was complimenting them on each area of improvement, the butler called us from inside the mansion.

It was time to go.

Miss Karina and I rode in a carriage behind that of the retired Count Worgoch and his wife.

Our destination was the airship landing area.

There was already a great deal of old capital nobles gathered there when we arrived.

"It's rather small for an airship, no?"

"That's true. But it's likely more agile, and its armor is made of mithril alloy."

Miss Karina and I watched as the airship touched down on the ground. The AR display labeled it the **king's private high-speed airship**.

"Is His Majesty aboard?"

"Yes, I believe so."

As I nodded at the anxious-looking Miss Karina, I referred to the information on my map.

We were here today with the other nobles to greet the king arriving on his private airship. It wasn't necessarily mandatory, but I did want to see what the monarch looked like, which was why I came along.

Temple representatives had come, too, but I didn't see Sara or the head priestess of Tenion Temple.

I hadn't been able to see Sara since the soup kitchen incident, but from what I'd heard at a few of the tea parties, she was lying low in the sanctuary to avoid the prince's courtship.

With all these nobles and officials gathered in one place, it would have been a likely target for a terrorist attack. However, most of the remaining Wings of Freedom members in the old capital had been hunted down; there weren't enough of them left to try anything.

Word at the banquet had been that the king was here to attend the wedding of Tisrado, the duke's grandson and eventual successor, and the granddaughter of Marquis Eluette, whose territory was on the western edge of the kingdom.

From my impression of the bride-to-be at Marquis Lloyd's dinner party, she was a beautiful, ethereal girl.

The wedding was in five days, and I'd been invited to cook for it already.

"Is that His Majesty the king?"

Raising my head, I saw a man with silver-gray hair descending the airship's ramp. Oddly, his beard alone was pure white.

The AR display appeared next to him, so I read the text there. He was fifty-five years old, younger than I thought.

The next bit of information surprised me: This wasn't the real king but a body double.

The minister behind him seemed to be real, though.

The nobles around us kneeled reverently, and I followed suit.

We stayed on our knees as the duke's heir approached to give a few words of welcome, and then until the king was out of sight.

The heads of the more powerful noble families and other influential people headed into the duke's castle, but that was the end for the rest of us, so I returned to the mansion.

"Satou."

Mia, who'd been reading a spell book with Arisa in the living room, trotted over to me and latched onto my waist. In her hand was a message addressed to me.

"Scrolls."

"Thank you, Mia."

The card was a notice from the scroll workshop that part of my scroll order had been completed.

"Prr, prr." Mia was imitating a cat's purr as she hung off me. I gently detached her.

"Mrrr."

Patting her head to alleviate her bad mood, I announced my latest errand.

"I'm going to Viscount Siemmen's place for a bit."

"'kaaay."

Arisa was too focused on memorizing Space Magic spells to give much of an answer.

"Hurry back."

"Of course."

Mia came to the entrance hall to see me off, and I patted her again.

"I'm just picking up the scrolls and saying hello to Tolma, so it won't be long. Then we'll all have dinner together, okay?"

"Mm."

For a moment, I felt like a father with a young daughter. Then I headed out to Viscount Siemmen's place nearby.

Mr. Djang, the workshop manager, presented me with the scrolls I'd prioritized highest: Remote Stun, Shooter, Standard Out, and Graphic View.

"Mr. Djang, Mr. Djang! Is Mr. Knight still here?!"

"Quiet down, Natalina!"

Natalina rushed in, waving around two more scrolls.

"Oh, perfect! Ta-da—I stayed up all night finishing Fireworks and Fireworks Illusion!"

The bags under her eyes suggested she was running on a post-all-nighter high as she thrust the scrolls toward me.

"Thank you very much, Miss Natalina."

"Hee-hee, no prob! ...So hey, I was thinking, maybe you could sell us these spells..."

Natalina put on a show of fidgeting and winking bashfully.

"Stop it, Natalina. You don't have the assets for that."

"You're sooo mean, Mr. Djang!"

Djang shook his head and turned to me with a serious expression.

"We'd be willing to pay this sum for the Fireworks and Fireworks Illusion spells."

Glancing over the contract he handed me, I raised my eyebrows when I saw the sum at the bottom.

"...Has there been some mistake with the number of zeroes?"

A hundred gold coins seemed like way too much for just two spells. Besides, selling the full chant for the spell with explanations and the rights to resell it didn't mean I couldn't use the spell myself anymore or that I couldn't sell it elsewhere. It wasn't an exclusive deal.

"See? I told you, Mr. Djang! This magic's worth way more than that! It's lesser magic—anyone can use it, you know?! And even from a scroll, it still makes beautiful fireworks... If we could finish it in time for Lord Tisrado's wedding, our orders would go through the roof! We'd make our investment back in a year, tops!"

Natalina seemed to have fallen in love with my Fireworks spells.

Still, the wedding was only five days away. I doubted they could mass-produce it before then.

...*Wait, what?*

Did they think I meant a hundred wasn't enough and wanted *another* zero?

"Good point. A hundred gold coins would normally be enough to buy one new spell, but these will surely be popular with nobles. Let's talk to Lord Hosarris and see if we can raise our offer to five hundred."

"Hooray!"

They were planning to buy them for a hundred gold coins *each*? I would've sold them both for ten, honestly...

Neither one took more than a day's work to create, so getting five hundred gold coins per spell would feel unjust.

"Wait a moment, please. If you really value my humble spells so highly, I'd be happy to sell them at your original price."

"Oooh, really? Yay! In that case, we've gotta start mass-producing them right away! Mr. Djang, we can halt production on other products for now, right?"

"Yes, that's fine... Except for Sir Knight's order, of course."

"Well, duh! But everything else is getting tabled for firewooorks!"

With that, Natalina bolted out of the room at top speed. Then she reappeared moments later.

"Thank you, Sir Knight!"

After a quick bow, she darted away again.

That's a lot of energy.

"I'm sorry. She can be a handful."

Mr. Djang and I sorted out the difference between the sale of the new spells and the price of my order, and he gave me a bundle of scrolls.

I made out like a bandit, if you ask me.

Once my business at Viscount Siemmen's estate was finished, I headed to Tolma's house nearby.

The maid guided me to a gazebo where, surprisingly, Tolma's family was enjoying tea with Miss Ringrande.

"Pardon me for intruding, Lord Tolma."

"Hey, Sir Satou. Come on in. You don't mind, right, Rin?"

"Certainly."

I had intended to simply thank Tolma for the information he'd given me and leave, but it would've been rude to refuse his invitation, so I came in and took the empty seat next to Ringrande.

"How's your social life going?"

"Very well, thanks to the wisdom you were kind enough to share with me."

"Glad to hear it. So, you've got some marriage proposals, too, right? Going to take a few of them up on it?"

I knew polygamy was common among nobles in this kingdom, but I couldn't get used to the idea of having multiple fiancées.

"No, I feel that I'm still too young for marriage."

If I settled down, I wouldn't be free to travel the world.

At a few of the tea parties, I had met young ladies around the same level of beauty as Sara or Miss Karina, but with Lulu and company around all the time, I was confident I wouldn't fall in love that easily.

"You sure? You must be popular with the ladies, right? If you at least marry your fiancée Karina, you'll become a viceroy of Muno Barony for sure, and then you'll have as much income and power as a senior noble. Then you could make Sara your second wife and probably find two or three more besides. If you take on some concubines, too, you'll have ten women easily!"

So you're talking about a literal harem? Seriously, what kind of kingdom is this?

Tolma's wife, Miss Hayuna, looked as appalled as I was, but the reaction of one particular individual was especially intense.

"Satou! So you *are* after Sara, then? And what's this about a *second* wife? She wouldn't even be your first?!"

Miss Ringrande stood up furiously and grabbed me by the collar, her love for her sister burning in her eyes.

"Please, calm down. Lord Tolma is letting his imagination run away with him. As I said in the temple, Sara is a dear friend of mine and nothing more. Besides, Karina and I aren't even in a relationship, never mind engaged."

I put both hands up in front of me.

"…You swear?"

"Yes, on my honor as a hereditary knight."

Miss Ringrande's suspicions hadn't subsided, but she at least let go of me.

Please stop believing everything you hear about me, people.

"I'm sorry. Something upset me earlier, so I'm still a bit on edge."

Miss Ringrande clenched her fists, trying to control her anger.

She must have remembered whatever that "something" was and gotten mad all over again.

Sensing the tension in the air, baby Mayuna started crying.

"Oh no, I'm sorry! There, there…"

The baby's cries softened Ringrande's rage immediately.

"Uncle Tolma, could we use your garden for a bit? Come with me, Satou."

With that, Miss Ringrande drew her sword briskly and insisted on sparring with me for almost an hour.

"You two must be thirsty, right? Why not drop the training for now and come have some wine?"

Tolma already had the wine in hand as he invited us back inside.

Miss Hayuna had returned to the house to put Mayuna to bed. The only other person left in the gazebo was a maid.

"…Can you believe that? I'm supposed to throw the fight in front of the whole city? And to that awful Prince Sharorik, no less!"

Drunk on the wine, Miss Ringrande leaned into me as she complained about what had been bothering her earlier.

It certainly felt nice on my arm, but it added to her flushed face and the scent of perfume mixed with sweat was threatening to make me dizzy.

"Why should I have to have some mock battle with the prince just because His Majesty will be present?"

Ah, and here comes round number three.

"And His Highness's sword is the Holy Sword Claidheamh Soluis. It's supposed to be the symbol of victory, the embodiment of the Shiga Kingdom, you know? So I don't…" She trailed off.

As it turned out, the third time was the last. She'd fallen asleep.

I eased the wineglass out of Miss Ringrande's hand and quietly put it on the table.

I let her lean on my shoulder as she napped, and Tolma and I chatted awhile and deepened our friendship with her light snoring in the background.

The Day of the Finals

Satou here. There are a lot of different beliefs concerning omens before natural disasters like earthquakes and such. When birds and small animals start making noise in anime and manga, for example, you know something bad is about to go down.

Tama had been acting strange all morning.

She kept pacing back and forth between rooms, pestering the other girls and rolling around on the floor.

They'd all noticed her unusual behavior.

"What's going on with you, Tama?"

"Dunnooo? I feel kinda itchyyy."

"Tama's being weird today, sir. I don't like it, sir!"

Hmm? Pochi was unusually temperamental, too.

Tama shoved Mia aside to curl up in a ball on my lap.

What's going on? Tama was usually so laid-back. It was unlike her to get pushy.

"Mrrr?"

Mia looked bewildered, too.

Petting Tama on the back seemed to calm her down slightly, and soon she fell asleep with a grimace still on her face. Pochi relaxed as well, wrapping herself around Nana's airship plushie like a hug pillow and rolling about with it.

Nana watched them enviously, perhaps wishing her physique would allow her to do the same.

"Say, master..." Arisa crept up behind me and whispered in my ear. "Didn't they act like this when we first went into Muno Castle?"

"Did they?"

Thinking back, I remembered they noticed something weird about the floor, but they hadn't lost their cool like this as far as I recalled.

I suppose they were uneasy in both cases, but...come to think of it, Tama had particularly good intuition in the Seiryuu City labyrinth, too.

Maybe they sensed that something ominous was going to happen today.

"I'll look into it."

With that, I opened up my map search.

Gah, these guys again?

Noticing yet another wave of cultists had invaded the old capital, I felt more irritated than worried.

Thanks to the territory map I gave the duke, more than 90 percent of them had been wiped out. How were there still enough to get up to anything?

I scanned the whole territory again to be sure. Evidently these guys were the last of the members remaining in the duchy.

There were only eight of them, and they were pretty low-level, 25 at the highest, so I doubted they could accomplish much. However, I didn't like that their current location was underground directly beneath the arena.

Because the king was visiting the stadium today, every noble with rank in the old capital was already there.

On top of that, today was both the tournament finals and the exhibition match between Miss Ringrande and the third prince. The arena was full to bursting with spectators.

Now that was a very likely target for some kind of terrorist attack. If they just had a short horn or two, it'd be no big deal, but if any of them had a long horn, it could be a serious problem.

Many of the nobles I'd befriended in the city were attending, too, not to mention Miss Karina and her brother. No way could I just turn a blind eye.

"Something smells fishy here...," I muttered.

"Seriously?" Arisa exclaimed, and all eyes in the room turned toward us.

"I'm just going to take care of it."

I slid Tama off my lap onto the sofa and stood up.

"Master, please allow me to come with you."

"Master, permit me to accompany you, I entreat."

"I want to help, too, sir!"

Liza, Nana, and Pochi gazed at me with hopeful eyes.

"You have to be a noble to enter, so I'll need to go alone." They were probably high enough level that it would be safe to take them along, but they'd be in danger if the Wings of Freedom had long horns or explosive magic items, which was why I made an excuse. "You'll get to show me the results of your training soon, don't worry. For now, I'd like you to protect Lulu for me."

As I tried to reassure the girls, I debated whether to go out as Satou or dress as Nanashi the Hero.

"Mew!"

Tama jumped up suddenly from her slumber, her ears and tail standing on end as her gaze darted around wildly.

And then, a tremor rippled through the old capital.

It wasn't an earthquake. Just the feeling of a magic wave passing through.

But that amount of power clearly wasn't normal.

"What was that?"

"Something went *bong*, sir!"

"A signal?"

"Master, we must prepare for battle, I report."

About half my party members had obviously experienced the same thing.

Tama must have been acting strangely earlier because she sensed it coming.

Liza started putting on the new equipment I'd given her. Before long, Pochi and Nana were changing clothes, too.

The sight of Nana's curves drew my eyes as she stripped off her clothes with no reservations whatsoever, but I forced myself not to stare.

Instead, I had Lulu put a partitioning screen in front of them.

"You change, too, please, Tama."

"'kay."

Tama pulled herself away from her restless gazing out the window.

Meanwhile, I continued searching the map.

Just as I suspected, the arena was at the center of the disturbance.

Searching for demons, I found that several short horns had appeared in the very spot where I'd seen the collection of Wings of Freedom members gathered. Clearly, it was no coincidence that the number of missing cultists was the same as the number of demons that had appeared.

"What happened?"

"Demons again."

"Aw, man! C'mon…"

I had to agree with Arisa. I was getting pretty tired of it myself.

Nearly twenty people at the arena were over level 40, including Miss Ringrande, the prince and his accompanying knights, and some of the duke's military officers. They would probably be fine without my help, but given the strange magic ripple that had just occurred, it was better to be prepared.

To be safe, I had Lulu, Arisa, and Mia change into the new equipment I'd recently fashioned for them as well. I also gave everyone fireproof cloaks made from hydra wings.

Just as everyone was almost ready, a warning bell resounded throughout the old capital.

Almost immediately, one of the maids rushed into the room.

"Sir Knight! That's the emergency alert bell! Please, follow me to the shelter nearby."

She quickly explained that there were underground bunkers beneath all the nobles' homes in the old capital for evacuation in case of attacks by demons, large monsters, or other disasters.

As we followed the maid, three more waves of magic power washed over us.

Something was definitely going on.

"Seems like there's still some trouble. Everyone, please evacuate to the shelter ahead of me. I'm going to scout things out."

I opened up a second map search.

According to it, another foe had appeared in the center of the arena. And he was a level-71 greater hell demon, at that. He didn't have any Unique Skills like the demon lord did, but he had "Summoning Magic," "Psychic Magic," "Blaze Magic," and other troublesome skills. *I'd better take care of him fast, before he summons anything.*

"Arisa."

"Yes?"

"If things get really dicey, I'll contact you with the Telephone spell. And if that happens, I want you to teleport everyone underground to the labyrinth ruins immediately, all right?"

"Okeydoke!"

I had a quiet conversation with Arisa as we continued toward the shelter.

"Tell the maid I went to the arena to check on Lady Karina, all right?"

"You got it."

Entrusting the rest to Arisa, I left the estate alone.

Once I confirmed on the radar that there were no witnesses around, I transformed into Nanashi the Hero and set out toward the arena.

As I traveled, I used my new Clairvoyance and Clairaudience spells to see what was happening at my destination. A window opened in the corner of my vision with an AR display that showed me the chaos.

"Demon! No—demon lord! Prepare to meet your doom!!"

Striking a dramatic pose like an actor, the prince shouted at the yellow-skinned greater hell demon.

The yellow demon had two heads and horns coming out of his shoulders that reminded me of a water buffalo's. I bet he used the extra head for chants, like the other greater hell demons I'd seen.

Clairvoyance and Clairaudience were sure handy for keeping an eye on a far-off situation.

"THAT SWORD IS CLAIDHEAMH SOLUIS, IS IT NOT? THEN YOU MUST BE A DESCENDANT OF YAMATO."

With that, the demon summoned monsters to sic on Miss Ringrande and the prince and company.

The summoning spell seemed to be continuous, too; monster after monster flooded into the spectators' seats.

The former ranged from levels 30 to 40, but the latter were weaker, level 20 at the most.

There were plenty of eliminated tournament contestants in the audience, so they should be able to handle the weaker monsters, but in all the mayhem, they weren't coordinating properly.

"Brave warriors! You must protect your neighbors! Now is the time to prove your worth in battle!"

The clear, ringing call was probably Miss Ringrande's.

Realizing the foolhardiness of their behavior, the warriors began to work together to defeat the monsters. They were even protecting the citizens and helping them escape.

Next, I turned my Clairvoyance toward the nobles' seats.

"The duke has brought His Majesty back to the castle! We must protect the nobles!"

The duke seemed to have used the power of the City Core to teleport himself and the stand-in king to the audience room of the castle.

His heir and other upper-class nobles still remained, though. There must be limits to how many people could be teleported.

Miss Karina and Orion appeared frightened but otherwise unharmed. With Raka, Miss Karina probably didn't need me worrying about her.

"The barrier! Put up a defense barrier! Can't we evacuate?!"

"A lesser demon self-destructed and destroyed the passage. We'll have to secure another escape route!"

High-level knights, priests, and sorcerers protected the nobles, so I figured they were safe, too, as long as the greater hell demon didn't attack them directly.

Currently, he was half-heartedly fighting Ringrande and the prince while scanning the arena as if in search of something.

The passage for the general seating seemed to be intact. Audience members were pushing one another as they fled.

Trying to shake off the images of red stains and motionless bodies in the stands, I used "Warp" to hurry toward the arena.

I minimized the Clairvoyance window so that it wouldn't obstruct my view.

As I approached the stadium, the streets became increasingly crowded with fleeing people and carriages.

Some of them were even branching out into the back alleys where I was running. I decided to take to the skies with "Skyrunning."

Finally, I got within view of the arena's outer wall and the yellow demon.

The prince and other warriors probably wanted to handle him themselves to gain prestige, but I had friends in the arena. I wanted to finish things up quickly.

First, I chose the Light Magic spell Laser to defeat the enormous yellow demon.

But just as I was about to put my plan into action, something happened.

A ripple of light appeared in the sky, and a sleek silver spacecraft (or so it appeared) materialized.

Hey, you can't just switch to sci-fi all of a sudden!

According to the AR, the ship was called the **dimensional submarine *Jules Verne*.** Since it was named after a famous author, I had little doubt that someone from my original world was involved somehow.

A section of the ship opened, and a number of things that looked like gun barrels protruded from it.

Moments later, heavy booms filled the air as it fired countless high-speed firebombs to shoot down all the airborne monsters.

They didn't seem to work on the yellow greater hell demon, but they still packed a considerable punch.

Then a man in blue armor appeared on the stern—revealed by my AR to be **Hayato Masaki the Hero.**

Clad in armor, sans helmet, his face in profile struck me as stalwart and masculine, his black hair cut short like an athlete's. He looked young for twenty-five, with the kind of understated handsomeness that some girls would probably secretly go crazy for.

He was level 69, too, so the yellow demon should be easy enough for him to handle.

"Look upon me!"

The hero must have used some sort of taunting skill with those words, as the monsters below all turned toward him.

When I looked back, a face guard hid his features.

"HAYATO THE HERO, IS IT? HAVE YOU COME PREPARED TO DIE THIS TIME, THEN?"

"I'm not the same man I used to be! Today I swear to enact my revenge!"

I could probably still use Laser to defeat the demon in an instant, but I would've felt bad doing it after that dramatic backstory.

"Stay out of this, you Saga Empire dog! I shall prove that your empire is not the only one that can produce a hero."

That must've been Prince Sharorik. He should really just leave this to the professionals.

"*<Dance>, Claidheamh Soluis!*"

The "dance" bit seemed to be a magic word; the Holy Sword flew out of his hands to attack the yellow demon.

So I guess the painting at the museum wasn't outright fiction, just a bit of an exaggeration.

...Oh. The demon batted it away.

Is that all you've got, Claidheamh Soluis?

"*Your Holy Sword weeps, Prince. This is one of the generals of a powerful demon lord of old—the Golden Boar Lord. He's a demon of the highest caliber who's survived for hundreds of years. If you wish to live, you had best retreat.*"

The hero readied his own Holy Sword.

"*<Sing>, Arondight!*"

As soon as he said the keyword *sing*, the Holy Sword Arondight emitted a powerful holy light.

Did my Holy Swords have special keywords like that, too? I didn't remember seeing anything like that in their descriptions.

I quickly checked Durandal's info, but it was a no-go. Once this whole mess was over, I'd have to take my time and investigate properly.

While my mind wandered a little, the hero's comrades emerged from the ship.

Out of curiosity, I used "Telescopic Sight" and "Amplification" to take a peek at his party members.

A beautiful woman dressed like a Shinto priest, with big breasts and a gentle air about her, cast strengthening magic on the party. She had a sexy beauty mark under one eye.

A long-eared female warrior, evidently from the long-eared Booch clan, fired an arrow that turned into ten arrows at the monsters coming toward the hero. What a great fantasy weapon.

The monsters that escaped her shots jumped and landed on the ship, but this time, an agile fighter and a dual-wielding swordswoman took them down in an instant.

They were beastfolk, like Tama and Pochi. The tigerfolk woman with curly hair and the wolffolk woman with a short bob both had lovely features, and their armor suggested they had the proportions to match.

The last member to emerge was a woman with a short staff, luxurious blond ringlets, and an enormous bust. They weren't quite as large

as Miss Karina's, but they could probably give her sister Miss Soluna a run for her money.

The information in the blond woman's AR display surprised me.

Her name was Meriest Saga, the twenty-first princess of the Saga Empire.

The "princess" part surprised me, but not nearly as much as "twenty-first" did. *You must be a busy man, Mr. Emperor.*

At any rate, the hero's entire party consisted of glamorous, gorgeous women, enough to make me wish death on him just a little bit.

The group got into formation to take on the yellow demon. There was hardly any difference in their levels, so I could afford to let them take care of things here.

So I decided to just help out with rescuing people from the arena and eliminating the small fry instead.

There was a time and a place for everything, after all.

Hero Summoning

No matter how dark the hour, we will never give in to despair. For Hayato the Hero will always be the last beacon of hope. As long as we have him, we can overcome anything. (Ringrande, follower of the hero)

All of us "followers of the hero" carry a protective talisman granted by the goddess Parion.

This sacred treasure draws power from the prayers of the people and the lives of the followers to perform miracles.

I had never encountered a situation so bleak that I had to use the talisman.

And I never imagined that morning that I would have to do so in my own hometown…

That day, I woke up in a melancholy mood.

It was the day I was scheduled to have a fake battle with Prince Sharorik to entertain His Majesty the king and the rest of the audience at the tournament finals.

I should have waited and come with Hayato and the others instead of going on ahead. *Have they left the Gray Ratfolk Emirate on the* Jules Verne *yet?* I wondered.

"Lady Ringrande, it is time. Please proceed into the arena."

I returned to reality, thanked the young official who'd summoned me, and rose to my feet.

Waving at the audience as they cheered my name, I strode toward the battlefield.

"Truly, what a farce this is…"

I never knew how heavy my heart would feel over a battle I was *forbidden* from winning.

The weight of the magic armor—called Chaftal, which I'd received when I joined the hero's party—felt especially great, and my footsteps dragged.

I wished I could be doing something else, like sword training with Satou. The boy was young, but he absorbed techniques with astonishing speed. His skills had vastly improved in the short time from our first meeting on the ship to our encounter just yesterday. Perhaps he would even join Hayato's party someday and accompany me at the hero's side.

As I daydreamed about such a pleasant future, I entered the circle that designated my starting position.

Seeing my arrival, a valet called for His Highness, who appeared from a waiting room.

The shrieking young girls filling the stadium had no idea of his true nature.

With a smooth metallic *shing*, the prince drew the Holy Sword Claidheamh Soluis from its blue sheath.

…It was beautiful.

I had never seen such a fine sword.

The otherworldly blue light radiating from the blade made it all the more mesmerizing.

Bewitched by the magnificence of Claidheamh Soluis, I thought back to my beloved hero Hayato and his Holy Sword Arondight.

In my memory, it glowed a vivid blue that called to mind dependability rather than beauty.

"The exhibition match between the Witch of Heavenly Destruction Lady Ringrande and the Bearer of the Holy Sword Prince Sharorik shall now commence."

The referee was dressed like a jester as he announced our names.

The prince scowled, likely displeased with the order in which our names had been read. Ill-tempered as always.

On the starting signal, I supplied my armor Chaftal with magic power.

Its enchanted circuits granted me Body Strengthening and created several layers of physical defense magic over the armor.

It wasn't terribly efficient with MP, but I could face grave injuries if I didn't use it against a Holy Sword.

Next, I infused my lightning broadsword with power to invoke "Lightningblade."

I'd obtained this powerful weapon by defeating a floormaster in a labyrinth. It wasn't quite as strong as a Holy Sword, but it still boasted higher performance than any ordinary Magic Sword.

"■ ■ ■— Ah!"

Sensing danger, I cut my strengthening magic chant short and leaped aside.

Fireballs blazed through the spot where I'd been standing, flames exploding over my back.

...A Fire Rod? No, at that speed, it must be a Blaze Rod.

Wasn't that a military weapon? What was that stupid prince thinking?

"Brings back memories, doesn't it? You made it yourself at the academy."

The prince's Holy Sword left blue traces in the air as it sliced toward me.

So fast! Maybe the legend that Claidheamh Soluis could fly really was true.

I blocked the Holy Sword with my broadsword.

What a heavy blow! I was going to injure my wrists at this rate.

Instead of transferring onto the Holy Sword, the lightning on my blade scattered into the air.

If it were an ordinary sword, it would've easily paralyzed or even knocked my opponent unconscious.

As payback, I swung my blade toward the prince's legs, but the barrier generated by the prince's white armor stopped it.

Of course. His armor was a legendary item made in the era of the ancestral king Yamato, after all. It was no surprise that it would have similar defenses to Hayato's Holy Armor.

I added more magic power to Chaftal to enhance its defense.

For the moment, I let my armor protect me from the prince's sword and focused on attacking.

Use skill: "Strike."

My accuracy would be lower, but my attacks would be more powerful.

Use skill: "Spellblade."

My sword glowed with red light.

I didn't generally like to waste magic like that, but this was no time to be conservative.

Use skill: "Sharpblade."

I didn't intend to kill him, of course, but I had to come at him with all my strength if I wanted to break through his defenses.

"Whirling Thunder Blade!"

I wasn't sure why, but I shouted the attack name without thinking. Hayato's foolish habits must be rubbing off on me.

I'd assumed the prince would block the attack, but instead I landed a direct hit, piercing through his armor's barrier.

Damn. If I didn't stop now, I would win the match.

I managed to kill my blade's momentum and stopped just before dealing the prince a deadly blow.

But of course, he couldn't miss an opening like that.

Claidheamh Soluis hit me square in the side, and I went flying across the arena like a ball.

Cheers, screams, and boos jolted me awake. I must have passed out for just a second.

Through my hazy vision, I saw fireballs flying at me in rapid succession.

Stopping my attack must have hurt the prince's bloated pride. The rage in his eyes was alarming.

I used the short Explosion Magic spell Quick Burst to blow up the fireballs.

But our battle ended there.

It was interrupted by the howls of strange figures that burst out of the floor beneath the audience seats...and the summoning circle they created in the sky.

WE'RE ALL IN DANGER.

My instincts set off a warning so strong it felt like my skull would crack.

I quickly started a Magic Blast chant.

"■■■■■ ■■—"

"Giving up on the sword and resorting to magic, are we, Ringraaaande?!"

The prince came charging at me with his Holy Sword.

This wasn't good. He hadn't noticed the summoning circle above us; I was the only one who saw it.

I had to stop my chant to dodge his attack.

I should have finished him off with my sword before. Now he had prevented me from stopping the summoning.

Clawed yellow feet descended from the summoning circle, followed by the rest of the enormous body.

It was a demon—a greater hell demon.

Suddenly, I remembered something Hayato told me before.

He had once been forced to flee from an opponent: a yellow greater hell demon.

Bitterly, he'd said that half his party had sacrificed themselves for his escape. Back then, I couldn't believe anything could defeat Hayato's unbelievable power, but now I understood.

This creature was on an entirely different level.

Were demon lords truly stronger than this?

Once he'd completely emerged, the demon dropped to the ground. He was more than three times larger than any human, and the tremors when he landed were almost enough to knock me off my feet.

The sheer physical difference made my heart quaver.

Impossible.

I could never defeat him. I couldn't even wrap my head around his existence.

My soul screamed at me to run away.

But just as my heart was threatening to break, an unexpected voice stopped me in my tracks.

"Demon! No—demon lord! Prepare to meet your doom!!"

The prince shouted at the yellow demon without a single ounce of fear.

He wasn't bluffing, either. If he was brave enough to bluff in a situation like this, I might not have ended our engagement.

…He doesn't realize how strong our opponent is.

The yellow demon tilted his two heads, then looked down at the prince's sword.

"THAT SWORD IS CLAIDHEAMH SOLUIS, IS IT NOT? THEN YOU MUST BE A DESCENDANT OF YAMATO."

Underneath his harsh voice, I could hear something like a howl.

Ah! His other head was chanting while he spoke.

In an effort to interrupt his casting, I rapid-fired Quick Burst shots at the heads.

But he was able to fend off the weak lesser magic with his hand. Speed alone wouldn't be enough.

I activated "Chant Reduction," then started invoking Explosion.

I probably wouldn't make it in time. But I wasn't about to let him cast a spell so easily. I could at least rob him of his chanting head in exchange.

The yellow demon's chant finished, and a summoning circle appeared on the ground to produce large monsters. There were scorpions, mantises, and two-horned beetles, all of them powerful enemies.

Shortly after the monsters emerged, my Explosion spell struck the demon square in the head.

Unfortunately, when the loud boom faded and the dust settled, the demon was by all appearances unscathed.

Clearly, I hadn't done much damage. The demon must have high magic resistance.

"HMPH, THAT STUNG A LITTLE."

Ignoring the yellow creature's mockery, I glanced around at the stands.

Monsters were still overflowing from the summoning circle and surging toward the spectators, as well as the prince and myself. I wanted to rescue them, but the yellow demon would never let me take my eyes off him.

Just then, inspiration struck.

There were warriors from the tournament among the crowd; they could handle the monsters.

I used the "Amplification" skill to address the fighters.

"Brave warriors! You must protect your neighbors! Now is the time to prove your worth in battle!"

Hearing me, most of the warriors started to fight to protect the other citizens. However, some of them were too overwhelmed by the chaos to think straight and started releasing attack spells despite all the people nearby.

"Magic users, focus on strengthening the warriors, not on attack magic. Work together to defeat the monsters!"

My words seemed to reach them, and they began cooperating to turn the tide of the battle.

These men and women were strong. As long as they kept their wits about them, they should have no problem with monsters like these.

I swung my lightning sword to dispatch a charging tentacled centipede monster.

A lance beetle tried to attack while I was distracted, but it flew right through the illusion created by my magic armor Chaftal.

Seeing the number of monsters I was fending off, some of the warriors climbed over the audience barrier to aid me.

They could handle the rabble. I had to do something about the summoning circle!

With the precious seconds they bought me, I chanted Break Magic to destroy the summoning circle.

"HMPH, NOT A HERO IN SIGHT, IS THERE? WHAT AM I TO DO WITH THE GIFT I BROUGHT?"

The yellow demon cast buff spells on the summoned monsters as he muttered to himself. He didn't seem concerned in the least that I'd broken his circle.

"HOW STRANGE IT IS. I THOUGHT THE BLUE ONE OR THE RED ONE WOULD SHOW UP RIGHT AWAY IF I MADE A FUSS."

A centipede devoured one of the warriors holding off the monsters for me. I hurried over to help, but we couldn't seem to recover the front lines. As I pushed forward, the severely injured warriors retreated.

If only Hayato and our friends were here to help...

"Ah-ha-ha! Having trouble there, little lady?"

"Don't get distracted, boy. We must go help His Highness."

The young boy knight and Sir Reilus of the Eight Swordsmen passed by on their way to assist the prince. Without slowing down, the boy knight sliced off a few of the centipede's legs.

While the monster was distracted, I stole a couple of seconds for a chant and used three Explosion spells to defeat it.

Each one took a long time to invoke, but thanks to the spell's stun and knock-back effects, I managed to find success.

"The legendary demon general... Truly a worthy opponent!"

Sir Reilus's shout drew the demon's attention to him and his Holy Shield. He'd probably used the "Taunt" skill on his voice.

The demon fired a red torrent at the older knight.

Incredible.

Reilus didn't falter for a moment, protecting the prince and the other knight from the Inferno spell.

He must have been aided by magic, but I still hadn't imagined that anyone but Hayato could block such an attack.

"OH? THAT SHIELD BRINGS BACK MEMORIES. HOW ABOUT THIS, THEN?"

A ball of white flames flew toward Sir Reilus.

The surface of the Holy Shield warded off most of the flames, but a few angled streaks licked around the shield and the knight behind it.

I couldn't let him be killed. Without Reilus, there would be no one left to hold the front lines.

If Hayato were with me, I...

As if inspired by my thoughts, blue light welled up from my chest through the gaps in my armor.

...Maybe now was the time.

I undid the clasps of my breastplate and pulled out the glowing blue talisman.

When wishes for a hero join prayers to the goddess Parion, the talisman can create a miracle.

And that miracle is called "Hero Summoning."

If the wishes and prayers are not enough, the miracle will consume the life of the user in exchange.

I didn't want to die, of course.

But if I wanted to protect my hometown, I could only pray for a miracle.

"O, Great Parion! Please, use my wishes and my life to enact a Hero Summoning!"

This was no magic chant...

"I am a follower! I am Ringrande, follower of Hayato the Hero!"

...It was a prayer to the young goddess Parion.

In response to my wish, the talisman on my chest blazed bright.

Now, Jules Verne, *come quickly.*

Bring the hero to the battlefield!

Hayato the Hero

It was the spring of my second year of high school when I was summoned to another world as a hero, nine years ago. At first, I didn't know what to think when I was told I'd be a hero who defeats demon lords, but I ended up agreeing anyway. The young goddess was very cute, for one thing! (Hayato the Hero)

"So, Hayato. Where do you think the demon lord's going to appear?"

"Who knows? Don't ask me tough questions."

We had just finished investigating the Wilde Labyrinth in the Gray Ratfolk Emirate when Meriest brought up the topic. We were about to depart for our next destination, meeting up with Ringrande in the Ougoch Duchy.

"If a demon lord appears, we get there as fast as we can and take it out. That's our job."

By now, I had gotten used to speaking arrogantly. As silly as it felt at first, I had to sound confident and full of myself if I wanted to protect my friends from the greed of others.

"Ah-ha-ha, that's our hero for you."

"True enough. They say it's been hundreds of years since the Oracles all pointed to different places."

That was the tigerfolk Rusus and the wolffolk Fifi.

They leaned on the back of my captain's chair, so I reached up and touched their ears. They really were a nice texture. We'd been working together for five years now, but it took three of those to let me touch their ears.

"I'd imagine it would be somewhere like the Living Labyrinth in Shiga Kingdom's Labyrinth City Celivera or the Illusion Labyrinth in the Weaselman Empire."

As always, our priest Loleiya spoke in a calm voice.

Without our secretary Nono and Magic Swordsman Ringrande, Loleiya was the only person left who could have an intelligent debate with Meriest.

According to them, Yowork Kingdom's labyrinth had only recently been revived, Ougoch Duchy's labyrinth was dead and in ruins, and Parion Province had never had a labyrinth to begin with; those three weren't strong contenders.

The seventh candidate from the Oracles was on another continent and would take some time to reach, so we decided to investigate all the others first.

Noticing that I was lost in thought for a change, Loleiya hugged my head from behind.

"Too heavy."

"Aww!"

I pushed Loleiya's heavy breasts off my head.

Inexplicably, she looked happy about the rough treatment.

Breasts were just sacks of fat, you know. A pervert wouldn't understand that.

"You're as stoic as ever today, Sir Hero."

Loleiya murmured, pressing her hands to her red cheeks.

Honestly. You're supposed to be a woman of the church...

Ah, why was I cursed with a party full of busty women? Couldn't I have at least one little girl?

I did have one silent type, at least, but Nono was twenty-three years old and, worse, an E cup. If a silent little girl wanted to join me, I'd welcome her anytime.

That middle school–aged girl I rescued a while back was pretty cute, though. If we'd met five years sooner, I probably would've proposed.

Just then, a regularly scheduled message arrived.

From the communications seat, the long-eared Weeyari looked over with her report.

"Hayato, we've received a scheduled transmission from Nono in Celivera. It says, 'All quiet.'"

"Good."

Meriest and Loleiya estimated that the Labyrinth City Celivera was the most suspicious candidate, so I was worried about leaving a non-combatant like Nono there, even with guards.

"Could someone go trade places with Nono in Celivera?"

"Whaaat? No waaay. I wanna stay with you, Hayato."

"Exactly! It's too hard to fight without Hayato by our side."

Rusus and Fifi insisted that it would be too stressful to stay in Labyrinth City if they couldn't go into the mazes themselves. I could definitely see them getting fed up and charging in anyway.

About half an hour later, we received our regular communication from our spy Seina in the Yowork Kingdom as well.

"The message reads as follows: 'This crummy little kingdom is peaceful today as usual. I'm sooo bored.'"

Like Nono, I'd like to have someone take her place, but Seina was the only one of us who could infiltrate the place safely. She was just going to have to tough it out.

As a hero, I couldn't say this out loud, but I secretly hoped the demon lord would appear in Yowork Kingdom. They deserved to suffer for sacrificing my honey to resurrect their labyrinth.

When I heard the adorable purple-haired princess Arisa was sacrificed, the world around me went dark. I still deeply regretted that I'd been leveling up in the Saga Empire's labyrinth and thus didn't hear about the fall of Kuvork Kingdom until it was too late.

Come to think of it, that was when I decided to hire a secretary to give me the information I wanted instead of depending on the empire.

"We haven't gotten anything from Rin yet?"

Ringrande was always punctual, so this seemed unusual.

As Loleiya had said earlier, the labyrinth beneath Ougoch Duchy was inactive. It was highly unlikely that a demon lord would appear there.

It was probably just a mistake that the Oracle had mentioned it at all, then, but it was Ringrande's home. Plus, her brother was getting married soon, so we decided to send her anyway.

"You're sooo forgetful, Hayato!"

"He really is! So what's he forgetting?"

Rusus and Fifi were the last two people on earth to accuse someone of being forgetful.

"Rin said she had business she couldn't get out of. She'll contact us later instead, remember?"

Oh, right. She'd been complaining about her exhibition match with that idiot prince of the Shiga Kingdom.

Just then…

The scenery outside the ship turned dark gray.

"…We're traveling through dimensions?"

Meriest gazed out at the gray expanse in surprise.

If the ship was being warped without permission, then…

"Someone must have used a talisman!"

"Not just someone. It must have been Rin!"

"Oh no, oh no! Is she okay?"

All my comrades had reached the same conclusion at once.

Damn! If she'd used the talisman for Hero Summoning, she could take years off her life span—or even lose her life entirely.

"Everyone, get into your positions!" My voice was rough with worry.

Everyone quickly slid into their seats, donning their headset-like magic items.

"Calm down, Hayato! We have to have faith in Ringrande!"

Even so, Meriest's voice was shaking with anxiety.

I took a deep breath, forcing myself to calm down and figure out what to do.

"I'll wait on the stern. Wee, you're in charge of navigation."

"Of course."

I hurried to the stern of the ship with Arondight in hand.

The ship passed through the world of gray and back into this one.

Beyond the canopy, I saw a swarm of monsters.

Is Ringrande safe?!

As I searched the ground for my friend, I gave the necessary instructions.

"Wee! Open fire from all mobile turrets!" I shouted into the headset.

A roaring sound and a flash filled the sky, and charred monster corpses began falling to the ground.

Meriest reported in over the hatch's speaker.

"Rin is safe."

Thank goodness for that.

"The enemy is…" Meriest trailed off.

Looking around, I saw what Meriest was trying to say.

I had a dark history with this opponent; I never expected to see him here…

It was in my third year of being a summoned hero that I met him.

That yellow freak defeated the party I thought was unbeatable. If my friends hadn't sacrificed themselves to buy me time, I would've been killed, too.

But I'm not the same man I was back then.

And now I had the chance to prove it.

No holding back. I was going all out from the very beginning.

I activated my Unique Skills "Unstoppable Spear" and "Invincible Shield." Finally, I activated "Infinite Regeneration."

"Infinite Regeneration" was a trump card I could use only once a month, so I would have preferred to save it in case of a demon lord battle, but I couldn't be stingy if I meant to defeat this demon.

I wanted to use an Accelerate Potion, too, but I held off, since that could come back to bite me if the battle went on for too long.

I jumped over the canopy and sprang onto the battlefield.

There, I gave my usual introduction.

"Look upon me!"

Yep, that felt good. The fear that threatened to shake my heart when I saw the yellow demon was swallowed in wrath and determination.

In response to my "Taunt," the monsters attacking Ringrande flocked toward the *Jules Verne* instead.

I thrust my Holy Sword at the armadillo type leading the charge.

The blue light of my Unique Skill "Ultimate Spear" created a field in front of the Holy Sword that pierced the monster and split it apart.

Black thorns like a sea urchin's shot toward me, but my "Invincible Shield" created an invisible barrier that warded them off.

I was at the top of my game, as usual.

"HAYATO THE HERO, IS IT? HAVE YOU COME PREPARED TO DIE THIS TIME, THEN?"

"I'm not the same man I used to be! Today I swear to enact my revenge!"

Leaving the smaller monsters for my friends to handle, I focused on the yellow freak.

Once my party had descended, the *Jules Verne* flew on autopilot and disappeared into a dimensional gap.

We couldn't afford to lose our precious ship now, after all.

"Stay out of this, you Saga Empire dog! I shall prove that your empire is not the only one that can produce a hero."

...What was that?

Looking for the source of the blue light, I found Prince Sharorik of the Shiga Kingdom and his Holy Sword Claídheamh Soluis.

Still, I wasn't impressed in the least.

If anything, I felt bad for the weapon with such a pathetic master. He couldn't tap into its true power at all.

"Your Holy Sword weeps, Prince. This is one of the generals of a powerful demon lord of old—the Golden Boar Lord. He's a demon of the highest caliber who's survived for hundreds of years. If you wish to live, you had best retreat."

That's right—just you watch!

I'll show you how to really use a Holy Sword!

"<Sing>, Arondight!"

The blue glow of the Holy Sword in my right hand intensified.

I activated my flying shoes and leaped toward the yellow demon.

Arondight was on fire today!

◆

...How long have we been crossing swords now?

I thought the yellow demon specialized in magic, but seeing his skill in close combat was shaking my confidence a little here. Whatever it might be, this yellow light extending from the demon's claws was dangerous. And it kept growing back no matter how many times I broke it, which was downright unfair.

According to my "Analyze" skill, our levels were almost the same.

So why couldn't I reach him?

I warded off the bastard's flame attacks with my "Invincible Shield" and used the strength of "Unstoppable Spear" on Arondight to shatter his defensive barriers. However, breaking through the scale-shaped defenses weakened my strikes.

It was just like the "Gold Scale Barrier" the Golden Boar Lord had in the legends of Yamato the Hero.

On top of that, even if I did manage to damage him a little, the three floating spheres around him would heal him right away. And if I tried to destroy the spheres first, he could summon a new one while I was crushing another.

At this rate, things were looking grim.

Just then, Meriest called out to me with concern.

"Hayato, don't try to fight all alone! We're a team, you know."

Shoot. I got carried away there.

Just as Meriest said, I couldn't defeat powerful enemies unless I worked together with my friends.

Fortunately, most of the other monsters were now on the side of the arena near the Shiga Kingdom warriors, who took care of them.

As an infrequent visitor to the Shiga Kingdom, I never knew how impressive their fighters were. They were doing a great job keeping both themselves and the monsters away from the yellow demon.

Almost as if someone has the whole thing under control...

The thought crossed my mind unbidden.

No, that was ridiculous. Those monsters might be small fry in this situation, but their levels were still in the 40s.

If anyone here had the ability to do that, I'd want to scout them for our party.

The magic users in this kingdom seemed just as skilled as the warriors.

Several Practical Magic users were using Magic Hand to relay the injured people from the audience seats out of the arena.

It must take dozens of sorcerers to transport people in such a ridiculous way, not to mention years of extreme training. Whoever they were, they definitely had my respect.

As I contemplated this, someone shot out the wings of a beetle that was trying to attack my party.

There must be a talented archer here, too, to penetrate the barrier-protected wings of a two-horned beetle. They must have both a powerful bow and skills as high as Weeyari's to pierce the wings of a flying beetle in a single shot, at that.

Just how many combat masters are there in this kingdom?

If I didn't know better, I'd think they could have defeated the demon lord without even Hero Summoning me.

Oops, but I guess letting other people do the work would make me a failure as a hero.

I had to be sure my party and I were the ones who defeated this guy, at least, or I'd bring shame on my Hero title.

Before charging back into the fray with the yellow freak, I shouted some orders to my party.

Rusus and Fifi appeared to be having trouble with a centipede demon.

"Rin! Give Rusus and Fifi some backup!"

"Understood!"

Ringrande wasted no time starting to cast Explosion Magic.

Loleiya's support magic chant seemed to be almost done.

"Wee, hold off the two-horned beetles for now. I'll send Rusus and Fifi to help you as soon as they can."

"All right, Hayato. Leave it to me."

Come on, Weeyari. I wanted you to say, "Can't I just bring them all down myself?" I thought archers were supposed to be cooler than this.

"IS YOUR LITTLE STRATEGY MEETING ALMOST OVER?"

Tch, I wondered why he wasn't attacking…

We'll make him regret not taking us more seriously.

"Meri, I'll buy you some time! Give him the biggest shot you've got!"

"Of course! Don't do anything too risky, Hayato!"

If my attacks alone weren't enough to break through, Meriest and the others could use their war-grade attack magic to bring down his defenses and let me finish him off.

"HUMAN MAGIC IS SO VERY SLOW."

The yellow demon scoffed as his other head howled.

His attack magic came raining down at me in the form of fierce white flames. .

Using my Holy Shield, enhanced with "Invincible Shield," I warded off the attacks easily.

"HOW IMPRESSIVE. YOU MUST HAVE GROWN MUCH STRONGER TO BLOCK MY WHITE INFERNO. HEROES ARE EVER SO INTERESTING."

Ignoring the demon's self-important praise, I gave my companions the signal.

Their targets felled, Rusus and Fifi rushed over to give Weeyari backup.

"Ringrande, Loleiya, let's begin the chant."

At Meriest's words, all three of them started invoking a spell with their talismans.

The talismans have many convenient functions, not least of which is the ability to synchronize chants and increase the power and precision of battle magic.

And the spell they chose was…a forbidden curse?! And a war-grade forbidden curse, at that?

I know I said "the biggest shot you've got," but that seemed like overkill to me. It was going to cause some lasting property damage, that was for sure.

However, nothing short of greater magic would work on this demon. If we wanted to destroy the Cure Balls, his lesser demons, and cause some serious damage, a powerful forbidden curse might be our best shot.

I felt bad for the locals, but we had no other choice. Hopefully, Ringrande's grandfather and his men evacuated them quickly.

Depending on the damage, my name as a hero might get dragged through the mud, but things would go from bad to worse if this freak cut loose. My reputation was nothing compared to human lives.

"HOW STRANGE INDEED. WHY DO RED AND BLUE NOT APPEAR?"

The yellow fiend surveyed the arena curiously.

I blocked his absentminded attacks with my "Invincible Shield."

This seemed like a one-in-a-million chance, but I couldn't afford to separate myself from my party.

"OH WELL. HERO, YOU AND YOUR FRIENDS TICKLE ME DELIGHTFULLY WITH YOUR ATTACKS, BUT I SHOULD LIKE TO TASTE YOUR FEAR AND DESPAIR SOON."

"Hmph, you masochistic freak! Me, afraid of you? I'd like to see you try!"

"VERY WELL, THEN. I HOPE YOU ENJOY MY LITTLE GIFT."

Tch. He was definitely up to something.

An ominous premonition sent a shiver up my spine.

I gulped down an Accelerate Potion in preparation for his attack.

The liquid was bitter, but I drank it all. As it went into effect, the movement around me gradually slowed.

The effect would last for only a short period of time, and when it wore off, I'd be exhausted, but this seemed like the right time to pull out all the stops.

A huge summoning circle appeared behind the yellow freak.

Like I'm going to let you summon something that easily!

"<Sing>, Arondight! <Play>, Tunas!"

I invoked the divine incantations of my Holy Sword and Holy Armor.

With my magic power as the catalyst, the philosopher's stone that formed the core of my magic armor began producing huge amounts of energy that surged through my body and into my Holy Sword.

I was ready before the yellow demon's summoning was finished.

"Shining Blade!"

What was the point of a special attack if you didn't shout it out?

I swung Arondight at subsonic speed, emitting a powerful blade of light that shot toward the summoning circle.

Dammit.

The bastard threw one of his floating Cure Balls into the path of the Shining Blade.

I fired another one, but this time he blocked it with one of the monster corpses at his feet.

Despite my best efforts, the summoning was complete.

"...Are you for real?"

Floating in the sky was the enormous monster fish, Tovkezerra.

It was bigger than the gunboats I'd seen in the Saga Empire—meaning it was over eight hundred feet long?!

"Th-the giant monster fish?!"

"No way! You mean that's the thing the Golden Boar Lord used?"

"The legendary floating fortress..."

The three members of my party who weren't chanting exclaimed in surprise.

The giant monster fish.

Despite its somewhat stupid name, the monster was level 97.

It was just barely within the range of my "Analyze" skill. I wondered if that might be a mistake, but the number was the same no matter how many times I tried it.

I gave myself a firm slap on the cheek in an attempt to pull myself together and stave off the fear.

It'd be nice if Meriest's forbidden curse could finish it off along with the yellow freak, but this wasn't a "two birds with one stone" situation.

I had to protect Meriest and the other casters from the freak's attacks, so the only option we had left to fight off that giant fish was the *Jules Verne*'s main battery.

I was concerned about the damage it might cause to our surroundings, but it would probably still be better than another war-grade forbidden curse.

"We won't back down, no matter what we're fighting!"

I struck an exaggerated pose and shouted instructions to my frightened comrades.

"Wee, Rusus, Fifi! Summon the *Jules Verne*!"

I'd hidden the precious ship in another dimension to protect it, but now wasn't the time to worry about things like that.

Sorry, Emperor. I might not be able to keep my promise to bring the ship back unharmed.

"I'm giving permission to use the main battery. Take the *Jules Verne*'s master key with you."

I took the glowing blue key out of my Inventory and tossed it to Weeyari.

While I was at it, I pulled out a healing potion to cure my body of the exhaustion brought on by the Accelerate Potion.

"YES, YES. THAT IS THE FEAR I WANT TO SEE."

Enjoy it while you can, yellow freak. As soon as Ringrande and the others finish their chant, it's all over for you.

I drank the potion in one gulp and looked up at the sky.

For some reason, the giant fish was staring fixedly at one corner of the arena, ignoring the rest of us.

Well, that worked for me. Maybe the yellow demon had failed to control his summon.

"HMM. A DASH OF HOPE MIXED WITH THE FEAR RATHER RUINS IT."

Hope? That's easy. I just have to think about something fun.

Once this battle was over, I'd go pay a sympathy visit to the orphanage—maybe they'd let us take a bath together or a nap or something. Anything was possible.

All right! My heart's full of hope now. We can do this!

"As long as I'm the hero, there will always be hope."

"HOW ABSURD."

The yellow demon scoffed at my determination and pointed to the sky.

The shadows over the arena began to block out the sun.

I didn't notice.

The summoning circle the giant monster fish had emerged from was still floating in the sky.

I should have realized what that meant.

The summoning circle wasn't finished. More enormous fish appeared, one after another. Including the first one, there were a total of seven.

So this is how I die, huh?

Hey, Miss Parion...
This world of yours is way too hard.

Nanashi the Hero

Satou here. Hardships often come up out of nowhere, but I think it can go very differently depending on whether you rise to the challenge or just accept it as part of life.

While the hero battled the yellow demon, I set about rescuing people and defeating the small-fry monsters.

Observing the seats from the spire overlooking the arena, I noticed that Miss Karina and the other nobles hadn't escaped yet.

The Wings of Freedom terrorists and the lesser hell demons had been taken care of, but removing the debris from the exit was proving harder than expected.

I jumped from the spire to the seats, approaching under cover of shadows.

A thorn-shaped monster was silently swooping down toward the nobles.

"Everyone, a monster is approaching from above."

A young woman with pink hair spoke up next to Miss Karina.

The magic users and knights around them hurried to counterattack, but it didn't look like they were going to make it in time.

I didn't want anyone else to get injured, so I grabbed some rubble and flung it at the demon to throw him off course.

The monster crashed into the ground harmlessly a little ways away from the nobles in a plume of dust and rocks.

Miss Karina and the shield-bearing knights warded off the flying debris, and as a result, nobody was hurt.

"Thank you, miss."

"O-oh, don't mention it."

Miss Karina turned bright red when the pink-haired girl thanked her.

Hey, she might just manage to make a friend after all. Maybe it would even turn into a *yuri* situation.

No other monsters were approaching, so I checked the state of the blocked passage on my 3-D map and used Magic Hand to start clearing away the obstacles.

So far, I'd only used Magic Hand for things like pranks and making those chain necklaces, but being able to control a hundred and twenty at once meant I could actually accomplish some heavy lifting with it.

With strength equivalent to about sixty grown men combined, my Magic Hands had no trouble with the ton of rubble.

At any rate, as far as I could tell, I was the only person who could transport this much at a time. The magic users working on the rubble could only move about a sack of rice's worth.

"Wh-what?!"

"Whose magic is that?"

Naturally, the people working on clearing it started raising a fuss, but I ignored them and kept removing the blockage.

They, too, seemed more worried about protecting the nobles than figuring out who was helping them. Once I'd removed a big enough chunk, they quickly got everyone to safety, Miss Karina and Orion included.

As the evacuation of the audience members was just about finished, I searched for anyone else who needed rescuing or any warriors I could assist.

"Waaaah!"

Hearing a child's cry, I saw a familiar-looking spearman battling a beetle monster with his cross-shaped spear. It looked like the monster's horn had stabbed the man while he was trying to protect the boy.

Worse yet, the scream had drawn the attention of the smaller insect monsters buzzing around the arena, and now a group of cricket-like creatures was closing in on the pair.

"Daddy!"

"Golao!"

The child was crying for help, but the father was already on his last leg.

Oops, I shouldn't waste time just watching.

I used Toss Stone from the magic menu.

Stone spears sprouted from below the audience seats, impaling the crickets one after another. The monsters wriggled and flailed, but they couldn't attack the child from that position.

The innumerable spikes pierced the beetle the spearman was fighting, too, and crushed its horn.

"Whoever you are, thank you for your help!"

The spearman finished off the beetle with his cross-shaped spear. Then his knees buckled, weak from the blood loss.

"Daddy!"

Staying in the shadows, I used the healing spell I'd just learned on the spearman, then lifted him and his son, Golao, out of the arena with Magic Hand and deposited them safely outside.

Conveniently, this spell had a pretty wide range.

The boy's screams as he was lifted into the air pained my heart, but their well-being was my top priority.

Aside from the warriors still fighting the monsters in the seats, there was still a handful of civilians here and there.

The civilians weren't the only ones whose lives could be in danger, so I used Magic Hand to lift them to safety like I had with the father and son.

At first, the other warriors were alarmed by the shouts of the people being lifted into the air, but by the time the battle was over, nobody paid them any mind. Humans could really adjust to anything.

While I was at it, I moved some of the monsters so they couldn't reach the warriors.

"Whoa, the monsters are floating around in midair!"

"Tch, damn mages. That's a big help and all, but I wish they'd tell us what they're going to do first!"

Some of the fighters complained, but they didn't seem to mind as much as they claimed.

With the people evacuated and the battlefield rearranged, it was time to move on to dispatching with the weaker monsters.

In total, there were seventy-six monsters without an opponent. I fired Remote Arrow in sets of five to take them out quickly.

Now that they were used to the screaming of the evacuees, the fighters didn't even attempt to figure out who was defeating all the extra monsters.

That did make things easier for me, but I couldn't help feeling a little silly after all the trouble I went through to keep myself hidden.

Before long, the coast was clear in the audience seats, so I turned my attention back to the main battle in the center of the arena.

The hero and friends were struggling more than I expected, but they were still persisting in their fight against the yellow demon.

However, because of a certain unwelcome intruder, the rearguard of the hero's party seemed to be having a hard time using their attack magic effectively.

"Foul creature! How dare thee deflect the attack of my Holy Sword?!"

"Your Highness, behind you!"

"Graaah!"

By "unwelcome intruder," I meant Prince Sharorik.

Despite the huge difference in their levels, the prince had evidently been flinging himself at the yellow demon undeterred this whole time.

A lizard-shaped demon knocked the prince and his young knight aside dramatically, but their lives didn't appear to be in any danger. I ignored them for the time being.

The older knight with the large shield had been severely wounded while defending the prince not long ago, and he was being carted off.

"Wee! You gotta do something about that two-horned beetle!"

"Yeah, we can't fight the centipedes like this."

"Impossible. It's moving much too fast for my arrows to hit."

The three beastfolk members of the hero's party were struggling with the beetle monster buzzing around above them.

Is it really that hard?

The whine of its wings was annoying, and I pulled a Magic Bow out of Storage and shot at the base of the appendages.

See? Direct hit.

I was only using ordinary arrows, but after a few more shots at the same spot, I was able to tear off its wings and send it plummeting to the ground.

I'd feel bad stealing all the prey from the hero's party, though. I decided to leave the rest of the monsters to them.

*   *   *

With that, I was out of things to do, so I consulted the map of the area and confirmed that everyone had evacuated into the nearest shelter or the duke's castle.

This way, even if the yellow demon used area-effect magic, no one should die.

With nothing else to worry about now, I decided to observe the hero's party's battle. Maybe I'd learn a thing or two.

Now that the meddling prince was down for the time being, the rearguard seemed to be able to use their attack magic properly. The battle was going much more smoothly than before.

Judging by the conversation I overheard between him and the hero, this yellow demon seemed to be a friend of the "Indeed" and "Yes" demons I'd fought before the demon lord.

Still, those three balls floating above its head were pretty impressive. No matter how much damage the hero and friends did, they healed the demon almost instantly.

According to the AR, they were actually demons called **Cure Balls**, not just a product of some spell. He must have used summoning magic.

Whenever one of the hero's rearguard destroyed a Cure Ball, he'd immediately summon another one. Pretty tricky.

Because I didn't want to insult them by butting in, I forced myself to stand by and watch for now.

...*Huh? My "Sense Danger" skill is going off overhead.*

When I looked up at the sky, I saw a summoning circle.

Whatever the yellow demon was trying to summon, I would defeat it as soon as it popped out. It'd be the perfect opportunity to test my intermediate attack magic.

But what appeared was...

A whale?

It was airborne and almost a thousand feet long.

But it was definitely a whale.

It was about ten times the size of the full-size blue whale model I'd seen in an aquarium in Japan, but that wasn't important right now.

What was important was this:

Whales were delicious.

On the ground, the hero and company forgot their battle and gaped up in shock.

Well, I couldn't blame them.

If the hero was Japanese, too, he must be familiar with the taste of whale. Once I secured the meat, I'd have to share some with him.

According to the AR display, it was a monster called **Tovkezerra**, so I doubted any activists would get mad at me for killing it.

This was pest control, and securing a valuable source of protein at that.

Ah, it's been so long since I've had whale...

As I stared at it, I almost started drooling. I couldn't even imagine how many servings I'd get out of something so enormous.

What should I make? Would simmering it with soy sauce be too obvious?

As I looked up at the giant monster fish and contemplated the best way to cook it, it somehow ended up staring back at me. Maybe it sensed that its life was in danger.

The last thing I wanted was for it to run away on me. I needed to finish it off in one blow.

Well, I'll be damned, Mr. Yellow Demon. Maybe you're good for something after all!

I was about to break into a little dance, but then things got even better.

Believe it or not, six more whales came out of the summoning circle.

This was the best battle ever. Who would have thought that such gourmet ingredients would deliver themselves to me just like that?

I waited a little longer, but that seemed to be the last of them. Just in case, I decided not to destroy the summoning circle so that they could call for reinforcements if they wanted.

Now, I didn't want to spoil any of the meat in the process. After I beheaded them with the light magic spell Laser, I put the corpses in Storage straightaway.

Ideally, I would've liked to show off Excalibur's sharpness, but the whales were just too big for that.

Laser was relatively weak for an intermediate spell, but I could fire several at once like Magic Arrow. I figured I could use the light magic spell Condense to make several lasers into one big one and power it up that way.

Switching my map into 3-D, I was able to simulate the best possible trajectory for the lasers.

According to my calculations, the exposure time wouldn't be quite long enough, so I decided to imitate a pulse laser by continuously switching it on and off. That way, I could take out all seven with one attack.

I could've just done it one at a time, of course, but I didn't want to let any of them escape through the summoning circle.

My strategy decided, it was time to go into action!

There was a powerful flash of light coupled with a strong ozone smell.

With the help of my "Light Intensity Adjustment" skill, I aimed at the whales through the flash, guiding the trajectory of my fake pulse laser.

The light beam beheaded the first one easily, shooting past them into the clouds beyond.

The other whales were looking down at me, same as the first, and conveniently formed a circle that made it easy to slice through all of them at once.

Even if they tried to flee now, it would be too late.

Without slowing down, my laser kept moving and sliced through the heads of each of the six remaining whales in rapid succession.

Perfect, got 'em all in one shot!

It'd be a disaster if I let those huge bodies crash to the ground, for various reasons, so I immediately got closer with "Skyrunning" and "Warp," used Magic Hand to reach them, and slipped all the whales into Storage.

The air was a little hot near the whale meat. Maybe they got slightly toasted in the process?

Even though I used lasers, there was a lot of fluid in the air. Liquid or not, it was a considerable mass, and it might injure the people below if I let it fall.

Making a snap decision, I used Magic Hand again to grab all the liquid in sight and put it away in Storage.

Because there were a few parasite-like creatures left in the air when I stored the liquid, I used the laser to destroy them (starting with the ones that were falling toward the arena) and stored those, too.

I wasn't able to hit all of them due to the angle I was firing from, but they landed near the prince. He could probably take care of those.

Once I finished that up, I noticed that the once-chaotic battlefield had gone totally silent.

...Erm, well.

If you ask me, it's the whales' fault for being so delicious!

> **Title Acquired: Organizer**
> **Title Acquired: Unseen Supporter**
> **Title Acquired: Ruler of the Battlefield**
> **Title Acquired: Giant Monster Fish Slayer**
> **Title Acquired: Light Master**
> **Title Acquired: Sky Chef**

...Whoops.

I might've gone a little too far in my determination to get that whale meat.

It felt like everyone was staring at me. Fortunately, the evaporated whale blood formed a mist that should hopefully keep anyone from seeing me clearly.

Besides, it didn't seem like anyone was using Clairvoyance like me.

It was too late to hide now, but I was dressed as Nanashi the Hero. I doubted there would be much trouble if people did see me. However, if anyone figured out that Nanashi was actually Satou, that would be a problem.

Clearly, the time had come for the "Nanashi Version III" persona Arisa and I had come up with during our midnight magic training.

I "Quick Changed" into a new set of clothes and used my "Change Voice" skill to create the kind of voice a female actress would use to play a young male character.

Now, it was time to act as rude, overly familiar, and un-Satou-like as possible.

Thus far, I'd been holding off from doing anything to the yellow demon, but Version III would never be polite enough for that. I should go with something more proactive.

I zoomed down free-fall-style toward the ground, using Remote Arrow to destroy the last few monsters and the demon's Cure Balls.

The extra arrows steered toward the yellow demon, but he intercepted them with Blaze Magic.

"Who are you?!"

"AND WHO MIGHT YOU BE?"

The hero and the yellow demon both shouted in unison.

They were keeping their distance from each other, but both were acting wary of me as well. I lowered my altitude some more, hovering about thirty feet aboveground.

"Hey, I'm Nanashi. Nice to meetcha."

I was careful to adopt a tone that disguised my age and gender.

—DANGER.

My "Sense Danger" skill alerted me to a threat from the direction of the women behind the hero.

Come to think of it, it had been two or three minutes since they started their chant. They must be charging up some kind of greater magic, and from what "Sense Danger" was telling me, it wasn't the kind you should be using within a city.

No—I have to stop them.

This was the first time since the demon lord battle that my instincts had reacted so strongly. Glancing at the log, I didn't see any kind of Psychic Magic affecting me.

The ideal route would be to persuade the hero to get them to stop, but I could tell we didn't have time to argue. I was going to have to resort to a little brute force.

Firstly, I used Break Magic to shut down their magic chant.

Of course, with the composition of the spell broken, the magic power they'd built up began to overflow in all directions.

I knew this was coming thanks to all my midnight experiments, so I used Mana Section to protect the women.

It wasn't an incredibly strong defense spell, but it did the trick.

However, the forced interruption of the spell created some recoil, which left the young women crouching on the ground.

"What are you doing?!" The hero rushed over to the lovely young women as he shouted at me.

"Sorry, sorry. That spell was gonna be a little too dangerous. I had to go ahead and stop it, 'kay?"

I shrugged, keeping my attitude light.

Really, a hero like him should be more careful about causing damage to his surroundings in the first place. Didn't he ever watch *Captain Tsubasa* reruns?

"WELL, THIS IS MOST AMUSING. SQUABBLING AMONG YOUR-SELVES, ARE YOU?"

The yellow demon sneered and began making new Cure Balls.

"YOU MUST HAVE USED SOME WITCHCRAFT TO SEND THE GIANT MONSTER FISH BACK THROUGH THE GATE, CORRECT? WHAT A WISE LITTLE EGG WE HAVE HERE."

Huh? So that's how you're going to interpret it? And what was "egg" referring to, exactly? Maybe it was some kind of code word.

Anyway, I guess the sight of a single laser attack taking out the whales must have been so unbelievable to the yellow demon that he dismissed it as an illusion.

Then, "Sense Danger" alerted me to another new hazard.

It was the hero's silver ship, which appeared to be emerging through a rift in space.

The bow of the ship seemed uncertain which way to face at first, but before long, the glowing white end of the main battery fixed directly on me. It must have seen me arguing with the hero and decided that I was the enemy.

You guys are way too hasty.

I couldn't help criticizing them in my head, but objectively, maybe I did seem a little suspicious. I guess the mask didn't necessarily make it obvious that I was a good guy.

With a rather futuristic sound effect, a beam shot out from the silver ship.

My light magic spell Condense redirected the ray into the sky.

Judging by the impact when it bounced off, that attack was probably four to six times more powerful than my Laser.

The gun firing the rays was getting red hot; it would have to stop attacking soon. Just deflecting it seemed like a waste of energy, too, so I decided to divert its shots to take out the yellow demon's newly summoned Cure Balls.

"YOU CAN BEND THE LIGHT OF THE LIGHT BOAT? I THOUGHT YOU WERE AN EGG, BUT PERHAPS YOU HAVE ALREADY BEEN HATCHED."

If that was an insult, I didn't really understand it.

The "light ship" must be referring to the hero's silver vessel.

The hero was shouting something to his friends aboard it, but I didn't think they could hear him.

"What a worthless hero you are! <Dance>, Claidheamh Soluis!"

...*Huh?*

Clearly the prince was still up and about.

As if the silver ship wasn't enough, now the prince seemed to think I was an enemy, too. His sword flew into the air and shot toward me. Maybe the rain of whale blood on him had offended him.

I leaned my head to one side to avoid the Holy Sword, then grabbed its hilt as it flew past.

At first, it thrashed about in my hand, but that stopped as soon as I had sucked all the magic out of it.

Really though, Prince. You've seen better days, haven't you?

His armor was half-broken, and his exposed skin was covered in what looked like bite marks. I was surprised he hadn't died of blood loss.

Those must be marks from the parasites that had landed near him earlier.

I'd assumed the prince and his Holy Sword could handle them easily enough, but judging by his current disastrous state, it must have been more of a struggle than I thought.

Beyond him, the boy knight had returned to the battlefield and was cackling madly as he hacked away at monster corpses with his sword.

While I was distracted by this whole spectacle, the yellow demon set about making a summoning circle at his feet to make his escape.

Oh, you're not getting away.

I quickly destroyed the circle using Break Magic.

Then I used "Warp" to get closer and cast Mana Drain to steal away the creature's magic.

Sadly, it wasn't possible to take all of it at once. The max was apparently three hundred MP at a time.

"*GRRGH! HOW DARE A MERE CHICK LIKE YOU STEAL AWAY MY MAGIC POWER SO EASILY?!*"

So am I an egg or a chick or what? I really don't get it. I mean, I like chicken and all, but I'd rather not be treated like one.

When the yellow demon tried to retreat out of range of my Mana Drain, I chased him around with "Warp," stealing his MP all the while.

At level 71, he should've had around 710 MP, but even after three

Mana Drains, the demon showed no signs of running out. Guess demons must get more than humans.

Plus, after ten rounds, I couldn't use it anymore. This stupid yellow jerk must have more MP than me.

Since I stole more MP than I could hold, I used the excess to charge Claidheamh Soluis, which I happened to still be holding.

As I poured magic power into it, the blade grew until it was too big to hold with one hand. If Arisa were here, she would no doubt be snickering inappropriately.

The Holy Sword stopped growing when I'd put about 500 MP into it. Now it was just about the size of the replica at the museum. Evidently, that replica was based on reality after all.

"GRRR. SO YOU ARE DESCENDED FROM VAMPIRES, ARE YOU, YOUNG CHICK?"

So now I'm a vampire, too...?

Because I couldn't steal any more magic, I destroyed his defensive barriers with Break Magic and struck him instead. The demon kept going on about something or other, but I was ignoring him at this point.

Once the yellow demon's barriers were mostly gone and his HP was down to about 10 percent, I flung him to the ground in front of the hero's party.

"...GAH!"

The hero didn't hesitate to lop the yellow demon in half with his Holy Sword Arondight. The two halves promptly turned into black dust and vanished.

I guess without a barrier to protect him, a demon could easily be defeated by a Holy Sword.

Maybe I should try to develop a new spell that could break up multiple spells at once.

As the yellow demon was destroyed, he shouted something like *"I DEMAND A REDO!"* but I still wasn't sure what exactly he wanted a redo of.

Still holding the Holy Sword Arondight, the hero strode up to me.

"What are you playing at?"

"C'mon, you had a grudge against that guy, right?"

"Hmph. Don't expect me to thank you."

"That's fine. You could've beaten him with that forbidden curse anyway."

The yellow demon's attitude had indicated he had a plan to deal with the curse, but I suspected it would be rude to point that out.

Still, this persona was a mistake. It was easier to communicate than when I tried to keep quiet Mia-style, but it still made talking difficult.

"By the way, that idiot prince is about to die over there. Shouldn't you help him?"

At the hero's words, I turned to see the roundworm-like monsters tormenting the bloodied royal.

...*Strange.*

Sure, the hero was splattered with blood and guts, but I thought he'd been holding his own well enough until now. Obviously, he had no intention of helping the prince directly.

I didn't feel any particular obligation to assist him, either, but those monsters were also the last in the arena, so I reluctantly decided to lend a hand.

Although these monsters had been level 20 and under when I first saw them, now some of them were as high as level 50.

They must have been using the "Life Drain" skill to steal levels and life force from the prince and other creatures.

Oh. That would explain why the prince's hair had turned white.

He was more wrinkled than before, too, and his level had dropped from the upper 40s to somewhere in the 20s.

The boy knight was in a similar state, though not as severe as the prince. His level was still barely in the 30s, and though his hair was white, his face hadn't aged yet.

. If the prince hadn't thrown Claidheamh Soluis at me, he probably would've had an easier time of things.

I'd better defeat those monsters before those two kick the bucket.

Remote Arrow probably would've been fastest, but since I had this Holy Sword and all, I figured I might as well try it out.

"<Dance>, Claidheamh Soluis!"

The Holy Sword shot out of my hands and multiplied like a scattering stack of papers.

...*Whoa!*

As I watched in surprise, Claidheamh Soluis split into thirteen thin blades, all shining with blue light.

An aiming scope appeared in my AR, not unlike when I used Remote Arrow.

It looked like I could set its trajectory in the same way. I wasted no time firing the blades toward the weaklings.

The blades sliced through the monsters one after another, wiping them all out in the blink of an eye.

Next, I supposed I should probably heal some of the prince's wounds before he bit the dust. I preferred not having the guilt of essentially MPKing him.

I didn't want those pesky parasites reviving themselves, either. I grabbed them in my Magic Hands and put them in Storage, then used Water Magic to heal the prince who was left lying on the ground.

I had planned to heal them only a little, but I accidentally restored his and the boy knight's HP in one go.

The white hair and other aging effects weren't reversed, but I had no intention of showing that much kindness anyway.

He was a big-shot prince. He'd be able to find some kind of temple or medicine or whatever to fix that himself.

Both of their clothes and armor were in tatters, so I threw a few cloaks over them that I'd taken from some thieves a while back.

Not long after, a group of birdfolk scouts flew into the arena.

The military had finally arrived. From what I could tell on the map, a force of forty-five iron golems and three thousand people, mostly knights, was surrounding the arena. There were even a few movable turrets.

"Tch, so now they show up, huh?"

"Hey, Hero, I'll be on my way now."

I gave the frowning hero a wave. I hoped to avoid getting caught up in any trouble here.

"I don't want to get too close to the rich and powerful," I added.

Sorry. The truth is, I already am one of those people.

"I get that. Hey, you probably know this already, but I'm Hayato Masaki the Hero. Just to be clear, Masaki is in fact my last name. You must be Japanese, too—no, if your hair's anything to go by, you're a reincarnation. But you were Japanese, right?"

"You don't really need me to tell you that, right? I'm Nanashi the Hero. Maybe we'll meet again on the battlefield sometime."

I'd already announced myself once, but since Hayato introduced himself, I followed suit.

I'd never heard a Japanese person speak so arrogantly, though.

"Wait a second!"

I started to leave, but the hero stopped me.

"What is it?"

"Sorry my friends tried to fire at you. And...thanks for helping us defeat the demon."

Huh? Apologies aside, I thought he said he wasn't going to thank me.

The hero seemed to guess what I was thinking.

"...I don't intend to take credit for defeating that demon. I didn't want to thank you for sticking your nose into it, either, but your help was the reason we defeated that greater hell demon without any of my comrades getting hurt. So, I thought I should thank you for that, at least."

Ah. Letting him deal the finishing blow must have wounded his pride as a hero.

"I see. Well, I accept your apology and your thanks."

"Hang on! Why don't you join me? I want you with me next time we fight a demon lord."

Yikes.

At least phrase it like "I want your strength" or something, please.

Really, I'm glad I had the "Poker Face" skill and managed not to make any weird faces.

"Was that a proposal? Thanks, but I'll have to pass."

"Th-that's not what I meant!"

The way the hero turned red from my teasing made me all the more suspicious.

I'm not homophobic or anything, but I'm definitely straight. A male love interest was the last thing I needed.

Just then, the sound of heavy boots filled the stadium, and the army's vanguard appeared in the audience seats.

"Well, see ya."

With another little wave, I took off into the sky.

"Right, we'll meet again when we fight the demon lord!"

Whoops, forgot to mention that I defeated that guy already.

"If you mean the one who appeared in this duchy, I took care of him."

In my haste, I'd left my title as Hero instead of True Hero, so I quickly changed it to the latter.

"Huh?!"

The hero's eyes widened.

"What do you mean?!" he shouted, but the cries of the army unit drowned him out.

"The ancestral king!"

Wait, what?

I was confused at first, but I understood when I looked at myself using the Clairvoyance spell.

With Claidheamh Soluis floating around me in thirteen pieces, I was a dead ringer for the picture of the ancestral king Yamato from the museum.

They must have mistaken me for his second coming or something.

If I remembered right, though, Yamato was an enormous man who swung a six-foot-long sword. That didn't fit with my current slender appearance, but maybe they couldn't tell my stature because I was so far away.

The atmosphere was almost unbearable. I decided to leave without delay.

I ascended hundreds of feet with "Skyrunning," then used the Wind Magic spell Air Cannon to accelerate onward.

It was very fast—over a hundred and twenty miles per hour. I'd have to experiment with its max speed later.

A Whale of a Party

Satou here. They say you can tell how old someone is by how whale meat was prepared in their school lunches, but since that can differ depending on the area, I don't think it's a hard-and-fast rule. All that really matters is that it's delicious.

"Hooray! We're having a real Japanese-style lunch today!"

Dressed in a *yukata*, Arisa got especially excited when she saw the lineup on the dining table.

Today's meal included rice with bamboo shoots, miso soup, *chikuzen* stew, *kobumaki*, simmered soybeans, edamame, fried tofu, cold tofu, meat simmered with soy sauce, and a pile of fried meat for the carnivorous beastfolk girls.

"Japeeese?"

"Japanesey, sir!"

Tama and Pochi didn't know what "Japanese" meant, but they were still hopping up and down with joy when they saw the pile of fried meat. As long as they were having fun, that was fine with me.

Miss Karina and the other girls also looked eager when they saw all the food. We were having a full Japanese-style day today, so everyone was dressed in *yukata* like Arisa.

Arisa had dressed Nana and Miss Karina with extra care, which meant there wasn't a single hint of their ample chests.

How disapp— I mean, how wholesome.

"What could this scent be? It is different from ordinary fried chicken."

Liza narrowed her eyes at the mountain of meat, and Tama and Pochi promptly lined up at her side, sniffing the air excitedly.

In front of Mia's seat, I'd placed a new kind of fried food.

"Vegetable *katsu*?"

"That's right. I used veggies like asparagus and lotus root, just for you."

"Satou!"

Mia hugged my waist with a rare smile.

She'd never been able to hide her envy when the other kids ate fried chicken, so I thought I'd give it a try, but her reaction was even happier than I expected.

"Master! There are yellow stars floating in the miso soup, I report!"

Nana had her face close to the miso soup as she waved me over frantically.

I'd cut steamed sweet potatoes into star shapes for the soup. Cutting around the stringy parts had been quite the undertaking.

All the extra effort was worth it to make everyone happy, though.

"Wow, I've never had such a feast!"

"Erina, remember, we're here as Lady Karina's guest. Be sure to show some restraint."

"Right, right."

Since we were celebrating a windfall of valuable ingredients today, I'd invited Miss Karina's escort maids, Pina and Erina.

Now I was just waiting for everyone to take their seats so we could get started, but Arisa was too hyperactive to sit down.

"Oh man, simmered soybeans! Ooh, and edamame, too! Oh my gosh, if there's ginger and green onions to top that cold tofu, I might just lose my mind!"

"Oh, Arisa, that's enough celebrating for now. Can't you sit down? We're all waiting for you so we can start."

"Whatever you say, my dear sister."

Still hyper, Arisa made a gesture of surrender to Lulu and sat down.

Then she led the group in a chorus of "thanks for the food," and the meal could finally begin.

"Nyummy!"

"This is the ultimate deliciousness, sir!"

"Amazing… Each bite is overflowing with savory flavor."

Tama filled her cheeks with the fried meat.

Pochi seemed to have improved her vocabulary just to convey the tastiness.

And Liza appeared to be on the verge of tears.

"Master, this meat is incredible. I feel as if every bite is filling me with power."

"Oh, Liza, you always exaggerate. Just pass me some of that fried stuff, please!"

Chuckling at Liza, Arisa opened her mouth wide and popped in some of the fried meat.

"Ooh, wait, this is gooood. I've never had anything so... Huh? Wait, it's kinda familiar..." Arisa furrowed her brow seriously as she chewed. "Mm? What kind of meat is this? It's not chicken, and it's not pork. I've eaten it before, but I can't quite remember..."

She tilted her head thoughtfully.

"...Wait, I've got it. This is whale, isn't it?!"

I knew she'd get there.

"I used to have it simmered in soy sauce or fried *tatsuage*-style in my school lunches. How did you even get whale meat, though?"

"Let's just say I got lucky."

Today was very fortuitous indeed.

There was no other way to describe it, since high-quality ingredients had delivered themselves right to me.

"Want to try it simmered, too?"

"Oh-ho-ho-ho! You know I do!"

I gave her a small bowl of the whale meat simmered with soy sauce. Much to my chagrin, nobody else had tried it yet. Did it look that unappealing?

I would've liked to simmer it with red sauce, too, but I hadn't been able to get any tomatoes in this world yet.

"Whale really is the best—"

Arisa was happily filling up on the simmered meat when her face suddenly froze.

"...Wait a minute. Whale?"

Was the seasoning not good enough?

"...Master. Didn't you say you fought some kind of greater hell demons today?" Arisa whispered into my ear after immediately plopping herself down beside me.

I fought a lot of different monsters today, but I had a feeling I knew what she was asking, and I responded in a low voice, "Yes. Giant monster fish."

"S-so by giant monster fish, you mean…those, uh, flying whales that were in the pictures of Ancestral King Yamato?"

I nodded slightly. I'm sure King Yamato enjoyed the whale meat, too.

"Giant monster fish… The floating fortress…"

Arisa sat stock-still.

Huh? Did it bother her that the meat was from giant monster fish?

"…Well, it's delicious, so no harm done!"

After chewing her lip for a moment, she hopped up and declared her ruling.

"Innoceeent?"

"Not guilty, sir!"

Tama and Pochi pulled out fans from their *yukata* and danced next to Arisa.

Arisa must have been teaching them some weird jokes.

"Arisa! Don't put your feet up on the table!"

"Yes, ma'am! Sorry, ma'am!"

Arisa, who'd posed with one foot on the table in her excitement, quickly bowed apologetically to Lulu.

Liza scolded Tama and Pochi as well.

Though her comment was forgotten in the wake of Arisa's dramatic reactions, I realized later that Liza's intuition had been correct.

With the help of Arisa, who could monitor her own skills, we later discovered that eating the fried whale meat temporarily increased some stats, like strength and stamina, by about 10 percent.

Because I couldn't reproduce the effect with ordinary ingredients, it must work only with certain kinds of monsters. I'd have to investigate further as soon as I had the chance.

At any rate, the fried whale was very popular with the whole group.

"With every biiite…"

"The meat is practically still moving, sir."

Okay, Pochi. I get that you like it and all, so please just calm down and eat without the creepy comments. Otherwise I'll get flashbacks to creepy meat monsters from those old horror games.

"Sir, was this meat perhaps very valuable?"

Liza looked anxious.

It was valuable in that there was no way to buy it no matter how much money you had, but each of the whales also weighed several tons; we would probably never run out of it.

"Do you like it? There's plenty more where that came from, so don't worry about it."

"…Yes, sir."

Liza clenched her fists and nodded solemnly. *Just relax and eat, please.*

Some of the other girls, like Karina and the beastfolk duo, were wolfing down the fried whale at a remarkable rate.

Miss Karina and her maids were too absorbed in chewing to speak.

"Tama, Pochi, I am taking command of this fried meat. Those two pieces on each of your forks will have to be your last. Ah, Lady Karina, please try to savor the taste more before you swallow it so quickly…"

Really, Liza, calm down.

The rapid disappearance of the mountain of food must have alarmed her.

There was a maid standing by the wall and watching with a warm smile, and I asked her to bring more fried whale from the insulated magic item I was storing it in.

Of course, the other dishes were well received, too.

"Bamboo shoots."

"Yes, they're tasty, aren't they?"

"Mm. Yummy."

"Mia, the *chikuzen* stew is delicious as well, I report."

"Gimme."

The other girls were enjoying the food at their own pace.

"Mia, there isn't any fish in the *kobumaki* with the red wrapping."

"Satou!"

Mia smiled happily as she reached out with her chopsticks.

"The fried stuff is great, but so is the stew! And the fish in this *kobumaki* is amazing! Oh, cold tofu, it's been so long! With the ginger and soy sauce on top, it's almost too powerful…"

Arisa seemed to have her own way of enjoying things, so I decided to leave her to it.

She sounded sort of like an old man, but I didn't want to rain on her parade.

Personally, the smiles on everyone's faces were what made the food truly exceptional for me.

◆

After a delightful dinner, we had a certain visitor.

When the maid told me we had a guest, I assumed it must be an acquaintance or someone connected to the hero.

But the person the maid brought into the parlor was someone I'd never met—a young girl with pink hair and turquoise eyes.

I had seen her before. If I remembered right, this was the girl who'd been standing next to Miss Karina during the fight against the yellow demon earlier that day.

"Black hair... Japanese..."

Looking at my face, her eyes sparkled.

With the dreamy sigh of a maiden in love, she gave a very unexpected greeting.

"So we meet at last, my hero."

That was how I met Princess Menea of the small kingdom of Lumork.

Afterword

Hello, this is Hiro Ainana.

Thank you for picking up the sixth volume of *Death March to the Parallel World Rhapsody*!

Once again, I crammed tons of pages into this volume, so I've got only one page left for the afterword.

For Volume 6, I decided to restructure the story to feature Sara's older sister and the hero's follower, Ringrande. I also added more of Satou's interactions with the nobles of the old capital, and his entanglements with the prince are also different from the web version.

On top of that, there are plenty of extra side stories to add to the fantasy appeal. One character who was mentioned by name only in the web version and alluded to in Volume 5 makes an appearance in this volume. I hope you all enjoy that!

Finally, the usual round of thanks! Thank you to my editors Mr. H and new Mr. H, shri, and everyone else involved in the publication, distribution, and sale of this book! And most of all, thanks to the readers for supporting us!

Thank you very much for reading all the way to the end of the book!

I hope to see you again in the next volume for the Black Dragon arc!

Hiro Ainana

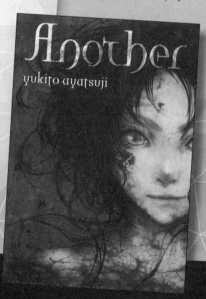